RIFTED HEARTS

M.A. GUGLIELMO

MERIT PTAH PRESS

RIFTED HEARTS

M. A. Guglielmo

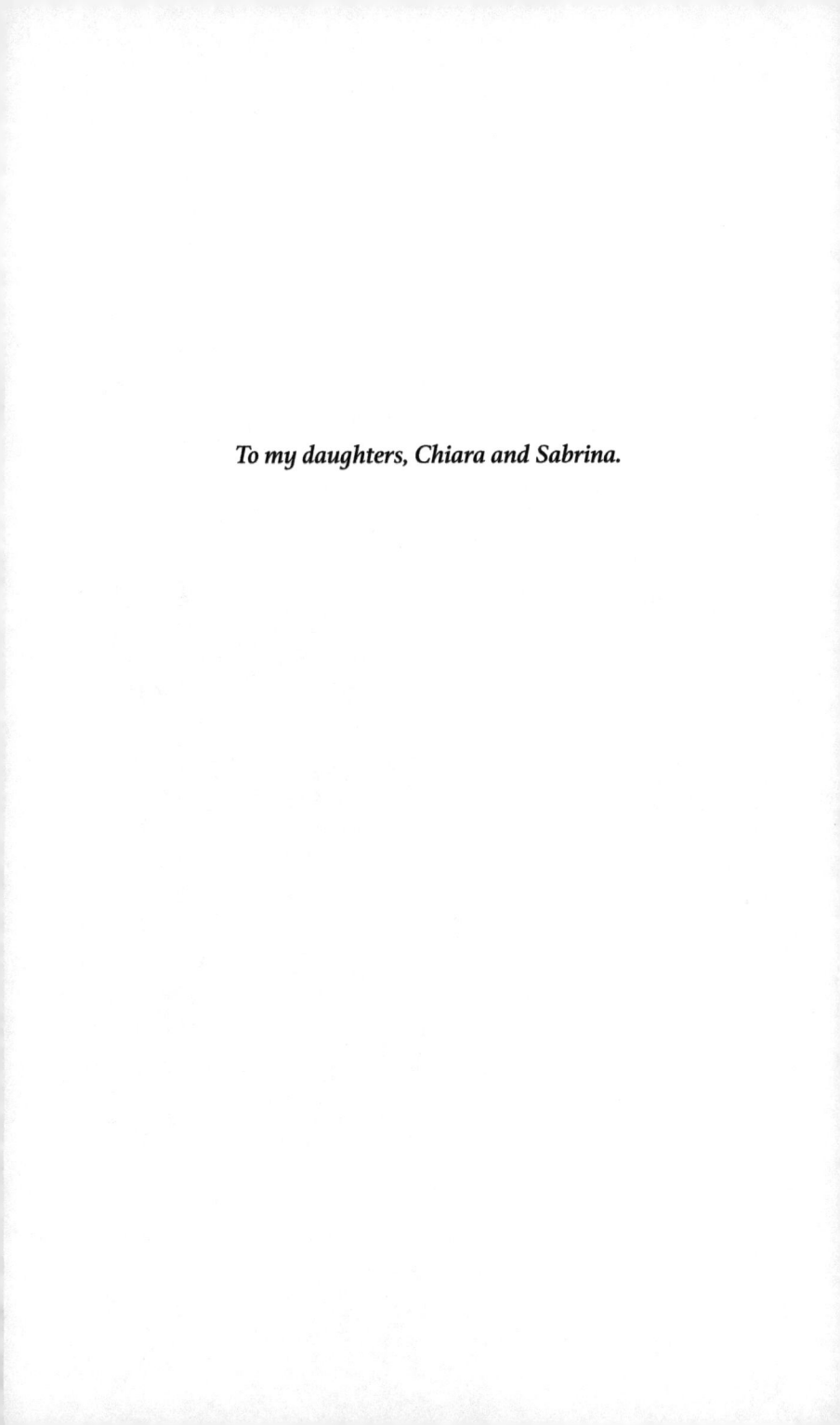

To my daughters, Chiara and Sabrina.

1

Kaveh Salehi knew a rift storm was coming—a bad one.

Worse yet, it might hit while the mare in the stall with him was giving birth. Amanita, who everyone else at Moon Star Ranch thought was an ordinary Camarillo White Horse, had been in the first stage of labor since late afternoon, her pale coat sweat-soaked and her breathing rapid. She would deliver soon, in the predawn hours, and Kaveh could only hope the horse kept her current shape throughout the birthing process. That would leave him managing what might be a typical foal—or might not.

He turned to his veterinary assistant, Katsuo Nakamura. Kat, as he was known, gazed at the restless horse in front of him with nothing short of adoration. The young wrangler had never met an animal he didn't like, and the more dangerous, the better. Rather like his taste in boyfriends. But if a rift storm was on the way, Kat needed to get out and leave Kaveh to handle this particular blessed event.

"I think it'll be a while before the foal comes. You should grab an early breakfast." Kaveh hated to lie, but Kat didn't know Amanita had alien blood, and frankly, he didn't want his assistant to find out. The young man had an unhealthy fascination with hostile Riftworld animals as it was.

Amanita had subtle signs she wasn't a normal horse, but on this side of the Saguaro Rift—a rippling portal in the Arizona desert that led into a fragment of the alien planet known as the Riftworld—she couldn't transform into her dangerous alter form.

Except during a rift storm.

"I'm off work later today anyway, so I don't mind staying." Kat turned to him with such enthusiasm and guileless joy Kaveh felt even more guilty.

Not guilty enough to tell the truth though. Kaveh pretended to look through his equipment. "I'm going to need some extra vials. I don't have enough for the lab tests I want to run on the foal."

"No problem. Tell me which ones you need, and I'll run over to the petting zoo to get them." Kat came over to join Kaveh in scanning the contents of his bag.

If he could get Kat out of here before the storm hit and Amanita's foal arrived, Kaveh was confident he could handle the situation. In addition to working as a large animal veterinarian, he was a specialist in the medical treatment of Riftworld species.

And like many of his patients, Kaveh had his own Riftworld blood. That was another secret he didn't want Kat or anyone else on the ranch to find out about.

Before Kaveh could come up with a list of equipment for his assistant to spend time collecting, the air itself shivered around him, and every electric light in the stable went out.

The storm had arrived, even earlier than he had anticipated.

Kat let out a yelp of surprise, but everyone who worked

at Moon Star Ranch knew how to react. While the deep, gong-like sound of the storm bell tolled, Kat located one of the phosphorescent lanterns that hung near every stall and shook it into activity. The living material within—composed of mushroom-like organisms that emitted phosphorescent light—began to glow. A rift storm meant Riftworld rules— and that meant no electricity or any complex human technology.

"It's the third storm this month." Kat moved the shroom light into position to give Kaveh a better view of Amanita.

The horse had rolled on her side now, and a stream of fluids gushed from under her tail, which Kaveh had wrapped up in preparation for the birth. At least she was still in her Earth form. That might not last, and now there was no practical way to get Kat out of the stable. Sheltering in place was mandatory during a storm. The protections around the buildings at the ranch—which Kaveh had personally overseen—were designed to keep human inhabitants safe until the danger from hostile Riftworld species had passed. That could take hours.

"Do you think they're getting more frequent?" Kat's face, which looked even younger than his twenty-one years, had a pale sheen in the light of the shroom lamp. The vet assistant had been born after the rifts, or "monster portals," had opened around the world, and he had grown up next to the one here in Tucson. Still, even humans accustomed to living near a piece of an alien world were unsettled by rift storms.

"Probably only a natural variation in timing." Kaveh hoped that was true, but the uptick in both the number and severity of the events had grown over the past six months.

Amanita climbed to her feet, and the foal's forelegs, covered in placental membranes, started to emerge. Kaveh put on a pair of gloves and approached the horse cautiously.

He could communicate with the mare telepathically, and in general she tolerated him better than she did the human inhabitants of the ranch. Still, he had only been present for her full transformation once, and it had been terrifying.

"You should stay back." Kaveh would have preferred Kat move to the opposite side of the stables, but he couldn't come up with a good reason to send his assistant away.

The owners of the ranch were on board with Kaveh's work helping injured or ill Riftworld animals who were no more dangerous than a domestic horse or a feral cat. They *would* have an issue with a transformed Amanita wreaking havoc on the ranch during a storm or trying to eat Kat, both of which she was more than capable of.

"She's reacted poorly to some medical procedures in the past," Kaveh finally said. Those procedures had involved him stopping Amanita from taking a bite out of him when she transformed while caught in a rift storm.

"Amanita likes me though." Kat put more optimism into his statement than might have been warranted.

Kaveh examined the mare, and everything looked good for the birth. The foal was in the right position and presentation. Amanita pawed at the hay beneath her feet then lay on her side again. He crouched down, ready to gently guide the baby's forelegs and clear the nose when it appeared. Once the shoulders were through the birth canal, the rest of the foal would come out quickly.

The storm hummed through Kaveh, enhancing his own alien senses and allowing him to perceive a shimmer over the mare's coat. Maybe if the foal came out before the full effects of the storm hit, Amanita would continue to look and act like a horse. She hadn't shifted into her alter form during the earlier rift storms that had hit the ranch, but judging by the way his body was reacting, this time might be different.

Kaveh tugged as Amanita pushed, and the foal came out, taking in normal breaths and sprawling out with gangly legs onto the hay. Even with the remaining membranes and fluid, the young animal's coat shone red in the glow from the shroom light.

"It's a boy!" Kat came over, ignoring Kaveh's earlier advice, and reached out to pet the newborn colt. The foal opened his mouth to reveal a set of fangs as long as Kaveh's index finger and shot out a black, forked tongue in Kat's direction.

Kaveh slammed his shoulder into Kat, sending him flying backward away from the colt. The animal tried to get up on its long legs, determined to bite Kat, before collapsing into an uncoordinated heap. The baby had certainly inherited Amanita's Riftworld blood. His skin under the afterbirth was covered in brilliant red scales, and the two nubs on his head were a reminder of the horns that would develop as he matured.

"That's—not a horse." Kat recovered enough to stand up, and instead of fleeing in panic, he inched toward the colt. "Wow, it looks like a baby dragon. Cool."

"Not everything with scales is a dragon, Kat." Kaveh let more irritation show in his voice than he should have. He turned his attention away from the foal and Amanita to make sure Kat didn't get closer. "It's a Riftworld animal known as a repoequus."

He was about to add in the part about the poison fangs when Amanita charged.

The hybrid mare had been lying on her side after the delivery of her monstrous offspring, but the creature who towered over Kaveh when he whirled back didn't look much like a horse. Amanita had transformed into the unholy sight of a full-size repoequus, her scales pearly white, and her deadly horns fully developed. She reared up. A glancing blow from her hooves sent Kat flying against the wall of the stall. He crumpled to the floor, and she turned her attention to Kaveh, opening her mouth wide. A single drop of venom glistened at the tip of one of her two fangs.

Without thinking, Kaveh flung his hands up, and green fire crackled toward the repoequus.

Amanita hissed, backing away and putting her body between her baby and the flames, as Kaveh shifted to stand in front of his unconscious veterinary assistant.

It took a moment for him to grasp what he had done. The flames crawling over his skin were *summ,* a poisonous fire he knew only from written accounts of Riftworld battles —and he had no idea how he had produced them. He concentrated on his hands, breathing deeply and trying to absorb the summ back into his body. He had to get it under control and convince Amanita he wasn't a threat. She was frightened and enraged, her focus on protecting her foal.

There was good reason for her fear. Summ was one of the most destructive weapons in the Riftworld, a power he should be far too young to use and one he didn't want. His hands and his mind worked together to help and heal, not to destroy. He focused on that positive image in his mind, then sent those thoughts out toward the repoequus—flash-backs of care he had given to other young foals and their mothers and the treatments he used to nurse Amanita herself back to health after he found her battered and bloodied in the desert.

The flames extinguished. Amanita snorted, then nuzzled her new colt's head as if she hadn't tried to kill Kaveh.

He backed away from the animals, his focus now on his injured assistant. Kat staggered to his feet, swaying as he did.

Kaveh put an arm around his shoulder, and the two of them stepped out of the stall. Kaveh closed the door behind them and leaned against it.

"Amanita turned into a mon." Kat stared back at him, his eyes wide. "A scary one too."

Kaveh waited for him to hurl the same name at him. He would have to leave the ranch and the animals and people he loved. The ranch might tolerate Riftworld creatures, even ones like Amanita, but Kaveh had pretended to be human. He'd tricked the owners and wranglers like Kat who trusted him. Even his Riftworld family might reject him if they found out he had the ability to kill any of them with a simple touch.

Kaveh was a monster even in a world of monsters.

Kat reached out to give Kaveh a hug. "You saved my life back there. How did you stop her?"

Kaveh hesitated then forced out a partial truth. "I talked to her about how I wanted to help, not harm her or the baby, and I think on some level she understood."

That wasn't a lie, as far as it went, but he knew Amanita had backed down because he had frightened even her.

"She's only half mon though, so she'll go back to normal when the storm passes." Kat, despite his near-death experience, was already craning his head to see back into the stall. "Her foal doesn't look anything like a baby horse."

No, he didn't, and Kaveh worried he might stay in his Riftworld form. If the ranch owners balked at keeping the two of them here, he didn't know what to do. He couldn't bring the recently foaled mare and her monster offspring back over the rift. His clan had little tolerance for the dangerous species, which was why he kept Amanita at the ranch.

Of course, if Kaveh's relatives found out he was capable

of calling up summ when threatened, the mother and son repoequus pair would be the least of their concerns.

"I'll have to talk to the owners." Kaveh didn't want Kat to get mixed up in his falsehoods, but if the full story of what had happened spread around the ranch before the owners heard about it, they might not react well. "If you could keep the details under your hat until I do, I'd appreciate it."

"I won't say anything." Kat rubbed at his scalp then winced. He hadn't been out for long, but even a short loss of consciousness indicated a concussion, hopefully a mild one. He would need to get checked out when the storm passed. "I don't want Amanita and her foal to get in trouble. She only wanted to protect her baby."

"Thank you." Kaveh's shoulders relaxed a fraction. "I'm not sure how I'm going to convince them to let Amanita and a baby repoequus stay here."

Kat looked thoughtful, which was never good. As sweet as he was, Kat somehow managed to get into a mess of trouble every time he came up with one of his ideas.

"Don't worry." Kat all but bounced with excitement. Kaveh needed him to rest and get a proper medical evaluation, but there was no stopping the young wrangler when he got this way. "I'll go with you to talk to the owners. I have a fantastic plan on how to convince them to let Amanita and her baby stay."

2

Remigio Gatti climbed out of the bright Arizona sunlight and into the rideshare truck's cool interior, flashing the lanky young man in the driver's seat his third-best sultry smile. A little flirtation went a long way—but with Remi's seductive powers, laying it on too thick might require him to find another form of transportation from the airport.

"Nice truck." Remi took in his driver's dazed expression and dialed back his allure before the guy passed out. He stowed his pet carrier under the dashboard in front of him and checked his wrist for the time. He had left the Rolex in Boston, since he needed his Bug watch for this job. "Hello, I'm Remi. Moon Star Ranch and Resort please."

"Sure, Remi." The young man blinked a few times then recovered enough from the state of overwhelmed lust Remi's psychic abilities had induced to reach for his cell phone. He furrowed his brow for a moment then turned the screen off before pulling out of the airport and heading to the highway. "Sorry, I almost forgot. GPS doesn't work out there."

"So I've heard." Remi stretched out his legs, ignoring the low growl that came from the carrier at his feet when the movement rocked the pink plastic crate. Lyall, the wheaten Scottish terrier inside, hated traveling in it. "I'm not too upset about giving up work emails and text messages for a week. Do you ever get any rift effects here in the city?"

"Some of the storms hit the northern neighborhoods a few times a year. I drive a horse-drawn rideshare when that happens." The driver's eyes were less dilated now, and he regained some semblance of conversational ability. "I'm Javier, by the way. Do you, uh, come here often?"

"It's my first time." Remi couldn't resist flirting back and even succeeded in not wincing at the clumsy line. Young, horny guys were too susceptible to his charms, and Javier had to be in his early twenties. Not even remotely a challenge. "In Arizona, that is. Not to mention my first time at a dude ranch."

"It's not easy to get reservations at Moon Star Ranch." Javier gave Remi's Italian silk suit an admiring glance before his cheeks flushed and he turned his attention to the highway. "Even if you've got tons of money."

"My work's paying for everything." Remi made it sound as if he was sharing this in confidence. His family had damn well better be covering his expenses for this trip. His father hadn't allowed him to take a vacation in over a year. He launched into his cover story. "I live-stream adventure travel on Apocalypse Data. My screen name's Wandering Monster, and one of my corporate sponsors set up this trip. After all, what could be more of an adventure than seeing real monsters up close and personal?"

"The ones at the ranch aren't dangerous." Javier shifted lanes, his eyes darting to Remi as if he couldn't help himself. Which, given Remi's psychic seduction powers, he probably couldn't. "There's a petting zoo—well, you might not want to pet everything in there, but those mons won't try to eat you or anything like that. You might see bigger ones on the rides closer to the rift, but the wranglers keep a close eye on the tourists."

Remi had no interest in watching annoying human children poking and prodding Riftworld creatures too stupid to avoid being rounded up and put on display. Not to mention that the entire concept weirded him out. He had a human mother and an alien father, not that either of them deserved to be called a parent.

A half-human member of the ratkind, as his father's Riftworld clan was known, Remi had inherited the psychic ability to manipulate sexual and romantic emotions. Like most of his father's people, he could also shift from a humanoid form—in his case, a quite attractive human man —to his rodent-like alter form. Many of his cousins looked like huge and terrifying rat monsters. Remi, unfortunately, could only transform into an oversized chinchilla.

Perfect monster petting zoo material.

"I heard the ranch has a veterinary clinic that treats mons." Remi shifted the conversation to a less fraught topic, hoping his driver might know something useful. He had many nefarious ways to get information out of people, but if simply asking worked, he might as well save his energy for the main job.

"Oh, they take in creatures from all over." Javier shrugged. "Some people in town call it Monster Ranch as a joke, but the owners and staff do rescue work with horses and normal animals too."

Javier knew more about the ranch than Remi expected, and the guy had a certain amount of clueless charm. He toyed with the idea of a brief fling, but he had limited time to get to his target and get the information Father needed. No time for seductions that weren't required for work. He'd have to wait until after this job for a fun hookup. Come to think of it, when was the last time he had sex with someone for no other reason than he wanted to? He couldn't remember.

Javier kept talking, rambling about information Remi already knew. "They have a veterinarian—Dr. K, everyone calls him—who specializes in things that come out of the Saguaro Rift. He even treats the big, scary mons. Like dragons."

"Sounds fascinating." Remi pretended not to be too interested in the main purpose of his trip and glanced out the window. They had turned off a long stretch of highway featuring billboards promoting everything from water conservation to post-Rapture mega-churches and were now on a two-lane dirt road with nothing but scrub brush and baked earth on either side. "Maybe I can get an interview with Dr. K. My subscribers would love that."

Remi had already arranged to be introduced to Dr. K— Kaveh Salehi was his full name—and he planned to do more with the veterinarian than live-streaming an interview. The dirt on Kaveh dug up by his family suggested he was a human minion of the Saguaro Rift clan of drakones—the Riftworld species humans called dragons. Remi's job was to seduce his way into the good doctor's confidence and discover the secrets the drakones hoarded like...well, dragons.

"He's a great guy." Javier had a note of hero worship in his tone. "I go out with him on guest rides close to the rift all the time, and he takes care of my sister's mothcat Flutterberry."

"A doctor and a cowboy." Remi rather liked the sound of

that. Maybe this particular job would be more entertaining than the last time he had been sent on a mission against the drakones. Then again, that was a low bar.

The truck came to a halt in front of a large gate featuring a horse rearing up with the moon behind it. Above it, a sign read, "Welcome to Moon Star Ranch and Resort."

Javier hopped out to grab Remi's suitcase from the back seat and even came around to open the truck door and hand it to him. "Remember to stay inside if a rift storm breaks out." Javier waved at the bungalows beyond the gate, charming southwestern-style small homes surrounded by drought-tolerant landscaping. "That's when the mons who like to eat people come out."

"I'll be sure to take that advice." Remi gave him a wink that left Javier staring at him with open-mouthed yearning.

Remi stepped out, grabbing the pet carrier and jostling it more than was absolutely necessary before setting off to the check-in desk. The driver might be cute, but Remi had a hot date with a cowboy doctor.

3

R emi didn't let Lyall out of the pet carrier until they reached the door to his cabin. That was sure to piss the dog off even more, but he'd been a dick since this trip began and Remi wasn't feeling charitable.

The Scottish terrier charged out of the pink crate then pulled up sharply before he poked his nose into a barrel cactus. The ranch's landscaping was beautiful—and very pointy. Lyall looked up at Remi and growled.

"Someone's in a bitchy mood." Remi bent down to give Lyall's collar a yank. "Try to bite me, and I'll leave this on for the whole trip."

Lyall bared his teeth, but after a huff of annoyance, he plopped his butt down and sat obediently—or at least the best approximation of obedience the terrier could pull off— beside the door mat.

"Now you're being a good boy, how sweet." Remi drawled as much sarcasm into his words as he could then rested his new leather carry-on on the ground and took out the key to his lodgings for the week. It was a real metal key too. Door card readers wouldn't work during rift storms.

Remi had checked in and flirted with the woman at the front desk, who had given him a fold-out souvenir map of the property. The ranch buildings had been set up in the shape of a horseshoe. The main building and dining hall were in the center of the half circle of guest cabins, with outlying structures including a pool, gift shop, and a corral used for mini-rodeo exhibitions every Friday. The monster petting zoo was marked on the map with a smiling cartoon dragon, which annoyed Remi almost as much as the concept itself.

The cabins were nice though. Each small building held an apartment-sized room, which in his case included a seating area near a king bed, a kitchenette, and a luxurious shower.

He walked inside, admiring the stucco walls, Western-themed wall art, and natural light. Far more tasteful than he expected. It smelled good too, with a faint scent of eucalyptus and lemon. Well, the website had said the staff used all-natural cleaning products.

Turning, he saw Lyall sitting outside the door, acting as if he was guarding Remi's luggage.

"Are you coming in, or do you want a formal invitation?"

Lyall drew back his lips, pulling off a wolfish grin. Then he lifted his leg and pissed on Remi's luggage.

"You little bastard!" Remi lunged outside to grab the terrier, but Lyall darted away, scampering between the artfully arranged cacti and disappearing in a blur of white fur.

Remi could have used a summoning connection with the collar to track Lyall down—the dog was his family's indentured servant after all—but he wanted to avoid using

Riftworld tech outside until he had a better idea of how savvy the ranch staff was about "alien magic." Hopefully, the ranch was full of clueless humans, tourists and staff alike, but having a veterinarian who cared for "mons," as Javier had put it, meant they had to have some knowledge.

Thinking of Riftworld tech made him remember Bug. He tapped his watch, and an image of a large beetle gleaming in cobalt blue and copper appeared. When that didn't work, he shook his wrist several times until the Riftworld insect embedded into the watch woke up. A pair of questing antennae came out first, followed by the head and body of the insect. The beetle enlarged its size as it emerged from the watch's sapphire crystal surface, reaching the size of Remi's palm. Bug lifted up his metallic outer shell to reveal inner translucent wings and flew off, buzzing around the room in erratic circles before landing on a bedside table to chew on a pen sticking out of a welcome basket.

"You're supposed to be searching the place for anything dangerous." Remi rarely tried yelling at the insect, since it did whatever it wanted and was obsessed with eating Earth plastics—which cost a fortune these days.

Between Bug and Lyall, Remi was quite fed up with his companions on this trip.

He pulled his bag inside, cursing the dog as he cleaned off the leather. So much for the room smelling nice. Once that was done, he took care to unpack immediately, hanging up his clothes and sorting out his personal care items. Other than the business suit he always wore on flights, he had brought along what passed for casual clothing in his wardrobe. Stripping down to his boxer shorts, he selected a neatly pressed pair of jeans and a polo shirt. He made a quick pass around the room, picking out inert shroom lights hanging on hooks near the bed, door, and bathroom.

Nothing too surprising about that. The ranch would need backup lighting when the electricity went out. He paused and looked up at the ceiling. It was done up in a rustic style, with dark wooden beams that contrasted with the silver vines accenting the windows and door frames.

"Bug." Remi used his most authoritative voice. "Check these out. Now."

Miracle of miracles, Bug actually listened to him, releasing the chewed-up pen and flying over to land on the stucco wall beside the door. It crawled over the vines, antennae waving. Finally, it paused, turned toward Remi, and made a series of loud clicking noises.

Remi let out a long-suffering sigh. He was quite good with Riftworld languages, but he didn't speak creepy-crawly.

Getting the hint, Bug flew back to his watch and plunged through the crystal surface like a diver into a pool.

Remi scanned the screen. The dead-appearing vines were guardweed, a semi-sentient Riftworld plant species that could be trained to violently attack intruders. Expensive stuff. Moon Star Ranch had some impressive defenses. Could Kaveh Salehi have helped them acquire the guardweed? That would be one of the many bits of useful information Remi intended to obtain with a little pillow talk.

The overly friendly woman at the check-in desk had told him the owner of the ranch would be available to chat with him in about half an hour, and if all went according to plan, Kaveh Salehi would be with him. It shouldn't take long for Remi to parlay that brief business meeting into a one-on-one interview that would end up with the two of them in bed.

Seduce the man, get the information his father wanted, then clear out.

It was his usual plan of action, and he nearly always

carried the seduction part off to perfection. At least there was one thing his father thought he did right.

A little more than thirty minutes later—Remi strove never to be too punctual or too late—he crunched his way down the gravel pathway to the main ranch house. Next to an outside fire pit, three men stood chatting as guests strolled by the front courtyard's two most striking features, an old-fashioned dinner bell and a large hanging gong, its surface featuring an etching of the same moon-silhouetted horse that adorned the front entrance.

An older man wearing a silver moon buckle on his belt had to be the owner, Garreth Hathaway. Along with his wife Chrissie, the two were a power couple in the hospitality business, running one of the most unique lodging properties in the world—a dude ranch featuring alien monsters. Next to him, a much younger man nodded shyly along with the conversation. With his stylishly mussed black hair, high cheekbones, and slender frame, he looked like a J-pop star dressed up in cowboy attire.

The third man was Kaveh Salehi.

Remi slowed his steps, eager to get a good look at his target before the man spotted him and Remi's powers crumbled Kaveh's intellectual and emotional defenses into dust. The pictures he had pored over during his preparation for this job had not done the veterinarian justice. He had intense hazel eyes under striking brows, broad shoulders, and a muscular frame nicely set off by well-fitting jeans.

Damn, the man was hot.

Maybe Remi could draw out the seduction and questioning stage a tad longer than he had planned. He plastered his best business-friendly smile on his face and approached Garreth first.

"Mr. Hathaway, good morning. I'm Remi Gatti, the live-streamer from Apocalypse Data. Thanks so much for inviting me here." Remi shook the man's hand with enthusiasm. "Your ranch has been on my bucket list for a long time. But I'm sure all your guests say that."

"We're delighted to offer you our hospitality." Garreth had a pleasant, deep voice with a faint twang. Not a bad-looking silver fox, but Remi couldn't afford any distractions on this trip. "I know you were interested in talking to our veterinary team, and they both happen to be right here." The owner gestured to the boy-band cutie first. "This is Kat Nakamura, one of our wranglers who's also a veterinary assistant." He beamed at Remi's target. "And here's Dr. Kaveh Salehi, the world's top expert on the medical care of Riftworld animals."

Remi deftly extracted his fingers from Kat's sweaty grasp as the vet assistant stammered out how pleased he was to meet him. He stuck out his hand to Kaveh and was rewarded with a warm, firm handshake. Not a boorish crushing grip, but the strength in Kaveh's fingers was still apparent. The good doctor was even more handsome close up, and Remi felt a pleasant electric tingle from the skin-on-skin contact even before he poured his seduction energy into the other man.

"Nice to meet you." Kaveh dropped Remi's hand and turned to Garreth. "I'll be heading back. I want to check again on Amanita. Her colt is eight weeks old today, and I'd like to reassess him one more time before we let the public see him in the petting zoo."

Remi stared at him in disbelief.

Kaveh wasn't even making eye contact. Granted, Remi had held back, but his allure should have been enough to have the vet hanging on his every word. It wasn't like his powers were having an off day. Garreth was smiling at him

—and Remi was *positive* the man was straight—and Kat had a flush on his cheeks and had become incapable of speech.

He hadn't directed any of his talents in their direction, and they were responding appropriately. Why wasn't Kaveh?

"I was hoping to spend some time talking to you about your work, Dr. Salehi." Remi sought out and caught the man's gaze, and this time he didn't hold anything back, sending waves of lust in Kaveh's direction. If that meant the man looked like a lovestruck fool in front of his colleagues, so be it.

"I'm sure Kat can answer any questions you have." Kaveh gave the barest of nods in his direction then began to step away.

What the hell was going on? Remi had never struck out like this in his life. Humans didn't have mental shields that could protect them against Remi's abilities. Most Riftworld species didn't either. His skills were the primary reason his father found Remi to be a useful member of the Colony, as his ratkind family was known.

A loud bark caused Kaveh to pause, and all four men turned to see Lyall bounding up to them.

Great, *now* the mangy pain in the ass made an appearance. If Kaveh could sense that half-human Remi wasn't who he appeared to be, Lyall would make him even more suspicious, perhaps even hostile. Remi didn't need that kind of trouble.

"Is he yours?" Kaveh crouched down to give Lyall a scratch behind the ears. "He's a gorgeous dog. Great conformation for a Scottish terrier." He patted the dog's head and stroked his back, showing far more interest in the goddamn mutt than in Remi. "He does need to stay on his leash outside the room, of course. What's his name?"

"My apologies. Lyall must have slipped out the door

when I wasn't looking." Remi tried to give Lyall a death glare, but the terrier was too busy wagging his tail and rubbing against Kaveh to even acknowledge Remi. "I'm sure Kat here is very knowledgeable, but hearing your stories about treating Riftworld mons would make for great streaming material. More views equals more business for the ranch."

"Animals, not monsters." Kaveh sounded curt. Damn it to hell, why weren't Remi's seduction charms working on him? He should be eating out of Remi's hand right now, and instead the vet was allowing Lyall to give him a wet doggie kiss on the neck.

Kaveh stood up, and Lyall moved on to sniff Kat's crotch.

Okay, Remi couldn't blame the dog for that.

"Our latest baby animal ambassador in the zoo needs my attention." Kaveh ignored Remi, instead directing a charming smile in the dog's direction. "Don't worry, Lyall. I'll get treats for you the next time we meet."

Kaveh strode off, which at least provided the consolation of checking out how nicely the man's jeans showed off his ass.

Remi forced himself to continue smiling then bent and picked up Lyall. He was sure the damn dog was laughing at him. "Well, I'd better get this little troublemaker back to my room."

AFTER STOMPING back to his cabin in a fury, Remi dropped Lyall onto the floor of his room, turned around, and slammed the door.

"That was a fucking disaster." He directed that comment behind him, where Lyall was supposed to be, but of course the damn dog had already jumped up on the bed, regarding Remi with an expression of smug satisfaction. "We are so not sharing a bed on this little adventure. Get off the covers. Now."

Lyall rolled around on the bed's wool coverlet, which had scarlet-and-black designs that would show every one of the coarse dog hairs he was rubbing on the fabric. He knew how much Remi hated that.

"I'm asking for help here, and you're screwing around." Remi collapsed onto the leather couch and threw a decorative pillow at Lyall, which the terrier dodged with ease. "Our target thought I was less interesting than a two-day-old cricket-protein sandwich, but he was fawning all over you."

Lyall nodded then stretched his paws out, sphinxlike, giving him an expectant look.

"I'll take off your collar if you tell me what happened back there." Remi held his palms out in a beseeching gesture. "Plus, I'll throw in some beef jerky. This place is a ranch—they might even carry the real thing, not the lab-grown stuff."

Lyall shook his head, his bright black eyes gleaming with mischief. Why did he have to be so difficult? Possibly because of the whole forced servitude thing, but that wasn't Remi's fault.

"I'll take the collar off and leave it off for the whole trip, not including the plane ride back because you have to stay in the carrier anyway." Remi hated being on the wrong side of a negotiation.

The dog kept staring at him.

Remi folded. "All right, no collar and I won't stop you going near the rift. Or tell on you when I get back either."

The terrier let out a bark of triumph, and Remi walked over to unsnap the collar. A moment later, Lyall sprawled out on the coverlet in human form—not wearing a stitch of clothing.

Ugh. This trip was getting worse by the minute.

Lyall's naked human shape was a twenty-something man with silver hair tossed back in an asymmetric cut, with wiry hair of the same color over his chest that formed a happy trail leading down between his legs. Remi found Lyall's incessant bragging about his cock size to be annoying, but he had to admit all that boasting had something to back it up. Lyall was hung more like a horse than a dog. He was shorter than Remi but had a compact muscular body Remi would have totally gone for had he not been—Lyall. The two of them had grown up together since Remi was fifteen, fighting constantly. Well, Remi had grown up, while the dog remained the same age. Lyall had been born in the Rift-world, so who the fuck knew how old he was.

Remi's father had won a mysterious bet with Lyall that led to the hellhound being an indentured servant to the Boston-based Colony, Remi's large and dysfunctional clan. Since the family business plan had been based on vintage Mafia films, Lyall's jobs involved intimidating enemies and working as a bodyguard—or as the dog put it, "Babysitting goddamn little rats like you."

"Put your living leathers on before I lose my lunch." Remi scrounged around in his carry-on and pulled out a leather cord with a large fang dangling from it. He threw it at Lyall, who caught it without looking. Remi's father had told him Lyall couldn't have any Riftworld tech on this mission, even the dog's bio armor, which could expand from the creepy necklace to cover his human alter form.

Well, what his father didn't know hopefully wouldn't come back to bite Remi in the ass. "Tell me what you know, you furry bastard."

"Your animal doctor smells like a drakone," Lyall said, "and they're resistant to psychic attacks. That's why your freaky mind sex thing didn't work, but he couldn't tell you're part ratkind. He certainly had no idea what I was, or he wouldn't have promised me doggie treats."

Lyall could transform into both an Earth dog and a full human manifestation, at least when he wasn't wearing his servant collar. His true Riftworld form resembled a huge canine monster from ancient human legend. He was awfully snippy when his unintelligible clan name was mispronounced, so Remi and his family called him what humans called the species—a hellhound. It was an apt enough description. Drakones and hellhounds did not get along, which gave Lyall exactly one thing in common with the Colony.

"Kaveh works for them, but he can't be a drakone." Remi flung himself back on the couch, wondering why he had agreed to such outrageous terms. Lyall had to be lying to him. Granted, Remi had only met one drakone in his life, a terrifying experience he had no intention of repeating, while Lyall had actual experience fighting them. "A lizard man impression, maybe, but not a perfect human transformation."

Kaveh had a damn perfect human body, in fact. Broad shoulders, big strong hands—

No, Remi needed to get a grip on himself. He seduced his targets, not the other way around.

"Mixed." Lyall rolled off the bed and rummaged around in the closet, throwing various pieces of clothing Remi had neatly hung up onto the floor before tossing on a pair of jeans commando-style over his bare ass. The necklace Remi shouldn't have given him was around Lyall's neck, but he still chose to steal Remi's clothes. The inert organism in the tacky rawhide-and-tooth jewelry, once awakened, transformed into impenetrable protection for his more vulnerable humanoid shape, at least according Lyall's endless war stories. Instead of activating it, the damn hellhound picked up one of Remi's favorite shirts and pulled it over his six-pack abs. "You're mixed yourself, rat boy. You should recognize one of your own."

Remi tried a breathing exercise his therapist in Boston had recommended. Lyall had this effect on him. He should have pushed back harder when his father had insisted the dog go with him as backup muscle. "Drakones don't fuck humans. Or ratkind like me. They also don't marry outside their clan."

"Not in the old country, sure." Lyall prowled around the room, probably looking for something to eat. A bottomless pit, no matter what shape he took. "But he's not much older than you. He would have been a child during the Sundering. Everything's screwed up here on Earth, what with the Matchmaker going haywire."

Remi didn't care about drakones and hellhounds clutching their pearl and fang necklaces, respectively, over the chaotic effect of Earth's natural laws. Over twenty years ago, entire chunks of the Riftworld split off, stranding multiple species on fragments of their home planet that opened only onto portals to Earth. Traveling to a different part of the Riftworld involved crossing into a world with wildly different natural laws, inhabited by a violent invasive species that was busily destroying the only planet they had.

That was the Sundering, as Riftworld people called it. To humans, it was the Monster Apocalypse, with inter-dimensional portals replacing areas around the Earth and alien "mons" pouring out of them. It might have been a bigger news event if there hadn't been six other apocalyptic-like events since then—seven, if you counted the US adopting the metric system.

Anyway, two alternate universes colliding had to cause some chaos, and the Matchmaker, a mysterious entity that selected marriage partners and altered reality until they met, was something that could easily be fucked up. Granted, being forced into a lifelong relationship with a random and entirely unsuitable partner by an ancient matchmaking sentience probably sucked. Fortunately, the Matchmaker targeted the so-called "higher peoples," not ratkind like himself.

The sex was supposed to be fucking awesome though.

"You think he's got enough drakone blood to have solid mental shields but not enough to figure out what we are." He still didn't believe Kaveh was part drakone, but Remi didn't face romantic rejection often—at least when it came to the sex part. Anything more long term than a few nights hadn't worked out, but he was fine being single, thank you very much. "What the hell am I supposed to do to get him in the sack? I don't want to go back to Father with my tail between my legs, and you don't want to go back to him at all."

"The ranch is showing off a new Riftworld animal tomorrow at the petting zoo." Lyall couldn't have said anything Remi wanted to hear less. "Kaveh will be there, along with a horde of gawking humans. Show up and do that video nonsense you enjoy so much. He'll love to talk to you about the ranch's new pet mon."

"Fine." Remi hated the thought of the zoo, but a live-stream with a new baby monster would bring in a lot of views. His vid streaming had started out as a cover story for a con, but Remi kept it up because he enjoyed filming his travel show. Plus, it made money. Remi had blown all of his first year's haul on a Rolex which he hadn't brought on this trip but otherwise wore every day. Legal income—a refreshing change of pace from the Colony's cash flow from various illegal enterprises. "What will you be doing to earn your kibble?"

"I'm going to check out the monstertown." Lyall getting close to a rift was a bad idea on many levels, but Remi had promised. "Might do a little hunting, get the lay of the land, that sort of thing."

"You want to figure out how to weasel out of your contract." Remi understood why Lyall wanted to get out from under his father's clawed thumb, but Remi wasn't willing to face his father's wrath if the hellhound succeeded in freeing himself. "Saguaro Rift opens up onto drakone territory. Not friendly terrain for either of us."

"I can take care of myself." Lyall's eyes transformed, glowing an unholy red. The dog was a badass fighter when he felt like it, which was why Father had sent him along. But even with the added power being near a rift would give him, the hellhound couldn't fight an entire clan of drakones.

Lyall strolled to the door then paused on his way out to give Remi more unwanted advice. "Worry about how to get into Kaveh's pants and let me do my job."

4

T he last thing Kaveh wanted was to be late for the petting zoo event. Not that he was looking forward to it. In fact, he had been dreading it every minute of the two months since he and Kat had pitched the idea to Garreth and Chrissie.

He shouldn't blame Kat. Wild schemes and overly optimistic plans were part of his vet assistant's charm. Usually, Kaveh played the voice of reason when Kat came up with yet another suggestion that might end in disaster. But Amanita giving birth to a foal who looked nothing like a normal horse had left Kaveh with few good options. He could only hope Kat's latest bright idea wouldn't destroy both his work and his relationships at the ranch.

Kaveh swung off Ranger and began to take off the gelding's tack, grateful when Javier came over to help him with the horse.

"I'm excited to see the new mon you and Kat are showing off, but Flutterberry's put out by all the attention this is getting." Javier, a part-time wrangler at the ranch, had a sister with a Riftworld companion animal—a mothcat—who often appeared at the zoo as one of what Kaveh called his Riftworld ambassadors. "My sister and Flutterberry got here early for it, and it's a good thing they did. There's already a bigger crowd than the owners expected."

"There is?" Kaveh's stomach lurched at that news. "I'm running late because of an emergency in my clinic, so if you don't mind taking care of Ranger, I'll head over to Amanita's stall and bring the colt over to the zoo."

"Kat already did that for you." Javier dropped that bombshell with a cheerful smile then continued blissfully relating more bad news. "Garreth and Chrissie are there with the mayor and a whole mess of reporters. Remi's live-streaming the whole event. He's that famous guy from Apocalypse Data I picked up at the airport yesterday."

Kaveh didn't wait to listen to the rest of Javier's updates. After mumbling a quick thanks, he strode toward the zoo at the fastest walk he could manage without appearing to be running in a panic.

He had made it clear that he would be the one to bring the colt over. The young animal had never shifted from his repoequus form into a horse. Although the animal hadn't tried to kill Kat since his birth during that bad rift storm, his poison fangs and fledgling psychic assault abilities still made him dangerous.

The petting zoo had originally been a barn with a fenced-in area containing kid-friendly Earth rescue animals such as goats, angora rabbits, and a few chinchillas. After Kaveh arrived, he had altered the space to accommodate a number of benign Riftworld species who either volunteered to interact with curious humans or who had no other safe place to go and at least didn't object to the arrangement.

Kaveh heard the crowd of people before the zoo came into view, but it was still a shock to see how many had shown up for the weekly lecture he and Kat held every Monday afternoon.

He spotted Kat standing on the small wooden stage they used for their talks, with a cockatoo wearing a leash perched on his arm. Kat had not only taken the colt over by himself against Kaveh's specific instructions; he had brought along Snow, of all the part-Riftworld animals he could have chosen. His sense of relief that his assistant was none the worse for wear after leading the repoequus colt away from Amanita was tempered by the sight of the bird, a force for chaos at the best of times.

Someone tapped him on the arm, and Kaveh turned to see the vid streamer Javier had mentioned standing next to him.

Remi, that was his name.

A small drone hovered in the air near the dark-haired man, and Kaveh realized with a jolt he was being—what had Kat told him it was called?

Live-streamed.

Kaveh flinched, even though no one could look at him and guess he wasn't human.

"And here's the man of the hour." Remi, without asking, put his arm around Kaveh's shoulder and grinned up at the drone, which darted into position like a dragonfly to capture both of their expressions. "Kaveh Salehi, monster veterinarian, who's revealing a terrifying new mon born at the ranch."

Kaveh took the man's arm off his shoulder, making an effort to keep his temper and not use any unnecessary force. "If you'll excuse me, I need to join my assistant to start the program."

Several other people encircled him, all with press mini drones of their own, and Kaveh glanced around him in astonishment. More reporters. He had met cadejos with less hungry expressions.

"Let's give the doctor some room, folks." Remi flashed a smile at the gaggle of press, and to Kaveh's surprise, they all fell back, lost interest in him, and began staring at each other. One woman reached out to take another woman's hand, giggling about something as they both blushed.

Kaveh took advantage of the opening and pushed forward. Remi strolled along with him, chatting at his drone and somehow succeeding in having the mass of people part around them.

Kat gave him a nervous smile as Kaveh walked through the open gates of the zoo's enclosure and joined him on the stage. Snow cocked his head, lifting one claw in a gesture that meant he wanted to jump onto his arm. The rescue parrot loved to flirt with humans, but he had bad habits that had led to him failing out of several adoptive families.

"No biting, Snow." Kaveh directed his comments at the parrot but included his assistant in a stern gaze before turning toward the audience. This was quite the crowd.

"You were a little late, so I took the colt over myself and put him in the barn—" Kat cut himself off as Remi waved his hand, his drone zooming up, presumably to get more footage for his online audience. "Oh, hi, Mr. Gatti. Did you have a question?"

Kat sounded even more flustered than he usually did in large groups. Kaveh was a born introvert as well, but between veterinary school and all the academic lectures he gave on his work, he had learned how to address an audience. He'd never been in front of the press like this though.

"We'll have a question-and-answer period after the main

presentation." Kaveh motioned to Kat, who was still staring at the vid streamer for some odd reason. Getting no response, Kaveh held out his hand toward Snow, taking care to keep his elbow bent and close to his chest. That made it harder for the bird to climb up to his shoulder, as he knew from painful experience that he did not want the cockatoo's beak near his ear or face.

"This is Snow, who's part cockatoo with one parent from a Riftworld species colloquially known as a phoenix." As the parrot hopped onto his arm, Kaveh showed him off to the crowd. "Like many animals of mixed ancestry, Snow has gifts from both worlds. He can not only mimic but understand human speech, and he can generate fire."

There was an interested buzz from the audience, and Snow perked up. He fluffed his wings, embers glowing red at the tips, and then hiccupped a smoke ring.

Kat, who had recovered from his odd distraction, clapped, and the audience politely followed suit. Snow had nothing like the fiery power of a true phoenix, but external validation of his limited pyrotechnic abilities was needed to avoid one of the bird's famous temper tantrums.

"Is the baby monster also a hybrid?" Remi piped up from the front row, despite Kaveh's clear explanation of when the Q&A would start. "I understand it's a rare species known for psychic attacks on humans using their own worst nightmares."

Had Kat told the vid streamer about the baby repoequus? Other than his assistant, the only other people who knew that information were Garreth and Chrissie, neither of whom was loose-lipped. He spotted the ranch owners off to one side of the crowd, standing next to a short woman in a fashionable pantsuit. Her cheerful smile appeared permanently plastered on her face.

The mayor of Tucson was here, and Remi had just blurted out that Amanita and her colt were a danger to the public.

"All of our Riftworld animal ambassadors have abilities they could use to defend themselves, as do humans." Kaveh did his best to ignore Remi's personal drone, which quivered, insect-like, in the air in front of him. "They have consented to be here on the ranch, interacting with humans so that all of us can learn more about our intertwined worlds."

Right on cue, a mini rift opened on the stage in front of them, and a large blue cat appeared out of thin air.

Flutterberry resembled a large Maine Coon cat, if one chose to ignore her silky teal fur, long-tufted ears, and the gossamer-thin wings on her back. The startled crowd surged forward to get a better look, with quite a few people making squees of delight and one child loudly asking if the cute kitty cat could fly.

Mothcats used their wings only for nonverbal communication, having chromatophores in them that were consciously controlled and could produce complex color patterns. The species could also translocate, a rare ability that allowed them to form miniature rifts that moved them instantly from one location to another, as long as it was within their line of sight. Some members of the species, like Flutterberry, had also bioengineered their vocal cords to allow them to speak human languages. The blue mothcat lived in Tucson as a companion animal with Javier's sister and her wife.

Or, as Flutterberry referred to them, her devoted servants.

"Flutterberry here is one of Moon Star Ranch's best-known Riftworld ambassadors." Kaveh couldn't keep the relief out of his voice. The mothcat adored human attention, and by the time he finished explaining the basics of mothcat physiology and Flutterberry chatted about the latest gifts her pet humans bought for her, everyone should have calmed down enough that their collective anxiety wouldn't provoke a response from the repoequus colt.

"Run away, humans." Flutterberry raised one paw into the air, her high-pitched voice resounding in the clear desert air. "A repoequus approaches, ready to flood your feeble minds with horrors beyond your imaginings."

The mayor's plastic smile faltered, and a shocked silence followed Flutterberry's unhelpful comments. Kaveh wracked his brain for the best way to explain away the mothcat's Cassandra-like prediction before confusion and fright swept through the crowd like a contagion.

His hesitation proved to be disastrous.

Amanita's colt barreled out of the barn, crashing through the bolted doors as if they'd been made of cardboard. The repoequus sensed fear from a large number of minds, and a simple Earth physical barrier wasn't going to stop him from seeking out prey.

The alien colt charged toward the stage and the open gate beyond it.

Kaveh had begun to get the animal used to a bridle, and the colt had one on now, the end trailing onto the ground. Kaveh dove for the end of the reins, planting his feet and holding fast to them as the colt tried to surge into the crowd.

Everyone else on the stage got out of the way. Kat scrambled backward and hopped off, and Snow flapped skyward and landed on the barn's roof. Flutterberry hissed and translocated back to her humans at the outskirts of the audience.

Kaveh pulled up short on the bridle, and the colt came to a halt.

Now close to 150 kilograms in weight, the animal certainly looked demonic, with scarlet scales gleaming in the sun, and small horns jutting out from his head. The colt opened his mouth and bared his poison fangs at the crowd, his forked tongue lashing out to taste the air around him.

Several children burst out into sobs, and members of the audience shrieked in distress, some clutching at their ears as if to block out the sounds they heard only in their minds.

Like all drakones, Kaveh had mental shields that made him resistant to psychic attacks. He could see the disturbing images the colt was sending toward the humans around him in his mind, but the overwhelming fear they invoked was blunted by his natural defenses.

The visions of terror had been ripped from the mass subconscious of the crowd. Undead zombies shambled across battlefields littered with bodies, a pit of snakes hissed and rattled, and a yawning abyss stretched far below a swaying rope bridge. Given the number of crises in the world today, from rising sea levels, super hurricanes, and sandstorms larger than some countries, the humans around Kaveh had rather unlikely primal fears.

Nonetheless, Kaveh had to stop the psychic assault. He flooded the colt's mind with positive thoughts that involved all the senses, from the warm scent of Amanita's fur to the sweet nourishment of milk from her teats, and then onto the playful whinnies of the colts and fillies the young repoequus had bonded with since his birth.

The colt lowered his head then turned back to let Kaveh stroke the reptilian smoothness of his nose.

"That was amazing." Remi's voice boomed out, loud and cheerful. The vid streamer came up to Kaveh and the colt, still talking at his drone. "Not only does Dr. Salehi have a demon unicorn on a leash, his little mon can live-stream horror flicks into people's minds."

Remi came up to the baby horse before Kaveh could stop him, hunching his shoulders and putting on a mock expression of terror as he hammed it up for his audience. The colt flicked its long, forked tongue at the vid streamer then went back to allowing Kaveh to rub his neck.

"Hey doc, what's this little mon's name?"

"We're planning a contest to pick one for him." Kaveh forced himself to steady his breathing.

No one was screaming or running away, and a few of the braver audience members took a few steps toward the colt. Garreth came the closest, and he gave Kaveh a slow nod of encouragement to keep talking.

"This is a repoequus, born to Amanita, one of our mares here on the ranch." Kaveh used his authoritative "I'm the doctor" voice, sounding calm and knowledgeable, even though his heart was pounding and the little he knew about the species of animal now nuzzling his neck came from drakone texts describing any Riftworld being with psychic powers as a menace. "As you guessed, Remi, the species has a mental defense mechanism that allows it to detect and magnify the fears of intelligent creatures nearby. Now that everyone is calm, the foal has settled down. Maybe your viewers could send Moon Star Ranch their picks for a name for our newest Riftworld animal ambassador, and our visitors here in person today could do the same."

Remi waved at the drone, once again placing his head next to the colt's in a selfie pose. Kaveh couldn't decide whether the man was too dense to realize the danger the repoequus posed to him or if he simply was willing to take the risk to get more views for his online show.

"Well, you heard the good doctor." Remi moved to stand next to Kaveh and once again draped his arm around Kaveh's shoulder without asking first. "Send in your votes to name Moon Star Ranch's first demon unicorn. This is Wandering Monster, signing off near the famous Saguaro Rift."

5

R emi sauntered into the bar for happy hour, projecting both confidence and a cheerful "I'm on vacation'" vibe, instead of the uncertainty and annoyance he felt.

He had made no progress with Kaveh today. Granted, the man had been distracted by a crowd of clueless humans and a juvenile repoequus—and, wow, Remi had not expected the petting zoo to feature that deadly Riftworld species. Did the ranch keep a great white shark in the swimming pool as well?

Remi's psychic abilities hadn't done *anything* to Kaveh, even with the added benefit of close physical contact. He wanted to do a lot more than put his arm around Kaveh's shoulder, but even that amount of touch should have helped him overcome whatever mental shields the man had. Instead, the only person turned on by those bro hugs had been Remi. He could still feel the warm muscles flexing underneath the vet's shirt and the sense of desire that had flared through him when their bodies touched.

He shook off that memory and tried to focus on his

mission. Plan A, walking in with his seductive powers blazing, hadn't worked. Twice. Time for plan B—attack a softer target.

Remi mixed with the ranch's crowd of guests, which included everyone from older clientele who clearly had serious money to a smattering of families with adolescent and younger children. All of the seats were Western-style saddles mounted on chair bases, and the alcohol and snacks were laid out on an honor system. He wasn't sure which one of those unique features was more shocking to his sensibilities.

He spotted Kat in one corner patiently answering questions from a girl about eight years old. Coming within listening range, he heard her rattle off a series of queries about baby dragons, magic cats, and of course, demon unicorns. Most of the vet assistant's answers were along the lines of "dragons don't live here on the ranch," "maybe if you ask politely, you can pet her," and "the baby unicorn is too dangerous to play with."

That was an understatement. As young as the repoequus appeared to be, the animal had still held about fifty human minds in thrall for short period of time. Remi had put serious effort into getting fewer than ten reporters randy enough to leave him and Kaveh alone.

If that was how powerful a juvenile was, Remi didn't want to meet an adult repoequus.

He considered bribing the little brat with candy to get her away from Kat, but an even younger and more excitable child swooped in to tug at the girl's arm, squealing something about a show with live scorpions, and they both ran off.

"You must get an earful of questions about the mons you care for here from the kids." Remi started with that as a conversation opener, not that he knew anything about children, human or not.

"I love showing the animals to the little ones. It's my favorite part of our zoo lecture every week." Kat hesitated then continued. "There's still so much we don't know about Amanita's baby, and today was the first time he was around that many people. I hope what happened didn't upset you."

"Are you kidding?" Remi hadn't made any progress on his goal of seducing Kaveh, but his Apocalypse Data account had raked in the cash, thanks to the repoequus. "My views on that stream were through the roof. And adding the teaser about naming the demon baby was genius. Now I need a killer follow-up interview with the doctor who delivered the little monster."

Kat looked confused, so Remi turned on a low buzz of sensuality, enough to keep the cute hottie focused on him but not enough to stun him into a state of dazzled lust. "Let's get some drinks, and you can tell me all about Kaveh."

Several minutes later, after Remi had 'bought' Kat a beer and himself a decent California Pinot by writing someone else's room number on the honor system card, he maneuvered the young man to a table outside.

"I've known Kaveh for about two years." Kat smiled as he answered Remi's questions. He spent far too much time smiling, in Remi's admittedly jaded opinion. He distrusted happy, open people on general principle. Of course, with Kat's looks, the guy could get laid any time he wanted, so maybe his sunny outlook on life wasn't unreasonable. Remi got laid pretty often as well, but using his charm to lure in a victim while under orders from the family wasn't fun—it was a chore.

Kat kept talking, mostly about medical topics that bored Remi to no end. "He did some work with Riftworld animals overseas, but he says his practice here is much busier, with a lot of different species." He wolfed down jalapeño poppers as he talked. "Thanks for streaming at our petting zoo today. The ranch website has been flooded with names for the foal already, and the mayor wasn't as upset as Kaveh thought she might be."

Remi did *not* want to talk about the zoo again. The only petting he was interested in involved him, Kaveh, and a lack of clothing on both sides. "I need my next stream to go deeper. My audience is interested in the mons at the ranch, and they want to know everything about the human veterinarian who's brave enough to treat them. That's why I need to know more about Kaveh as a person."

"Kaveh's super nice." Kat supplied that bland platitude with breathless admiration.

The vet assistant wasn't fucking Kaveh, that much Remi knew. He only idolized the man. Remi's abilities allowed him to pick up on emotions—well, as long as they were related to lust. He could tell Kat liked men but didn't want to get into Kaveh's oh-so-perfectly fitting jeans. Lucky for him because Remi's family had no compunction about getting rid of any obstacles that could mess up a job.

"He's awfully busy though," Kat said. "I'm not sure I can get him to spend time on an interview."

"What about his life outside of work?" Remi pushed his own plate of poppers over to Kat. He hated greasy food, and this close to a rift he spent a lot of time thinking about green salads. His Riftworld alter form, the chinchilla part of him he ruthlessly suppressed, was acting up. "I didn't see a wedding ring, not that it means much. Does he date men? I mean, he is awfully good looking. Totally my type."

Kat's cheeks turned pink. He was ridiculously pretty. Remi preferred his men on the rough-and-ready side of things, but if he hadn't been on a job, he would have been sorely tempted to take Kat to bed and find out what other parts of him blushed when he got embarrassed.

"Kaveh works a lot of hours and doesn't take as much time off as he could." Kat hesitated, and Remi sensed he was getting closer to dragging out some real information. Remi amped up his allure, and Kat blurted out, "He doesn't date men or women. Kaveh's ace, you know?"

It took a few seconds for that sentence to sink in. "You're telling me Kaveh's asexual and doesn't date or fool around or anything else?"

That was an unbelievably bad stroke of luck.

Remi was pansexual and seducing anyone for a brief fling, including straight men, wasn't much of a challenge. He had never met anyone entirely resistant to his psychic abilities, although most members of his family were too conscious of his powers to be influenced by them. The good news was this meant Kaveh didn't suspect Remi's true nature and hopefully wasn't the scary half-human drakone Lyall thought he was. The bad news was that he wouldn't fall for any of Remi's usual tricks. Remi would need to actually work to get Kaveh into bed.

"He's homoromantic, I think." Kat took another sip of beer and kept talking. Once Remi established a psychic link to someone he was targeting, getting information was simple. "Maybe demiromantic too. He mentioned he was in a relationship with a guy years ago, but they broke up. But if you're open to queer platonic relationships, you should ask him out. It would be good for him to get away from work once in a while. Kaveh's a brilliant veterinarian and a wonderful person, and I'd love him to get together with someone as nice as he is."

"Nice." Remi repeated the word in funereal tones. In the

Colony, nice was an insult. Even though Remi caught an endless amount of shit from his more powerful and dangerous cousins, no one ever accused him of being *nice*. He gritted his teeth and smiled at Kat, focusing his powers on him until the young wrangler's eyes glazed over. "I'd be totally interested in platonic-dating Kaveh. And you're going to help me with that."

"I HOPE you came up with something helpful with all of your sniffing around." Remi tossed a bag of beef jerky in Lyall's direction, threw his shopping bags on the sofa, and flounced onto the bed. It was around ten o'clock, the earliest Remi had retired to his hotel room in years.

After a surprisingly decent dinner—albeit served in family-style chafing pans—he had endured the after-dinner entertainment of cowboy singalongs and a trick roping exhibition. Afterward, he wandered the ranch property, finally arriving at the gift shop. As expected, the store carried jerky made from cows raised at the ranch and at a fraction of the cost non-lab-grown meat usually commanded. It also boasted a collection of rather fetching cowboy hats and various souvenir options. He had decided his retail therapy counted as a reasonable work expense.

"I ran into a cadejo who was willing to talk, for a price." Lyall was in his human form again since Remi had been desperate enough to agree to keep his collar off, *and* the hellhound was wearing more of Remi's clothes, damn him.

"What price was that?" Cadejos—one of many names humans gave to the ten or so Riftworld species who reminded humans of frightening monster dogs from legends—had a similarity to their counterparts in Earth myths. Some became obsessed with particular humans, following them around and protecting them. Most of them, though, simply ate any people they came across. The last thing Remi needed was a trail of partially consumed bodies to raise suspicion.

"I gave him my collar." Lyall laughed at Remi's shocked expression. "Yes, I know, it was a perfect swap."

"Setting aside the obvious issue that Father will skin me alive when he finds out I not only disengaged the damn thing but let you give it to a potential enemy, what would a cadejo want with it?"

Lyall waved off Remi's concerns. "I can come up with a fake collar, if necessary. Plus, I can't be released from my fucking contract with Arimanius merely by someone in the Colony taking the stupid thing off. Believe me, I've tried."

Remi was quite aware of Lyall's attempts to get out of his indenture contract. His father Arimanius, who wanted Remi to call him Ari and who Lyall always referred to by his full Earth name, had warned Lyall would massacre them all if the hellhound found a way out of the agreement.

Ari did love his drama.

"I don't understand why your creepy new friend didn't ask for something more typical, like the still-beating heart of one of the guests here."

"José's pretty chill for a cadejo." Lyall was already on a first-name basis with the locals. "He lives in the Saguaro monstertown with his human, and the two of them like to spice things up in bed. You know, she turns him into a cadejo, and he has to beg to get the collar off before the sexy times start. As long as they don't leave it on for too long, they'll be fine."

Remi tried to imagine himself voluntarily putting on a device that confined him to his chinchilla alter form and shuddered. That would not be sexy. It would be humiliating and not in a fun way.

"The Saguaro Rift is different from the one you're used to near home." Lyall always sounded so damn patronizing when he explained things to Remi.

No, Remi had not been born before the rifts opened up. He'd never even crossed over one. So what? He didn't care about the old country, as Lyall and his father called the fragments of Riftworld that lay on the other side of the rifts.

"Well," Remi said, "the Witch City Rift is in the goddamn ocean."

Lyall snorted. "Yes, I know we're near an air rift, not a water one. The interzone of this one is different. This ranch is in an outer interzone. Most technology works, except during storms. The Saguaro Rift monstertown is in an internal interzone, with some Riftworld natural laws applying, but human technology functions most of the time. The military base is sometimes behind the rift and sometimes in the interzone."

"Rifts don't move." Remi must be misunderstanding him. "Also, the military couldn't have built a modern facility on Riftworld land. Not unless the base is a glorified mud brick castle that was defended by archers and swordsman."

"When the base was constructed, the rift was stable. The expansion and contraction of Riftworld territory began afterward." Lyall narrowed his eyes at Remi. "What information did Arimanius tell you to seduce out of Kaveh?"

"He didn't tell me." Remi had a queasy feeling that his father, as usual, had neglected to tell him key details about the job. "Once I have Kaveh under control, I'm supposed to contact Father and wait for instructions."

There was an uneasy silence between them. Remi wasn't supposed to trust Lyall. Not that he trusted anyone, especially members of his family. But his personal security was the dog's job, and Lyall had to obey his contract. Besides, he didn't think the hellhound was making this up. Remi, a consummate liar himself, had an excellent sense of when someone was bullshitting him.

"Well." Lyall's tone turned sarcastic. Or rather, more sarcastic than usual. "I have a suspicion your father is interested in more important information than Kaveh's thoughts on horse deworming."

"You think the drakones have developed the ability to move rifts and expand their Riftworld territory?" Saying it out loud sounded preposterous.

But Lyall knew a lot about rift technology. Some older members of his species could translocate by creating mini-hellmouths, similar to the smaller portals mothcats generated. But Remi had never heard of technology that could move a rift. That sort of power could expand or contract the Riftworld's presence on Earth.

He tried to come up with reasons to disprove Lyall's theory. "Why wouldn't they have kept the larger territory if they have that sort of power?"

"Maybe they can only move the rift temporarily." Lyall shrugged. "Or maybe there's a price to pay to keep it in the new position. Either way, it means the Saguaro Rift drakone clan can control their rift. This has to be what Arimanius is after."

Plenty of people would pay any price for this secret, Riftworld or human. The military would be particularly interested. That part worried Remi, but multiple bidders made for a higher price and his father was the leader of the Colony. Or, as many of Remi's mafia-movie obsessed cousins called him, the Don. In the end, Arimanius would decide what was done with the drakones' secret.

"Could anyone in the monstertown be bribed to get us more information?" Remi had access to many things people coveted: local currency, alien tech like Bug, and an impressive collection of Riftworld porn.

"Unlikely." Lyall sounded definitive on the subject. "Having the drakones at their backs keeps them safe, and since the giant flying snakes leave the town alone, no one wants to endanger that arrangement. Especially because the drakones don't often lose when it comes to fighting. The townies want to be on the side of the winners."

Remi knew it wouldn't be that simple. Besides, the drakones would want to hoard their secret like they did everything else. Only someone close to them could help him. "That makes it even more crucial I get information out of Kaveh."

Which was not going to be easy.

"I get that the good doctor isn't falling for your usual slutty charms." Lyall crammed another piece of beef jerky in his mouth, chewing noisily as if he wanted to annoy Remi on purpose. Which he undoubtedly did. "Did that hot assistant of his have anything useful to say?"

Lyall usually had impenetrable mental shields, but Remi didn't need his psychic powers to know the hellhound found Kat attractive. Remi knew Lyall preferred men, since determining sexual preferences came easily to him, but the dog was too damn grouchy about his involuntary servitude to drool over cute humans. In fact, Lyall claimed he would never lower himself to sleep with one.

"Kat told me Kaveh is asexual." Remi allowed his arm to drop over his forehead in languid despair. "Well, maybe demisexual. And he wants someone...nice."

Lyall laughed so hard he choked on the beef jerky and had to cough up a piece into his hand. He popped it back into his mouth. "I've met full-blood kraken more softhearted than you."

Remi sat up, annoyed. "I can pretend to be nice for a week. Or at least a day or two. I'll rescue someone's cat or feed an orphan. How hard can it be?"

Lyall huffed in amusement. "I'm looking forward to seeing this plan of yours fail utterly. So far, the only thing that worked on him is me. Maybe I can pretend to have a cactus thorn in my paw."

"I'm not desperate enough to need your help getting a mark into bed." Remi forced himself to get up. Time to try out that luxury shower in the bathroom and not think about how fun it would be if a naked Kaveh joined him. "Kat signed me up for a slow ride near the rift that Kaveh's leading tomorrow morning. I can check out the area and hit on him at the same time."

"Good luck." Lyall strolled over and opened the door. Normally, Remi wasn't supposed to let the dog run off and stir up who knew what kind of trouble, but he had already taken off the collar that kept Lyall in his terrier form. Breaking more of Father's rules wasn't going to make things any worse if he screwed up this job. "Somehow I don't think that's the type of ride you're going to enjoy."

6

Kaveh wasn't pleased Remi Gatti had signed up for the afternoon activity to see the rift. It was the trail ride that brought guests closest to the rift, and he accompanied the wranglers every time as added security. Something about the vid streamer from the Northeast bothered Kaveh. Maybe more than one something. After all, Remi was a reporter of sorts, and Kaveh didn't want anyone looking into his past. Remi also had a cocky air about him, as if everyone he met would fall in love with him.

Still, Remi wasn't all hat and no cattle. Kat had been gushing about the streamer's stunning blue eyes and charming smile, and even Garreth had commented that he was a fine-looking young man. Of course, the ranch owner's positive opinion might have a lot to do with the good publicity Remi's numerous online subscribers could bring to his business. The ranch was doing well, but the extra money spent on helping Riftworld animals and keeping the normal horses and livestock healthy cut into profits. Garreth and his wife's tendency to be generous to a fault to employees and their families also didn't help, although those values were exactly what had drawn Kaveh to this place.

Kaveh sat on Ranger, an ordinary bay quarter horse who wasn't able to transform into a killing machine, unlike Amanita, and kept an eye on the vid streamer. Remi was waiting outside the corral where guests mounted their horses for the group ride. He had changed into more casual clothes, but even his T-shirt and jeans looked too well pressed and new for his own good.

None of that bothered the three other guests vying for Remi's attention. One was a teenage girl who found everything he said hilarious, and another was an older man whose frank stare at the man's body made Kaveh feel uncomfortable on Remi's behalf. The third, heaven help him, was Jeanette, a tall blond wrangler in her thirties who usually had a good head on her shoulders.

Remi flashed his quick smile at his admirers, appearing unfazed by all the attention. Kaveh couldn't understand the effect the man had on everyone, but then again, he never had a knack for recognizing sex appeal. The blogger was objectively attractive, friendly, and even had a charming pet dog. There was no reason Kaveh should be suspicious simply because everyone found him fascinating.

Yet he still was.

One by one, the guests stepped up onto a platform and mounted a waiting horse. Some of the regulars had particular animals they had bonded with on earlier trips, and others had been selected based on the guest's height, weight, and riding experience. Remi was almost as tall as Kaveh but with a much slimmer build. He had put down that he had little riding experience, and he did look uncertain as Jeanette encouraged him to take a seat on Pogo, a well-mannered Appaloosa who was a good choice for novices.

Pogo was not, as it turned out, a good choice for Remi Gatti.

As Jeanette was encouraging the streamer to swing his leg over to get into the saddle, Pogo turned his head and snapped at Remi, raising up and bucking at the same time.

Given his awkward position and the suddenness of Pogo's attack, Kaveh was surprised at how deftly Remi twisted away from the horse and managed to get both feet back on the platform, putting distance between himself and the animal.

Jeannette wrestled with Pogo's reins, and stammered apologies in Remi's direction.

Kaveh nudged his horse into a quick trot and rode over to give her a hand. Even Ranger snorted at the blogger, and Kaveh had to reach out with his mind, sending calming mental images to both animals.

"I don't know what's got into him." Jeannette was clearly embarrassed and baffled by the horse's behavior.

Remi, for his part, didn't seem startled or unsettled at all. There was a hard set to his mouth for a moment, a fleeting expression of annoyance, and then he was all smiles, dismissing the need for apologies and joking that the horse must not have liked his cologne. He turned his blue eyes in Kaveh's direction.

"Thank you for riding over to rescue me." Remi had an olive complexion a little darker than Kaveh's, with a spotless white cowboy hat set over his jet-black hair and enough stubble on his cheeks to look fashionable. He was, in fact, wearing cologne for a two-hour trail ride, a scent of sage mixed with rosewood, along with a faint whiff of fresh grass.

Kaveh's sense of smell wasn't as enhanced as his vision, but he could use it to tell that someone or something was wrong, and he might have been able to do that with Remi if not for the damn perfume.

"Jeannette, move Pogo away for a minute and I'll have Remi ride Ranger." Both animals had taken a strong dislike to the man, but Ranger's bond with Kaveh was strong, and as long as he rode alongside him, the bay gelding should behave. "Sorry about that, Remi. You can stay close to me until the animals settle down."

Kaveh swung down off Ranger and helped the man mount his horse. It could have been his imagination, but Remi seemed to become more awkward and unsure than was warranted, grasping on to Kaveh's arm with his slim fingers before he settled into the saddle.

"Well." Remi stretched out his long legs on either side of the horse as Kaveh adjusted the stirrups for him. "This is certainly a big horse."

"We have some Percherons who are even larger." Kaveh placed his hand on the horse's neck, calming Ranger down again. The horses' reactions to Remi were certainly unusual. Maybe keeping a close eye on him was a good idea.

"The bigger the better." Remi tilted his head toward Kaveh, as if he expected a particular response and was surprised not to get it.

"The larger breeds like the Shire and the Percheron were bred as draft animals." Kaveh was no extrovert, but he didn't have trouble making light conversation about animals with strangers. He had no idea why Remi was staring back at him with an eyebrow raised. Kaveh mounted Pogo, sending both horses relaxing thoughts as he urged the Appaloosa to stay close to Ranger and the vid streamer. "You may not be familiar with those names, but I'm sure you've heard of Clydesdales, another draft horse. They're strong, easily managed, and have great stamina."

"Oh, yes." Remi gave a little start as Ranger started to walk out of the corral but then settled into the saddle, following the line of mounted guests out to the trail. "Big, easily managed, and plenty of stamina. That's exactly what I'm looking for—in a horse."

It finally clicked that Remi was flirting with him.

It wasn't uncommon for him to miss these types of signals, but he always felt embarrassed when he did. He wasn't quite sure why Remi was interested, especially when the man seemed to have no shortage of admirers. Perhaps he flirted with everyone he met.

As he often did in these situations, Kaveh lapsed into silence, not certain how to respond.

Remi picked up the thread of conversation after another flicker of annoyance came and went across his face. "How close will we get to the rift? I thought the army had restrictions on civilians going into the interzone."

"When the military pulled out and abandoned their base, they stopped caring about people wandering close to the rift." Kaveh had been a child during the Sundering. That had taken everything from Kaveh—his parents, his birth clan, and any knowledge of his people, the Azdaha drakones.

Remi must be too young to remember that time, and of course humans saw the event differently. Media reports back then had screamed about monsters slavering for human flesh and described the rifts as the beginning of yet another apocalypse. The US military had wasted billions of dollars and the lives of many soldiers trying to wage war against the Riftworld, as had other countries. It hadn't worked. Human technology didn't function even at a distance from the rift when the storms blew in, and the powers Riftworld people possessed attenuated when they strayed too far from the barrier. That had led at first to a standoff and finally to grudging acceptance on both sides.

Now, twenty-five years later, the Monster Apocalypse was only one in a series of crises from the extreme weather of global warming to endless rounds of pandemics and the inevitable political unrest, and the rifts themselves were tourist attractions.

"The abandoned military base is past the hills." Kaveh pointed to the elevations in the distance. They were out amongst the saguaros now, the tall cacti interspersed with other plants evolved to thrive in the desert. It was a beautiful landscape, wild and unique, and Kaveh never tired of riding through it. "The rift expanded to include it after the army left."

He made it sound like a natural, unexplainable event. In truth, Kaveh's drakone clan had adjusted the border. Few knew that his people had learned how to manipulate the rifts, and that was a good thing. It was a dangerous secret.

"Is that where the dragons live?" Remi kept glancing from one side to the other as his horse brought him uncomfortably close to various cacti and their pointed needles. Kaveh sent another image to Ranger, this time of a nice crunchy apple if the horse got Remi through this ride without injury.

The question raised Kaveh's hackles, even if it wasn't unexpected. It was predictable Remi would ask about Kaveh's people, given that humans were obsessed with anyone or anything large and dangerous, and the drakones were among the most powerful species caught up in the

Sundering. They weren't as big a threat to humans as less flashy but more hostile species such as the ratkind, but such distinctions didn't mean much to the public.

"They're farther out, beyond another—barrier." Kaveh found that he didn't want to share even the most basic information with the blogger. It wasn't rational. Remi had come out here to write a travel post about Moon Star Ranch and the Saguaro Rift, and everyone knew the drakones were here. "The base has been resettled with wild Riftworld species. There's also a mixed settlement of humans and Riftworld people nearby that everyone calls the monstertown."

"I've been to the Witch City monstertown," Remi offered. "It's off the coast of Massachusetts, so the rift is in the bay. You'd be surprised to find out how many humans want to hook up with a water monster. Can't understand it myself, but I'm not going to kink shame anyone."

Kaveh didn't understand the overwhelming urge to have physical intimacy so many people—Riftworld or human—felt, an urge he didn't share. Attraction and love had come to him only once and likely would not come again. He was fine with that.

As for human-Riftworld marriages, Kaveh visited the Saguaro Rift monstertown frequently and had a clinic where he saw many patients in such relationships. He didn't talk about his work there even with his friends at Moon Star Ranch, like Kat and Garreth, and he certainly wasn't going to share that information with Remi.

"I suppose for some people it might work out," Kaveh said. "Love is strange at times."

Remi laughed at that. "I suppose that type of love could get quite strange indeed." Those words held enough innuendo that even Kaveh noticed. "The docudramas love to talk about the Matchmaker curse. You know, when some monster falls into obsessed love with a human and carries them off."

"I've heard of the Matchmaker, yes." Kaveh had heard far more than he wanted to. The Matchmaker was responsible for ending Kaveh's only romantic relationship. He certainly didn't want to talk about that with Remi, so he kept his gaze set on the path ahead.

They lapsed into a silence Kaveh welcomed. This man had a talent for finding topics of conversation that made Kaveh uncomfortable.

Marriage brokering in human society was an occupation for social busybodies who liked to bring people together, out of altruism or profit. The Matchmaker—whether it was a sentient creature or a set of natural laws which acted intelligently, scholars and the religious disagreed on this point—was viewed with deep respect in drakone society. It was a complex and ancient process humans would call magic and took into account factors no living individual could predict. The unions brought together by the Matchmaker might cement political alliances that would become critical decades later, or it might lead to warring factions reaching a mutually beneficial truce during times of conflict.

After the Sundering, the relationships brought together by the Matchmaker began to include inter-clan marriages that horrified traditionalists, including ones between rift people and humans. Ceto, the matriarch of a clan of aquatic drakones who lived offshore of Massachusetts, had recently been paired with a human man and was scandalously proud of her new husband.

The ride wove in and out of the famous saguaros, with shorter plants adapted to the desert climate interspersed at a distance that gave the impression the landscape had been planned out by an expert gardener. They climbed up a higher elevation, the horses picking their way through the rocks. The animals were extensively trained on the trails and could all but find their way out and back blindfolded.

At the summit, Kaveh gestured toward a cluster of cookie-cutter single family homes down in the valley. Other structures not resembling any human architecture sprouted amongst the buildings.

"That's the Saguaro Rift monstertown. It was a housing development in progress when the rifts opened worldwide. Now it houses about a thousand inhabitants." Kaveh pointed to the remains of the abandoned military installation, gray and gloomy against the tawny desert landscape. "The base is also home to numerous Riftworld species."

The ranch guests nudged their horses closer, chatting amongst themselves about monsters and if they might see one. An older woman with a professorial air about her asked a question about water rights, a fraught topic in Arizona and the West in general. Kaveh explained the interspecies agreement that allowed water to be shared across the rift, allowing both the monstertown and Moon Star Ranch to be fully supplied with the rare resource.

He left out that he'd been the one to negotiate the agreement. It wasn't a secret that Kaveh facilitated communication between the drakone clan and human society, but he didn't like to advertise it either.

Remi put on a pair of dark sunglasses, appearing uninterested, but Kaveh had the sense his eyes were assessing the settlement with more than the typical curiosity of a guest at the ranch.

"Do the mons there allow visitors?" Remi asked. "Salem's version gets quite a few tourists."

"By invitation only," Kaveh snapped back more sharply than he had intended. He tried to add a friendlier note as he started down the mountain slope to the final viewing point on the ride. "Except on Wednesdays. There's an open-air market and getting permission to visit and shop is usually granted for small groups."

"I'm not one to miss an opportunity to go shopping." Remi tensed as Ranger stumbled on a loose stone, swaying for a moment before moving faster to catch up with Pogo. Kaveh was certain the horse had done it on purpose. "I'm sure Garreth could get me in. Would you like to join me and tell me all about the scary townies we might meet?"

There was an intensity to Remi's voice, as if the words took an unusual effort to say, despite his light tone.

"I have a clinic in the afternoon." Kaveh didn't want to add that the clinic was in the monstertown and he could easily spend the morning there with Remi. Was this more flirting, or did the blogger genuinely want to learn about the community there? Maybe he was being too hard on the man, so worried about his own secrets being revealed that he was finding conspiracies where none existed.

They approached a turn in the path, and Kaveh was relieved to hear the amazed gasps of the guests in front of them. There was nothing like a first look at the rift to bring an end to an awkward conversation.

A few kilometers away, the saguaro forest ended in a rippling wall of light and color. The phenomenon had been compared to the aurora borealis, and it stretched up from the ground to soaring heights against a clear blue sky, extending hundreds of kilometers in length. The natural laws of this world didn't apply to it, so even though it was little more a meter in depth, entering it on either side meant traveling to the piece of the Riftworld that had been sundered from the whole.

It was Kaveh's home—and it wasn't. As much as he was

grateful for the care and protection the drakones there had given him as a child, he didn't feel he belonged among them. And since he wasn't human, he didn't fit in on this side of Saguaro Rift either.

Kaveh brought his horse to a halt alongside Remi and sent out more soothing thoughts to Ranger so he didn't try something while the blogger was distracted by the view. As he did so, a long shape appeared in the sky, and the guests began to exclaim and point overhead.

Above them floated a red-and-gold drakone, a massive serpent swimming through the atmosphere as if it was water. Xiang Jao —Kaveh recognized his clan matriarch in her stunning aerial form—twisted and floated in intricate patterns. Two more drakones came into view, Rhys and Tarasque, Xiang Jao's two husbands. The three of them must have decided to take a mating flight out past the boundary.

Well, today's guests were certainly getting their money's worth.

Kaveh was soon barraged by questions from the group, starting with why the drakones resembled giant floating serpents as opposed to the winged and fire-breathing reptiles depicted in human myth and legend. That led into explanations about marital relations among air drakones and their dual forms, one humanoid and the other enormous and aerial. The conversation took all of his concentration, and he only had a chance to see Remi's reaction after Xiang Jao and her husbands turned back and swam out of sight through the rift.

The blogger had been oddly quiet during the excitement of the drakones' appearance, and he cupped his hands around something when he noticed Kaveh's attention.

"I was trying to take a picture with my watch." He did an

excellent imitation of an embarrassed grin. "Silly, right? Everyone knows tech won't work out here."

Ranger snorted then gave a mild buck, little more than a wiggle, but Remi wasn't expecting it. He grabbed the saddle horn with both hands, and the watch he'd been holding tumbled to the ground.

Kaveh swung off Pogo and bent over to pick it up. There were reasons the ranch staff advised guests not to bring along Earth technology on a ride this close to the rift. Losing a smartwatch wasn't the worst that could happen.

He glanced at the object then froze.

The wriggling butt of an insect stuck out of the polished surface of the watch, disappearing into it as the organism fused itself with the human technology.

Remi had a cyberbug.

The Riftworld beetle-like animal bioengineered itself to merge with human electronics, and Kaveh was sure Remi had used his enhanced smartwatch to download the insect's visual memories of Xiang Jao, Rhys, and Tarasque.

Very few humans had access to cyberbugs, and most of those were in the military. Remi didn't strike Kaveh as the military type, and that wouldn't explain the odd reaction of both Pogo and Ranger to the streamer.

It was more likely that Remi, like Kaveh, wasn't fully human.

Remi had been able to hide his Riftworld parentage from Kaveh but not from the equine senses of Pogo and Ranger. The vid streamer could simply be reluctant to out himself as being mixed. Or maybe Remi was here for more than racking up views on his online program. He could have been sent by one of the drakones' many enemies.

He could be a spy.

Kaveh handed the watch to Remi and forced himself to

smile. There was no getting around it—he needed to find an excuse to spend as much time as possible with the blogger to find out who he was and what he wanted. His nonexistent flirting skills weren't of much use, but Remi had provided him with an obvious opportunity.

Kaveh needed to ask Remi out on a date.

7

Remi was feeling generous after dinner, pleased with how well the day had ended, especially given how badly it had started out. He even put his own name on the honor system bar for a cactus fruit margarita and took it back to his room.

Lyall was sitting at the edge of the bed, still in his human form and wearing more of Remi's clothes. It didn't matter. Remi was in a good enough mood to overlook these minor irritants.

"I thought you'd be out with your new cadejo friend." Remi relaxed on the sofa and waved his drink in the dog's direction. "Otherwise, I would have brought you a margarita. I've got good news."

"I can smell that fruity abomination from across the room, and that's not a real drink." Lyall sounded grumpier than usual. Honestly, the dog had no collar, no curfew, and had been doing nothing on this job. He should be in bad doggy heaven. "What's so good about it? Did you and Kaveh finally get busy?"

"Not yet." Remi tried to wrench his mind away from how

fine the vet looked on a horse, with those broad shoulders and muscular arms. The cowboy boots were also a plus. Maybe Kaveh could leave those on when they both got naked. "But he asked me out on a date. He's showing me the Saguaro Rift monstertown tomorrow. Plus, three of the drakones were banging each other in the clouds during that horse ride I had to go on. The matriarch Xiang Jao and her two husbands. I used Bug to get images of them, the entire monstertown, and the base area, all from a safe distance."

"There's no safe distance from a drakone." Lyall drummed his fingers against the bed, a sullen expression on his face. "You should know all about that, given you almost got eaten by one last summer."

Remi didn't want to relive the humiliation of that particular job. "Even I have a bad day every five years or so. I've got this one in the bag. I threw everything I had at Kaveh during that damn horse ride, and nothing seemed to affect him. But after watching some dragon sex in the clouds, he came around."

"I don't think you should go after Kaveh." Lyall sounded downright bossy. What, he didn't think Remi was capable of seducing the veterinarian without using mind tricks? "You're in over your head, and Arimanius shouldn't have sent you here."

"This is a simple seduce-and-run job." Remi had been feeling so happy about Kaveh asking him out. No, not happy, only pleased he had the mark's attention. "I'll have him wrapped around my little paw, and then I'll call Father and let him handle the rest."

"The same father who came close to getting you killed by Ceto, the most dangerous drakone on the East Coast." A little growl punctuated Lyall's words.

"That was Zale's fault." Remi's cousin Zale, a half kraken,

had totally fucked up a job near the aquatic rift offshore of Salem, Massachusetts, and Remi had nearly been eaten by a terrifying—yet insanely sexy—aquatic drakone.

Remi pushed those unpleasant memories away and flashed a grin and pulse of seductive energy in Lyall's direction. He never tried that stuff with the dog, but it would either annoy him enough to end the conversation or distract him from it.

Nothing would go wrong. Remi would go on a date with Kaveh in the morning and end up in bed with the hot doctor tomorrow night.

"I'm going with you to the monstertown." Lyall responded to Remi's sneak psychic attack by unexpectedly going into dad mode, not that Remi had any experience with his real father worrying about his welfare. "The drakones are trouble, and someone needs to watch out for your fuzzy little ass. Do you even know anything about them?"

"Of course I do." Remi did his best to sound indignant because he didn't know that much about drakones, other than that they were rich, powerful, and hated the Colony.

"No, you don't." Lyall was too damn good at seeing through Remi's lies. "First of all, the drakone clans aren't all the same."

"Some of them swim and some of them fly." Remi drawled that out, as if the conversation was tedious and unnecessary instead of terror inducing. He didn't want to know more about the drakones. He wanted to sleep with Kaveh—only to get information from him, of course—and get the hell back to Boston. "They can command the sea or the air in full Riftworld form or walk around looking like the creature from Black Lagoon."

"Air, water—and land. You're not including the most

dangerous drakones of all." Lyall sketched the Riftworld symbols for those elements in the air, and the pulsing red sigils remained floating above him until they gradually faded away.

Remi didn't like when the dog did stuff like that. Some Riftworld abilities were close enough to what humans called magic that even Remi used the term. Anyway, Lyall was dangerous enough as a fighter without adding in fancy tricks, and Remi had thought he couldn't do anything like those sigils with the servant compulsion in place. Maybe it would best not to mention it. If Lyall ever broke free of the Colony's hold on him, he would want revenge, being a hell-hound and all. And even though Remi wasn't even close to being the dog's most hated member of the Colony, he had no interest in being an incidental casualty of Lyall's wrath.

"How the hell do you know so much about them?" Remi asked.

"None of your goddamn business, so stop whining and listen to me." Lyall rolled off the bed. To forestall more arguing, Remi pulled a bottle of single malt scotch out of his shopping bag. He had picked it up as a bribe to improve Lyall's terrible attitude, and this seemed a good time to give it to him.

Lyall grunted and snatched the bottle from him then grabbed a water glass and poured himself a solid slug of the liquor. "It's about time you got me a real drink. Smelling that fruit punch you call a cocktail is pissing me off."

"Like you're ever not pissed off." Remi sipped his cactus fruit margarita, which was a little sweet, granted, but well deserved after all the hard work he'd put in today. "Okay, you're old and know a lot more about drakones than I do. Go on, dazzle me with your knowledge."

"Ceto is water, of course, and the head of Saguaro Rift

drakones, Xiang Jao, is air." Lyall sounded very sure of himself.

Remi's anxiety rose. Maybe it was only the mention of Ceto that made his inner chinchilla freak out.

"Xiang Jao is from the Loong clan. After the Sundering, she gathered together a group from other air clans and formed an alliance with Ceto and the water drakones. Dangerous enough on their own. But the land drakones— you can think of them as giant worms that can burrow up through the earth—are even more deadly. Their clan, the Azdaha, hunted everything, including other drakones. They're big, vicious, and some of them can call up a poisonous fire called summ. Even people in my war-crazy pack don't want to fuck with someone like that."

"I heard something about the Azdaha once." Remi didn't remember much about that conversation, possibly because he was excellent at ignoring information he didn't know how to deal with. "I thought they were one of the drakone clans left behind when the rifts opened."

"There's a rumor that Xiang Jao found a juvenile Azdaha caught up in the Sundering and brought them into her clan."

"Okay, so the matriarch may have a super-dragon fighter." Remi's head was spinning, and half of his drink was still in his glass. "It can't be Kaveh." There wasn't any way a killer dragon with poisonous fire that could terrify hellhounds was working as a veterinarian at a dude ranch. "This isn't a problem as long as I follow standard ratkind operating protocol and seduce, steal, or con my way to get what Father wants. I'm not going to provoke a full-blown war."

"A lot of people, human and not, would go to war if they thought they could gain power over the rifts." Lyall knocked back another slug of whisky and glared at him. "Anyway, I

want to check out the abandoned military base. I've heard
disturbing rumors about what lives there."

Remi considered his options. He could ignore the dog, of
course. But Lyall didn't often give out free advice, and
insulting a hellhound was never a good idea. He could force
the dog to stay in the cabin all day, which would infuriate
him, even if Remi could manage that type of compulsion
now that the collar was off.

A thought struck him. Why not manipulate Lyall into
doing what he wanted? After all, that was Remi's usual
modus operandi, and he was quite good at it.

"Look, I don't need a third wheel on this trip." Remi
reached out with his powers, this time aiming to increase
Lyall's sexual desire for a target the dog was already interested in. "But I could convince Kaveh to bring Kat along."
Remi wouldn't have missed the mental equivalent of Lyall
perking up his ears even without his ability to sense lustful
emotions. "I'll plant a strong suggestion he comes with us
and takes you on a little stroll around the base."

Lyall appeared torn for a moment, but in the end, he
listened to his heart, instead of his brain. Or maybe a
different organ. "That makes sense. You see what you can
learn from Kaveh, and there'll be a good reason for me to be
sniffing around if Kat is with me."

"Plus, you get to spend the day with the hottie vet
assistant." Remi raised his margarita glass in a toast. "A win-
win for both of us. Let's drink to it."

8

R emi hadn't expected to ride out to the monstertown in an air-conditioned limo— although it would have been nice—but he had forgotten that transportation in these parts involved getting on a horse.

He stood waiting for Kaveh near the stables, watching as the early risers among the ranch's guests saddled up for a morning ride and headed out. The horses had no trouble sniffing out his ratkind heritage, and like most Earth animals, they took a strong and instant dislike to him. He had tried using some of his magic on Ranger—yes, that was the brute's name—but the whole gelding thing made Remi's attempts to stir up the horse's lustful side less effective.

Sure enough, Jeannette was leading Ranger out of the temporary stables the animals were brought to in the morning. Remi recognized the animal by the white stripe on his nose, as well as the snort of fury Ranger gave when he got a good whiff of Remi. The cologne he put on to throw off Rift-world people who could pick up the ratkind by scent didn't work on Earth animals.

Kaveh walked out next, and Remi could feel his pulse quicken as the man strode forward holding the reins of another horse, this one all white. The vet patted the animal's long neck, murmuring something that sounded soothing even at this distance. Damn, those shoulders. Remi couldn't wait to see Kaveh with his shirt off, with everything off, in fact.

Well, maybe not the boots.

He was so busy running through sexual fantasies in his head about Kaveh that he paid little attention to the horse as he stepped into the corral and made his way over to the man, putting on his most flirtatious smile.

"Good morning." Kaveh gave him a brief nod, his expression more of anxiety than enthusiasm over their upcoming date.

Remi would have to work a little harder to get the man to loosen up.

"I thought you might want to try a different horse today. This is Amanita."

"She's so pretty," Remi said without glancing at the horse. He dug into his pockets for the treats the staff kept at the front desk. They were crumbly and smelled like stale cat food, but he was trying to blend in with the guests, who couldn't get enough equine quality time. "Maybe she wants a horse cookie."

He slid his gaze reluctantly away from Kaveh to the animal as he held out a treat.

The horse regarded him with liquid black eyes that appeared even darker against the animal's pale fur, and her nostrils flared.

Remi startled, pulling his hand back. He couldn't do much with his sense of smell, even on the rare occasions—rare as in once since adolescence—that he transformed into his ratkind alter form. Still, the scent of bitter almond mixed with burning metal was distinctive. And familiar. He had picked up the same smell at the petting zoo.

There were many rift species that could take on an equine form but only one with poison fangs that could sink into flesh and psychic powers that could melt brains.

Kaveh had brought the mother of the baby repoequus on display in the petting zoo for him to ride. Mixed, since she could hold the shape of an Earth horse, but still dangerous.

Lyall's warning came back to him, a nagging irritation from his subconscious. He pushed it away. Kaveh was human. He had to be. The drakones didn't mess around outside their clan. The vet took care of Riftworld animals, and maybe his bosses had given him a dangerous one to play with.

Remi gave Amanita a hard look, and she glared back at him. The species was rare, and Remi had never encountered one before coming to the dude ranch. They were known for confusing their prey with awake nightmares, having a toxic bite that could do damage even to a drakone, and possessing an all-around nasty disposition.

On the positive side, she didn't hate him for being ratkind, as a regular horse would.

Images assaulted the edges of his mind, views of blood and lightning, alternating with disturbing flashes of dismembered bodies of rodents strewn in sizzling pools of acid. A primal terror rose up in him, a sense of panic that he was stuck in a nightmare and couldn't wake up.

Remi's telepathic abilities revolved around emotions or images involving sexual attraction. He wasn't sure how his ability could block a psychic attack by a repoequus, but he was not about to let this damn demon horse ruin his date with Kaveh.

He pushed back at her onslaught with every horse porn image he could remember.

The awake nightmare of gruesome sights ceased, and Amanita huffed, which Remi chose to interpret as her being mildly impressed.

"Maybe Remi would prefer a different horse." Jeanette had come up to them, eyeing Amanita with concern. At least the pretty blond wrangler had some sense of self-preservation, unlike Kaveh. "She had a foal recently and might be a little...skittish."

The images from Amanita returned, this time tinged with fondness, and included a mental picture of the baby repoequus, complete with dripping fangs.

"Adorable." Remi said that out loud, since this telepathic exchange had stretched his abilities to the max. "I'm sure Amanita and I will get along just fine."

Remi directed that last part at Kaveh, who had been watching him with his head tilted, assessing him. Was this all a setup?

"Let me help you into the saddle." Kaveh motioned to the platform, and Remi trotted up the steps and waited as Amanita was brought around. Fortunately, the repoequus had decided Remi was her kind of monster. He settled into the saddle, wincing as he stretched his thighs out and let Kaveh adjust his stirrups. This trip was far more athletic than he had planned on.

Kaveh swung into Ranger's saddle, and the repoequus jerked forward to follow the real horse out of the corral without guidance from Remi. The vet glanced at him as they rode away from ranch. "You seem more comfortable on Amanita."

"I'm getting the hang of things." Remi decided to try to combine his seductive abilities with old-fashioned flirting, given that his encounter with Amanita had gone well. His voice grew sultry. "Although, if you have any suggestions on how I could move better, let me know."

Kaveh nodded, not showing a hint of reaction to Remi's best attempts to be suggestive. "Try to move with the horse. Sometimes we tell less experienced riders to sit as if they had a hundred-dollar bill in their back pocket they need to watch out for."

Remi gave a few pelvic thrusts, pouring waves of lust in Kaveh's direction.

"That's better." Kaveh gave him the barest of smiles then looked up and waved. Kat was riding toward them on a black-and-white-spotted horse, with Lyall trotting along beside him.

Remi held back a long sigh of frustration. He understood that Kaveh was ace, but he had never failed so utterly with a mark. Worse yet, the less his seductive wiles worked on Kaveh, the more his own interest in the man grew. That never happened. Yes, some of Remi's marks were more attractive to him than others, but the sex was a chore, yet another job his father assigned to him.

"The terrier's coming with us?" Kaveh's face broke into a smile for the first time as he gestured at Lyall, who sat, tail wagging. Damn the man. None of Remi's usual tricks did anything to the veterinarian's chilly exterior, but the dog only had to sit on command and Kaveh was fawning all over him.

"Remi suggested I take him, and..." Kat's adorable face scrunched in confusion, as his currently clear mind tried to make sense of his lust-dazed agreement with Remi's plan last night.

"If Remi's coming to the monstertown, Lyall might as well." Kaveh gave a smile that was as reassuring to Kat as it was concerning to Remi. He again wondered if this was a trap. Even if Kaveh was human, his drakone masters must have told him about potential threats. The drakones hated and despised the ratkind, and the feeling was mutual.

More importantly, how the hell had Kaveh remembered Lyall's name but barely exchanged a few words with Remi?

Remi was still stewing about that a half an hour later, when they descended the rock-strewn hill and headed toward the monstertown. The outer barrier to the interzone Lyall had mentioned had no visual manifestation, unlike the glimmering air rift in the distance. When they crossed the demarcation though, Remi sensed a shift similar to one during a rift storm, the natural laws of earth weakening, and his ratkind alter form coming closer to the surface.

Given how Amanita had tried to take off after a jackrabbit that crossed their path, the last thing Remi wanted was to reveal his chinchilla alter form, which could best be described as snackable, from the repoequus's point of view.

The monstertown was a gated community of sorts, with an eclectic collection of half-buried trucks, shipping containers, and hunks of concrete forming a wall around it. Paint peeled off an ornate sign from before the Monster Apocalypse that read: Cactus Flower Estates. Ornate, wrought-iron gates flanked by a pair of stone Chinese guardian lions led into the main street of the development.

Kaveh and Kat dismounted as they drew close to a lean-to structure with a trough of water and wooden posts located about sixty meters from the gate. Remi had planned to pretend he couldn't get off the horse by himself, but his heart wasn't in it.

He swung off the repoequus, sending more naughty horse images her way. A ripple of emotion came from her, dangerously close to amusement.

"I can't believe you rode Amanita out here." Kat took her reins and secured them to a post in the lean-to. "She was so well behaved too."

He took a leash and collar out of one of the saddle bags, and Lyall came running up to him, vibrating with pleasure as the vet assistant snapped them into place. The dog gave Remi a wink.

Lyall was such a horny little bastard.

"I'm going to take Lyall for a walk to see the old military base." Kat's perky expression faded into bewilderment again. Remi could almost hear his internal confusion—*why do I want to go there?*

Lyall pulled at the leash, tugging the cute vet assistant in the direction of the abandoned military installation. Remi had a brief flash of anxiety. If there was any danger in the monstertown, Lyall wouldn't be close if Remi needed help.

On the other hand, the dog wouldn't be close to Kaveh. Remi had never thought the surly hellhound would be competition, but Kaveh was a special case.

"The perimeter should be safe during the day, but don't get too close." Kaveh gestured toward the gray walls in the distance, about halfway to the glimmering light of the Saguaro Rift. "The dog may get too alarmed for you to get anywhere near the outer fence anyway. Earth animals are terrified of the phantoms' scent. As they should be."

Phantoms? More Riftworld mons Remi had never heard of. Maybe they were the source of the rumors Lyall had been talking about. Anything deadly enough to worry a hellhound wasn't the kind of trouble Remi was looking for.

He considered asking Kaveh about the phantoms, but the vet had turned to walk to the monstertown.

Remi hurried to catch up. He fell into step beside the vet, who was, yet again, aloof and unreachable. The strong and silent routine was getting old.

"Riding Amanita went well." Remi edged closer to the veterinarian as they walked toward the monstertown front gates. He smelled like leather and spring rain, and it was all Remi could do not to sniff him. "I take it she's the mother of that baby demon unicorn in the petting zoo."

"Amanita made a connection with you." Kaveh gave him a sidelong glance. "I thought the two of you might have something in common, and it seems I was right."

He didn't put any challenge in the words, but Remi was once again left wondering if the man suspected his true identity or was merely a terrible conversationalist.

Fuck it. Remi couldn't take this anymore. He gave up on his seduction magic and snapped back, "Like killer looks, a great body, and a charming personality?"

Kaveh chuckled, which Remi hadn't expected at all. "Two out of three maybe. Amanita has quite the temper."

"I never get angry," Remi said. "I get even."

That provoked a full laugh from the veterinarian, which was a hell of a lot better than anything Remi had achieved with his compulsion abilities.

They stopped in front of the gates, the late morning sun hot and yellow overhead. Kaveh bowed to the male dog lion then turned and gave a deeper bow to the female.

"Greetings, Dr. Salehi." The female dog lion turned her head, her stone-like skin wrinkling as she did so. "We see you have a guest."

"Remi Gatti. Nice to meet you." Remi didn't have to feign surprise at the discovery that the statues were living guardians. He had met a few Riftworld creatures with a similar gargoyle-like appearance, but these two were much more impressive. They looked like they could do a lot of damage to anyone trying to attack the town.

The gates swung open, and he and Kaveh stepped off the dirt road that led into the town and onto the paved surface of Main Street, Cactus Flower Estates.

Otherwise known as the Saguaro Rift monstertown.

The town looked like its history—part suburban housing development, part recycled military junk, and the remainder total bizarreness. Some of the inhabitants had tried to recreate Riftworld architecture, including one house-like structure with walls covered in scales that rippled from the muscles underneath and a roof covered in tufts of coarse hair.

"The farmers' market is in the main square." Kaveh gestured down the street to a central park.

There was a buzz of noise from that direction, and as they walked, a bicyclist with bright pink hair under a helmet decorated with dragon scales zoomed past them in the direction of the square. Remi couldn't tell if the person was Riftworld or human.

"It's early, so they'll be setting up," Kaveh said, "but I'm sure you'll get some great interviews."

Remi wanted to hear that laugh again, deep and joyful, but he had no idea what had brought that side of Kaveh out. Remi had acted like himself, which was so not the way to get a man. Still, Kaveh seemed to appreciate bluntness.

"What do the townies here think about the drakones?" Remi tried to slow down to match Kaveh's steady pace as they walked. They were close to the same height, but the vet's gait seemed deliberately slow, as if he didn't want to rush bringing Remi into the heart of the monstertown. "I'd think they'd be unhappy about having giant dragon overlords."

"The drakone clan would only intervene if there was a serious threat to the town's inhabitants." Kaveh answered his question with a solid finality. He was a loyal minion, that much was clear. "This monstertown abides by local laws and ordinances for the most part."

"That sounds like a big caveat." Remi wondered what information Lyall might bring back from his jaunt with Kat to the military base. He had better be focused on getting good intel and not on the twink who was walking him on a leash. Their cover would certainly be blown if Lyall transformed into his human form—or worse, his hellhound manifestation.

"With the exception of the clans who live inside the base, who have a limited understanding of human society, everyone here is interested in coexisting peacefully with their neighbors." Kaveh paused at the entrance to the park, where a mixed group of humans and rift people were setting up stands for the Saturday market.

Amidst carts for selling desert art and cactus fruit drinks, Remi spotted Riftworld displays featuring foods not likely to be appreciated or even digestible by human palates, along with textiles, furniture, and body decoration entirely alien to Earth. Remi preferred to keep himself as fully in the human world as possible, but shopping excursions that included these type of items didn't come along every day. He had been banned for life from the closest spot to Boston, the Witch City monstertown.

The two of them walked through the market, with nearly everyone calling out greetings to Kaveh or coming up to give him a hug. Remi tensed after every one, as if he was jealous—which was ridiculous. He hadn't even slept with the man yet, and Remi never felt possessive about the marks he was sent to seduce.

Somehow, Kaveh was different, and different wasn't a good thing. It was dangerous.

Remi had left his drone back in his room, not sure how reliably pure Earth tech worked in the monstertown. He gave his watch screen a discreet tap, getting a confirmation from Bug that the town's wi-fi was functioning. After sending a firm command for Bug to stay inside, Remi pretended he had an ordinary smartwatch and cobbled together a video stream by asking touristy questions of the vendors at the farmers' market. He ate cactus flower candy and filmed Kaveh smiling as he made the rounds.

They stopped by another stall, this one featuring a version of a Riftworld drink made with spiced milk. The two vendors were a couple known as the Goat Sisters. One was a cheerful human woman wearing a garish sundress, and the other was her wife—who wasn't human at all. She came from a Riftworld clan often called fauns, with a humanoid upper body and a lower body complete with hooves and a tail. The two of them had a herd of goat-like animals with mixed Riftworld ancestry who had suffered various ailments, all treated by Kaveh. The women couldn't stop talking about one newborn mon whose life the vet had saved. Remi got it all on the stream, switching from a funny bit where he made faces as he drank the milk to the poignant moment when the baby goat, now healthy, nuzzled Kaveh. The views were astounding, and Remi basked in the flood of effusive comments from his subscribers.

They finally moved on, after Kaveh's efforts to pay for Remi's drink were firmly rebuffed. It was a similar story with everyone they met—the stories of Kaveh's medical cures, anxious rift people asking him about new symptoms, and more full-body embraces that made Remi wish he could get away with hugging the vet.

After the first half hour, Kaveh started to relax. Remi had reined in all of his lust magic and hadn't made a suggestive remark the entire time. This was an unprecedented level of self-control on his part.

"You're a popular man," Remi said. "Rave reviews from all of your patients."

"I'm fortunate I can help them." Kaveh greeted yet another well-wisher, a young woman with purple hair and a dress covered in puppy designs. A large dog with black fur and glowing eyes loped next to her, and Remi had to hide his shock when he recognized Lyall's collar around his neck.

This had to be José and his pet human, only thanks to the collar, the cadejo was on a leash. Why were they walking around like this?

Remi tried to cover up a nervous swallow as he scanned the market for an escape route, his earlier bubble of happiness popping out of existence. This could be bad. If Kaveh connected Lyall's collar back to him, not only would Remi's mission go down in flames—he could personally be in danger. He doubted Kaveh would get violent if he suspected the truth, but the townspeople might not react well to a spy from the Colony with a hellhound bodyguard sneaking into their farmers' market to gather intelligence about the drakones. He could make an excuse to leave Kaveh's side and make a run for it, but the only option for getting back to the ranch was riding Amanita. Anxiety rising, Remi missed the first part of the woman's interaction with Kaveh, but her next words made clear what the problem was.

"It was fun at first, but now I can't get it off." The woman's oversized glasses were purple as well, making her look like a little kid dressed up in her grandmother's closet discards. "And José can't tell me how because he's in his alter form and can't come out of it."

Kaveh dropped down into a crouch, inspecting the collar with a frown. "Jessie, where did he get this?"

Remi tensed. But Jessie gave a helpless shrug, and the cadejo only let out a low whine. Lyall had created a disaster. Although the Colony's hold over Lyall didn't depend only on the collar, the tech it used was specific to binding and controlling a prisoner. If Kaveh brought José back to his drakone masters, they would undoubtedly recognize it, and the number of Riftworld clans with access to this type of construct was limited. Especially after the clusterfuck in Salem last summer, the drakones were on guard for more trouble from the Colony.

Remi could get the collar off the cadejo, but he had a hard time imagining how he would do that and keep up the pretense of being a clueless human taking a tour of a monstertown. If he didn't do something though, Jessie might give Kaveh enough details to incriminate Lyall and, with him, Remi.

"I'm great at getting these things off." Remi dropped down next to Kaveh and reached for José's collar, ignoring the cadejo's warning growl. "Lyall is always getting burrs under his."

Remi knew his babble made little sense, but he had to say something. He closed his fingers around the leather-and-metal-studded restraint device and sent the collar a mental image of a zipper being pulled down.

José jerked his head back, perhaps in preparation for sinking his teeth into Remi, but the collar was already off.

Remi wasted little time backing away, waving the now inert device in the air.

A snarl escaped the cadejo's jaws as he collapsed to the

ground, writhing about as the transformation from dog to human form played out. In a moment, a handsome, dark-haired man in his twenties climbed to his feet, dusting off his jeans.

Remi rearranged his expression from relief to the shock and awe that would be expected from a human with limited experience with Riftworld people. Inwardly, though, he was impressed with José's smooth transformation. Maybe the cadejo had a talisman similar to Lyall's living leathers but a more fashion-forward version.

"Thank you!" Jessie flung herself at Remi and wrapped him in an embrace before planting a kiss on his cheek. "Kaveh, your new boyfriend is awesome."

9

K aveh didn't know how to feel about Remi. He had gritted his teeth and asked the streamer out on a date, focused on his duty to protect the clan and uncover what Remi was up to, if anything.

So far, the date wasn't as awful as he thought it would be. After Remi had mercifully stopped with the flirtatious jokes that Kaveh didn't get, things had smoothed out. Kaveh could catch glimpses of the real Remi—sarcastic, intelligent, more than a little unsure of himself, and good at hiding it. Helping him stream a video about Kaveh's friends at the farmers' market had been fun.

But one thing was clear. Remi wasn't human.

Amanita's reaction had raised Kaveh's suspicions that Remi had a Riftworld background, given his ability to turn away her psychic attack. He felt guilty about standing by as the repoequus mentally assaulted the vid streamer, but perhaps she had wanted to challenge Remi. Amanita had done the same to Kaveh when they first met, but she only caused humans who came near her to feel unsettled and spooked. Remi, for his part, had done something back to the repoequus and clearly gained her respect. Aside from Kaveh, no one else on the ranch had been able to ride her, although she would tolerate grooming and snacks from Kat.

Any doubt that Remi was mixed had vanished when he deactivated and removed José's collar. The cyberbug fused on Remi's phone was suspicious enough, but the collar was Riftworld tech that a fully human individual couldn't have removed, which was why Jessie needed to ask for help. Kaveh had wanted to get a closer look at the device, but the cadejo had grabbed it back from Remi before Kaveh had a chance.

Now it was only Kaveh and Remi, alone together in the clinic office. The first-floor room had been kept frozen in time as a medical practice before the advent of computerized records. Shelves held patients' charts with color-coded tabs in alphabetical order, all with notes typed out on an antique typewriter sitting on a metal desk from the 1950s. The monstertown had universal internet some of the time, but Kaveh needed access to charts during rift storms.

Remi had offered to help out while Kaveh saw a few patients, so Kaveh put him to work cleaning the aviary cages in the back. They held rescue birds, mostly Riftworld hybrids who shouldn't have been kept as pets by humans in the first place. It was a dirty job, and Kaveh was surprised and somewhat impressed the streamer had agreed to do it.

"Those cages were disgusting. The one you warned me about, Snow, gave me a good nip when I took him out of his cage." The streamer slumped into a chair, holding up a swollen finger wrapped too tightly in blood-dampened Band-Aids.

He made a valiant attempt at a forlorn look in Kaveh's direction, but the attempt at puppy-dog eyes was so out of character that Kaveh burst into laughter. Remi stiffened for a moment, as if expecting to be mocked. Then he beamed back, the first genuine smile Kaveh had seen on him. It lit up his face, beautiful and wicked at the same time.

"I'm doing my best to get sympathy here." Remi stretched out his long and lean body in the mid-century modern leather chair Kaveh had found at a vintage shop in Tucson. "I'm not used to this much honest work taking care of little flying monsters."

"Let me bandage that properly." Kaveh opened a drawer in his desk and pulled out a scroll wrapped in scaly leather and tied with an elaborately knotted string. He untied and unrolled it, lifting off one of the many strips of cloth marked with red sigils. Kaveh was not a born healer—his drakone birth clan were known for the awful poisonous fire of summ, not saving lives—but he could use Riftworld medical supplies.

A wary look flickered across Remi's face as he spotted the bandage, but it was gone as quickly as it came. Kaveh gathered a few more items and pulled his chair around the desk so he could sit closer.

Remi held out his hand, and Kaveh unwrapped the mess of Band-Aids, cleaned the wound with alcohol, and inspected the wound. It was a solid bite, enough to cause some bleeding. Snow was up to his old tricks again.

"This is a Riftworld healing cloth." Kaveh found that he liked the brush of his fingers against Remi's cool skin. This close to him, the faint scent of mown grass and fresh hay was more pronounced, as if the cologne the man wore had worn off with the passage of time and sweat from cleaning out the cages. "Snow's bite isn't poisonous like those of some Riftworld birds, but this material will work better than a regular bandage on a wound from his beak. Are you okay with me using it?"

"I can't pass up a chance to see alien medicine."

Remi lied well, but Kaveh was beginning to distinguish between the streamer putting on a front and a genuine response.

"At the zoo, you said Snow was half cockatoo and half mon." Remi's eyes flickered down to his bandaged hand resting in Kaveh's and made no move to pull away. "Is he in your care because neither side accepted him?"

Kaveh wondered if he could ease this conversation with Remi into a discussion of the man's Riftworld ancestry. Normally, he would feel it was rude to delve into another person's background out of mere curiosity. But these were not normal times, and Kaveh needed to know who Remi was and if he was a threat to the clan or the monstertown.

"Having a mixed background is a challenge quite a few of my patients face." Kaveh chose his next words with care. "But they have much to teach us as well. We all have to learn to work together, now that there are two worlds on one planet."

"That's a nice sentiment." Remi didn't have to spell out how little he thought of this optimistic view of Earth-Riftworld relations. "But there are plenty of people who won't accept anyone who came out of the rifts and mons who feel the same about humans."

"That's why I have Riftworld ambassadors like Snow, Flutterberry, and even Amanita's colt." Kaveh had to believe that his work trying to demystify the Riftworld would make a difference in the long run, even if there would always be some on both sides who wanted to reject peaceful interaction and embrace conflict. "Granted, Snow's little love nips don't help the cause for coexistence."

The last words were out of Kaveh's mouth before he realized how that sentence must sound. Remi raised his eyebrows. In what must have been a heroic show of restraint, he refrained from any sexual jokes.

A knock resounded through the office. Kaveh straightened, his senses on alert. He realized he had held onto Remi's hand longer than was strictly necessary.

"Come in," he said, but even as the door opened, he knew one of his kind was on the other side. His parents and their clan had once hunted down and killed other drakones, and his ability to track others of his kind was an innate, if disturbing, skill.

A tall drakone in his humanoid alter form walked in, iron-gray scales covering his skin, with a proud gaze and slit-pupil eyes. Over six meters in height, he was dressed in a linen tunic over patterned trousers and wore a woolen cloak bright with red, blue, and yellow stripes. A gold torc hung around his neck. The only thing missing from his traditional Welsh clothing was the spear he carried around at formal clan events.

Kaveh sucked in a breath. Rhys was here.

It was never easy seeing his former lover. The memories of their relationship—Kaveh's only romantic relationship, in fact—were conflicted. Kaveh had been hurt and angry when Xiang Jao had told him that the Matchmaker had intervened, and Rhys would become her second husband. Of course, no one could defy the Matchmaker, but he had wanted his lover to at least be upset by the sudden end to their romance. Instead, Rhys hadn't even been the one to tell him.

The past was in the past, and Kaveh knew it. What mattered now was why Rhys had come to his office. The drakones of his adopted clan, unlike Kaveh, couldn't pass for human. They disliked traveling to the monstertown and relied on Kaveh to pass messages along to the town council and to handle any interactions with humans in the outside world.

"Greetings, brother." Rhys spoke in the drakone language, and judging by the irritated look he threw in Remi's direction, he did so because he didn't feel inclined to include a human in their conversation.

Kaveh made a point of answering back in English. "Good afternoon, Rhys. This is Remi Gatti, who's visiting the ranch. Remi, this is Rhys."

Technically, Kaveh should have introduced his fellow clan member as the second husband of the Saguaro Rift matriarch to maintain even the lowest level of courtesy expected in clan etiquette. But Rhys knew the reasons Kaveh chose to live in human society and also why he didn't want any of the humans around him to know what he was. His ex had chosen to barge in, speaking in the drakone language and interrupting Kaveh's conversation with Remi. Like the older members of the clan, Rhys was treating him as one of the rare children from a drakone and human relationship—scandalous, inferior, and in need of protection and supervision.

Kaveh was tired of that attitude.

Besides, if Rhys had wanted formal courtesies, he shouldn't have interrupted Kaveh at work without sending word he was coming.

Remi rose to his feet, and his smile looked forced. His body had tensed and gone still, as a prey animal might when confronted by a predator. Not surprising of course. Rhys cut an intimidating figure, with powerful muscles under his scaled skin. His facial features must have looked strange and alien to Remi.

"It's an honor to make your acquaintance." Remi sounded confident, even enthusiastic, but both of his hands were curled and stiff by his side. "I don't suppose you'd be interested in giving me an interview?"

"I'm here to talk to Dr. Salehi." Rhys added in the human courtesy title, perhaps to point out Kaveh's lack of formal introductions. "I would appreciate you giving us some privacy for our discussion."

That was rude even by Rhys's standards, but Remi put on a charming smile and moved toward the door. "Of course. I'll go check on the bird cages again. If you change your mind about the interview, please let me know."

Rhys glared at Remi's back as the vid streamer slipped out. "He's not a resident of the town, I take it. Why did you bring him here?"

Kaveh tried not to bristle. Granted, Rhys was older than him, and his position as the matriarch's second husband gave him added standing in the clan. But Kaveh found it frustrating to be treated like this when he was a grown man with a respectable position in human society. That was one reason he lived and worked at the ranch. The other reasons were more complicated, and Rhys was one of them.

"He's a bard, of sorts." Kaveh had no idea how to explain what a vid streamer was to Rhys, especially since he had a limited understanding of Remi's job himself. "He intends to share stories about the ranch and the monstertown with a large number of humans. Anything that puts Riftworld people and the drakones in particular in a positive light with the surrounding communities is a good thing."

"It doesn't matter what they think of us," Rhys snapped, then let out of frustrated sigh. "In any event, I didn't come here to argue with your beliefs about cooperation with humans. The matriarch asks that you attend services and the communal meal at the end of the week."

It had been a while since Kaveh participated in the religious observances of his adopted clan. They weren't onerous, and in fact often provided an opportunity for introspection and self-evaluation. They were far more pleasant than the dark rituals his biological Azdaha clan was purported to have carried out. But he had been avoiding his family. He should have told them about the summ and asked the matriarch for advice on how to control it. The awful green flames hadn't returned, and the longer he waited to tell them about his new Azdaha powers, the harder it became to tell the truth. His heart pounded, an irrational fear sweeping over him that Xiang Jao had discovered his secret.

"It's been a while." Kaveh knew such a reminder didn't warrant Rhys coming into the monstertown in his humanoid alter form. "Is that all you came to tell me?"

Rhys shook his head. "No, there's more. The matriarch has received word of another Matchmaker pairing and wishes to discuss it with you and the entire family."

This wasn't about the summ, then.

A chill of unease ran through Kaveh.

"She thinks the Matchmaker chose me." Kaveh's mouth had gone dry, and although he already knew the answer, his heart sank as Rhys nodded.

It had been difficult giving up his relationship with Rhys years ago, but he'd moved on and accepted he was unlikely to form a similar attachment again. Demiromantic, a term he had learned from his human colleagues, described him well. He hadn't been attracted to Rhys until they had formed a close relationship, and not having a romantic or sexual partner didn't bother him. He treasured his relationships with his friends and family, and that was enough. What would bother him was to be forced into a romantic relationship by the machinations of the Matchmaker. Could it be a match with someone in the clan? The few family members who weren't married were older and wouldn't be a good fit even if Kaveh wasn't ace.

Rhys tugged at the open-ended circlet of gold the Matchmaker amulet had transformed into when the ancient sentience paired him with the matriarch. The object was one of the most revered communal treasures of the Saguaro Rift clan. It transformed into a new shape when touched by a clan member who had been chosen for Matchmaker pairing and then would alter again when the drakone honored by the Matchmaker gifted it to their spouse.

He held it out to Kaveh, his expression conflicted. "She asked me to bring the amulet to you in order to confirm this."

Kaveh didn't want to look at the thing, much less touch it, but he forced himself to take the gold circlet. It reformed in his hand, turning into a bracelet molded into facing griffins, with lapis lazuli and other precious stones embedded into the gleaming metal.

There was nothing he could do about it now.

The Matchmaker had chosen him, and Kaveh had no choice but to obey.

Rhys stiffened for a moment, but the pull of tradition and etiquette was too strong. "Congratulations, Kaveh. The Matchmaker has honored you. The amulet is yours now."

Just as the ancient artifact that expressed the will of the Matchmaker had transformed into a Welsh torc for Rhys, the object now reflected Kaveh's background. His biological clan had adopted the symbols of the human civilization near an ancient rift opened millennia ago, in this case, the Achaemenid Persian dynasty. It would change its shape again when his intended spouse touched the object, and then Kaveh would know who the Matchmaker had chosen to be his lifelong partner.

"Does she know who I've been matched with?" Kaveh didn't try to keep the dread out of his voice. The only remaining eligible members of the clan had no understanding of how the human world worked and understood Kaveh's preferences even less.

"Not someone in our family." Rhys made this sound like an unfortunate turn of events.

Kaveh's initial relief twisted into more anxiety as he waited for Rhys to tell him more. He knew little about the handful of other drakone clans that had come through the Sundering to Earth. Perhaps being paired with a total stranger would be even worse.

"The Matchmaker makes its decisions with knowledge we cannot hope to fully understand. It's our fate and our honor to accept the one chosen for us."

Kaveh puzzled over that convoluted statement before figuring out what Rhys was trying to say. His next thought was that Rhys could have tried out this little speech when he had learned the Matchmaker had paired him with the matriarch, rather than not talking to Kaveh about it at all.

"I've been matched with a human, like Ceto's husband?" Kaveh had only met Ceto, an aquatic drakone who lived off the coast of Massachusetts, once.

Her Matchmaker pairing had been with a marine exobiologist, which made sense, but his relatives bemoaned the entire affair as unnatural. The fact that Ceto and her new human husband were thrilled with their marriage had sent the traditionalists in the clan into a frenzy.

Ceto's husband had at least studied and interacted with aquatic rift people before being matched to what most humans would call a sea monster. How would someone without that background react if Kaveh revealed he was a drakone and that the two of them had been paired up by a mysterious and ancient Riftworld entity? Most of his human friends thought of drakones as exotic alien dragons, not as people.

"That's the most likely possibility, but I don't think even she knows." Rhys spotted the open roll of medical sigils on Kaveh's desk and frowned. "I thought I sensed something off about this Remi Gatti you brought here. It must have been the healing parchment. It's not wise to give out these items so freely."

Kaveh had no intention of sharing his suspicions about Remi having a Riftworld background with Rhys. His former lover had little interest or liking for humans, and he could be downright aggressive where other clans were concerned. "Remi had a phoenix bite while helping me with my work. The sigils work better on those than human medical treatments."

"There's something odd about him." Rhys cocked his head toward the door as if he heard something, then gave a dismissive shake of his head. "In any event, now you have an activated amulet. The matriarch will expect you to focus on finding the spouse it will reveal. Perhaps you could start with the humans you know here and at the ranch. If your future spouse is close enough to activate your amulet, those would be the logical places to search. Your intended is likely to be someone you already know."

Kaveh didn't feel like searching for a wife or husband he didn't want in the first place, but as before when the Matchmaker upended his life, he had little choice in the matter.

"Thank you for coming to tell me this." Kaveh stepped forward and embraced Rhys. He wasn't often physically expressive, but he still felt fondness toward his ex and wished they had remained friends. "I'll be prepared tomorrow to listen to the matriarch and find out what I need to do next."

Rhys appeared pleased with Kaveh's display of affection, even hugging Kaveh back. Then his expression changed to one of worry. "A human match is far from ideal of course, but the sooner they are found and brought into the keep, the better. Our enemies could find such a person far too tempting. Ceto's husband was targeted by the ratkind only last summer."

The keep was home and fortress to the drakones, but it was hard to think of it as a comfortable place for a human who might know nothing of Riftworld customs and history.

Kaveh turned the gold bracelet over in his hand. Regardless of his personal feelings, his duty was clear. He would find the person linked to him by the Matchmaker and protect them. As much as he hated violence, if any of the ratkind tried to harm his intended, they would learn why the Azdaha were the most feared clan in the Riftworld.

10

Remi started to walk toward the aviary as soon as the conversation between Rhys and Kaveh began to wrap up. His ratkind hearing had allowed him to listen in to the conversation while loitering a few meters away from the door to the office. The spot made it easy to slip into the room that held Kaveh's winged patients and pretend he had been working with the birds instead of eavesdropping.

It had been a lucky break to come to the medical clinic with Kaveh. Rhys was condescending to Kaveh but didn't treat him like a servant or an errand boy. Lyall was right—Kaveh had to be part drakone and unusually adept at holding a human alter form. This would change his father's calculations about the operation. A half-human drakone who was accepted by the full clan was far more important than a human minion. The bombshell that Kaveh had been paired by the Matchmaker with an unknown partner was even more critical information.

Lucky bastard, whoever the unsuspecting spouse-to-be was. Remi couldn't help feeling a pang of envy. Kaveh was gorgeous, had an incredible body, and as a member of a drakone clan, was insanely rich. Not to mention that he was also smart and skilled with his hands.

Big, strong hands that had held Remi's a few moments too long.

No, this was all a ridiculous daydream, and Remi needed to get his head in the game. Kaveh had been a challenge to seduce even before this revelation, and now he would be focused on finding his one true love. Given the drakones and their tendency to hoard anything they coveted, the unknown human would be tucked away in a safe corner of the drakones' stronghold as soon as Kaveh figured out who they were.

Remi should contact his father and brief him on this new development. If the Colony could find the Matchmaker's choice first, they would have leverage over Kaveh and the whole drakone clan. A hostage like that would be worth a secret as important as how to control a rift, and Remi's mission would be a success. Remi could leave the kidnapping and dangerous parts to his violence-loving cousins and head back to Boston before things got ugly.

Before he had to face Kaveh after betraying him and putting his soulmate in danger.

He should sneak away now and try to send his father a message. Time-sensitive intelligence and all that. Instead, he chose to procrastinate, telling himself it was better to wait and see if he could learn more about the Matchmaker's choice. He stepped into the aviary, packed with cages and filled with the raucous screeches and cries of the animals inside. A pair of the winged, feathered reptiles called phoenixes, with brilliant red-and-gold plumage, called out challenges to one another while fire rippled along their extended wings. They were about the size of macaws, and

Kaveh had explained to him that the juvenile Riftworld creatures were recovering here from injuries. The vet had left out a few details, probably because he didn't want a human guest to know how dangerous they were. Mature phoenixes could erupt flames from their wings, growing larger and larger, and rain down fire and destruction from the air.

Remi's father had talked wistfully of buying a few to wreak havoc on their enemies, but Arimanius had never found a seller willing to let them go for a good price.

In a center cage, Snow, the half-phoenix cockatoo who had bit Remi, gripped his wooden swing and swung around in circles like a gymnast on the high bar. Other than a red glow at the tip of his white feathers, he appeared to be an ordinary Earth parrot. As Remi approached, the bird paused, his black eyes sparkling with mischief. He lifted a clawed foot and extended it out, begging to be allowed to hop onto Remi's arm.

Remi wagged his bandaged finger in Snow's direction. "You fooled me once, my little friend, but you're not getting me twice."

Snow gave a puzzled squawk, as if he had no idea what Remi was talking about. He hopped closer to Remi, using his beak to move along the sides of the cage.

"Treat," the bird said, cocking his head in a cajoling gesture.

Remi laughed. "You want a present after biting me? Totally shameless."

He held out one of the Brazil nuts Kaveh had cautioned him were only occasional snacks. Remi had given the devilish parrot four of them already.

"Kaveh told me you're half mon, like me. Prove it, and I'll give you this."

Snow pulled his head back, indignant, but then fluffed out his feathers. Their red tips glowed brighter, and a few sparks floated down to the bottom of the cage like falling firecrackers. He followed the display by gagging out a small puff of smoke.

"Pathetic." Remi gave the bird the nut anyway, making sure Snow had no opportunity to take a chunk of his finger with it. "I guess us mixed folk need to stick together."

"You dirty rat." Snow did his best James Cagney impression, which was pretty awesome.

"Not a nice thing to say, Snow."

It was Kaveh's voice.

Remi froze, wondering how much of the conversation the vet had overheard. All of it, probably. That might not be a total disaster, as long as he didn't realize Remi had been spying on him and call the big drakone back. That Rhys guy creeped him out, and Remi didn't have Lyall by his side if things went south.

"Did your dragon friend leave?" Remi turned around and mounted a full charm offensive. Less lust than his usual version of mind control but often quite effective. Oh, right. If Kaveh was even part-drakone, psychic powers wouldn't work on him at all. "I'd have loved to talk to him more."

"You couldn't get out of my office fast enough to get away from him." Kaveh smiled. It wasn't a dazzled, charmed expression. It was an "I'm not buying your bullshit" look. "I overheard your conversation with Snow. It's hardly a surprise to me that you're not all human."

Remi wanted to snap back that he had overheard Kaveh's conversation with Rhys and knew he wasn't fully human either, but that would be suicidal. He wasn't thinking clearly, mainly because the vet was so damn attractive it was infuriating. And even worse, the man was resistant to his best moves. He opened his mouth to come up with a better lie, but Kaveh cut him off.

"I'm from a Riftworld background myself." Kaveh stepped nearer to him, and with Snow and his beak behind him, Remi was more or less trapped.

This close, the scent of leather and rain that Remi had come to associate with Kaveh was downright intoxicating, and the man was close enough that Remi could feel his body heat. It would be so tempting to lean in and kiss him. No, if Remi's lust magic didn't work, simply grabbing the man and sticking his tongue in his mouth certainly wouldn't.

"Would that background have scales and a taste for golden treasure?" Remi kept his tone as light as he could, but all he could think about was running his hands over Kaveh's chest and unbuttoning his shirt. Maybe there were scales over those amazing pecs, and the thought of that sent heat straight to his groin. He needed to get a grip on himself —and not the part he was thinking with right now.

"I have drakone blood." Kaveh worked his mouth for a moment before continuing. "But I'm always as boring and human as I appear now."

Nothing about Kaveh was boring to Remi.

"No one at the ranch knows that about me, and I won't tell them about your background if you want to keep it private." Kaveh searched Remi's face, as if worried that Remi was going to run screaming out of the room. "You also don't need to tell me what clan you're from, if you even know. But I have a problem I need help with, and you might be the one person I could ask."

Remi, against his will, closed more of the distance between them. The room felt too warm, and his pants were becoming uncomfortably tight. It was as if his own manipulative abilities were being deflected back at him. He had never crushed on anyone this hard before, and why his body was reacting this way to a man who wasn't sexually attracted to anyone, much less him, was a total mystery. He focused again on Kaveh's words, not his body. They had entered into a negotiation, and Remi needed to keep his wits around him.

"What do I get out of this arrangement?" Remi once again went with honesty, which was totally unlike him.

"I could do an interview with you and tell you about drakone society." Kaveh took a deep breath. "It would surprise a lot of people, but I'm going to need to...move on, in any event."

If Kaveh's drakone clan planned to marry him off to whatever random person the Matchmaker wanted, they would also pull him back from his work in the monstertown clinic and the ranch. He'd be back in the drakone stronghold, with a bewildered and perhaps unwilling spouse, and all the people who depended on him for medical care for themselves and their animals would lose him. Remi rarely had reason to be grateful for his ratkind family, but at least members of the Colony didn't have their life partners assigned by the malfunctioning matrimonial process that ruled the love lives of the so-called higher clans.

"All right." Remi could hardly stay in character and not accept the offer. Any vid streamer would give up a limb for this sort of access. The drakones were beautiful, dangerous, and mysterious. An interview like this would be fought over by media outlets and be worth a fortune. "So, how can I help you?"

Kaveh pulled a metal object out of his pocket. It looked like loot from the heist of a Middle Eastern museum exhibit —a solid gold bracelet studded with jewels.

Remi had to shove both hands into his pockets. The temptation to steal it was that strong. But it was a Riftworld artifact, probably cursed, and trying to steal gold from a dragon was a good way to get dead.

Kaveh stared down at the priceless object in his hand as if the winged lions depicted on it would come to life and devour him at any minute. Then he lifted his head and locked eyes with Remi. "You said you knew about the Matchmaker. I need help finding the person it's chosen for me."

Remi and Kaveh rode back to the ranch mostly in silence. For once, that wasn't the vet's fault. Remi needed time to process the opportunity and risks that Kaveh's offer presented.

Kaveh had asked Remi to help him find his...well, soul-mate sounded ridiculous, but there were worse options, like assigned life partner. Remi knew a fair amount about the Matchmaker curse, as the Colony called it. He hadn't understood quite how important it was to the drakones, wrapped up in tradition and also part of their religious beliefs. Kaveh asking a virtual stranger to help him fulfill his obligations to the Matchmaker seemed risky, even desperate. It wasn't a step the vet would have taken if his relationship with his drakone family was as close as it should be.

Rhys had made marrying a non-drakone sound like a highly undesirable outcome, which might explain Kaveh turning to Remi for help. The drakones were known for their snobbery about who they considered beneath them—basically every other Riftworld species and especially humans. Maybe Kaveh had integrated into human society to find out more about that side of him and get away from his relatives. A drakone partner would be a step up for the vet, but Kaveh hadn't sounded happy about the development even before he had learned his arranged spouse was a clueless human. He was being railroaded into marriage, essentially.

Remi needed to stop worrying about Kaveh's feelings. His job was to help the Colony win against the drakones, and being asked to find the Matchmaker-assigned spouse by Kaveh was a huge stroke of luck. In fact, holding Kaveh's future spouse hostage might lead to a quick ransom deal and avoid conflict that could end up with a high body count. In a way, Remi would be the good guy in all of this.

Sort of.

"How will this Matchmaker deal with you being ace?" Remi asked, tired of trying to convince himself he wasn't a horrible person. The two of them were riding side by side through the saguaros, the late afternoon cooling off as clouds scudded in overhead. "I mean, if it's love at first sight and all."

"No idea." Kaveh shook his head. "I've only been in a relationship once when I was younger, and we had grown up together in the keep. I knew him for years before I felt attracted at all."

The drakones had raised half-human Kaveh in their stronghold across the second rift barrier and made sure he was protected. Interesting. Some clans didn't let their mixed children live with a con-artist mother skipping from one catfishing scam to the next and then call the kid in to do their dirty work when he turned fifteen.

Remi pushed away thoughts of his childhood and focused on the diamond mine of information Kaveh was giving him about drakone society. Then something clicked, a crucial detail the vet hadn't told him outright.

"Wait, if you grew up with the drakones, was Rhys your boyfriend?" Remi had immediately disliked the insufferable drakone when he had barged into the office, interrupting the first time Kaveh had touched Remi.

Damn, was he actually mooning over holding hands with a guy? Especially a guy who had an intended spouse Remi was going to help kidnap.

Kaveh stared down at his saddle for a long moment. Ranger gave a soft whinny, as if sensing the mood change in his rider. The vet gave his neck a fond pat before answering. "Yes, Rhys and I were together until the Matchmaker made their decision."

"The decision to have him break up with you and marry someone else." Remi couldn't say what he was thinking out loud. As bad as the Colony could be, at least the ratkind weren't ruled by the Matchmaker's power. If a human or someone from another Riftworld clan married someone from the Colony, they became part of the family, for better or worse.

Usually worse.

But saying that would be insensitive, even by Remi's admittedly low standards. Besides, Kaveh hadn't pushed for more details after learning Remi was only half human, and that was a good thing. Remi didn't have a solid cover story that involved a loving parent who wasn't associated with organized crime. "Who did he marry?"

"He's the matriarch's second husband." The words came out flat. "I'm hoping the person the Matchmaker has selected for me isn't already in a romantic relationship."

"And if they are, what will you do?" Remi asked. Kaveh might only be half drakone, but with the clan behind him, anyone currently banging the lucky dragon bride or groom would be smart to back off. "You could ride on in, throw them on the back of your saddle, and drag them away to your hoard."

Kaveh visibly flinched. "Absolutely not. I wouldn't want to break up a happy couple or, even worse, a family. But I can't leave the person the Matchmaker has chosen for me alone. The sentience involved has creative and sometimes unpleasant ways of bringing people together. Besides, Rhys is worried the individual might be in danger. The drakones have many enemies who might go after a human linked to our clan. There was a worrisome incident involving the ratkind in Salem, Massachusetts last summer."

"I think I heard something about that." Remi had, in fact, been the ratkind behind the incident in question. He meant to steal an amulet of immense power and value from a marine biologist married to an aquatic drakone. Ceto, the biologist's wife, did an excellent job of living up to the sea monster stereotype and almost eating Remi. It had been a disaster, and Remi was lucky Ceto's husband Jal had distracted his wife with a promise of some hot married sex.

The less he and Kaveh talked about the ratkind and the clusterfuck in the Salem monstertown, the better.

He decided a quick change in conversational topic was in order. "Enough about what you have to do. Tell me what you *want* in a partner."

"I'm hoping the person will know at least a little about Riftworld society and be open to accepting the clan's protection." Kaveh sure was focused on keeping this guy—for some reason, Remi hoped they were looking for a man—safe. But Kaveh continued to avoid giving Remi any clues as to what type of person he wanted to spend the rest of his life with. "Most people would have run screaming when Rhys walked into my office. If this person has had exposure to Riftworld culture, like you, this would be easier."

Not fleeing in terror was a pretty low bar for a future spouse. After all, the drakones were rich and powerful, and money and influence made anyone more attractive. Trying to gently lead Kaveh into sharing wasn't working. Remi decided to take charge of the questioning. "You're still not talking about you. If I'm going to help, I need information. Let's start with sexual orientation, shall we?"

"I'm homoromantic and asexual." Kaveh cocked his head toward Remi. "And you?"

"Pan and so, so allosexual." Remi grinned at Kaveh and was rewarded with a curve of the man's lips. "Okay, let's move on to my favorite topic—sex. Are you sex-favorable or sex-averse?"

"Indifferent, I guess." Kaveh let out a breath, as if relieved Remi knew something about asexuality. "I enjoyed making love with Rhys, even though he usually initiated sex. But after we broke up, I haven't missed being intimate with someone."

"What type of men do you think are attractive, even in an aesthetic sense?" Remi asked.

Kaveh mulled that over for a moment. "Well, you're very good looking."

"Absolutely correct." Remi tried to ignore the butterflies in his stomach after that statement. "And yet I've been throwing myself at you for days without any luck."

"I wasn't sure why you would be interested in me." Kaveh frowned. "Granted, I'm not good at picking up those kinds of signals."

"You must look into a mirror at some point," Remi shot back. "It would be hard for me not to be interested."

"You're a lot easier to talk to when you're too frustrated to lie." Kaveh tilted his head to look up at the sky.

The brilliant sunshine was gone, dimmed by dark

clouds. It rarely rained this time of year, the ranch's website had said, but it seemed they might get a little wet. Remi allowed himself a brief fantasy in which Kaveh was so drenched he had to take his shirt off.

"This was the first time I've ever asked someone out on a date, and I was dreading it." Kaveh truly was terrible at flirting, but he seemed to be saying that his day with Remi hadn't been all bad. Progress. "I have no idea how to find the person the Matchmaker has picked for me, much less how to court them."

That should have sounded old-fashioned and stilted, but instead Remi felt another stab of envy toward the eventual object of Kaveh's affections. "Well, I'm great at dating." Not so good at relationships lasting longer than the con he was pulling, but he kept that to himself. "You can practice with me while I help you find the person the Matchmaker has decided you're fated to marry."

Kaveh didn't answer right away, his eyes on the horizon. Remi tensed. He had pushed too much. The vet had asked him for help finding the right person, and this pretend dating suggestion had taken things too far.

"It's only a rainstorm." Kaveh turned back to Remi with a relieved expression as fat raindrops splashed onto the dry earth around them. "Rift storms have been coming with increasing frequency the last few months, and that can indicate a superstorm is brewing."

"No rampaging horde of monsters is on its way. That's good." Remi enjoyed seeing Kaveh when he was happy and liked the fact the vet was smiling at him even more. He decided to make an even bigger bet. "How about we go into town tonight for a practice date?"

11

K aveh walked into the restaurant Remi had picked out for their first fake date, already feeling uncomfortable. It wasn't that the place was overly formal—in fact, it exuded a studied casualness. The clientele was young and well-to-do, the decor avant-garde, and the menu prices ridiculously expensive.

He could have guessed that last part without the online search he had performed while waiting for Remi to get ready. There had been plenty of time to learn about Tucson's upscale dining options. Kaveh had cleaned himself up and put on a Western blazer over a button-down shirt with a bolo tie before walking over to Remi's cabin, only to find that his date for the evening hadn't even made it into the shower. Fortunately, Lyall, the Scottish terrier, kept Kaveh company. Remi's dog was a little wary of Kaveh when he first arrived, sniffing him with the air of a concerned parent meeting their child's prom date for the first time. A few doggy treats won him over though.

Remi finally emerged, wearing a version of Western

formal wear that looked like it cost more than Kaveh's secondhand pickup truck.

"Expense account," he had explained breezily when Kaveh asked if he had bought the clothing on this trip.

The two of them now were being ushered to a table toward the back, and Remi took the seat that faced the door, leaving Kaveh a view of the open-air kitchen and its busy chefs.

"I like to check out everyone when they come in," Remi said before Kaveh even thought to ask about the seating choice.

He was as charming and affable to the staff as he was to everyone, but underneath his polished exterior Kaveh sensed uneasiness. Perhaps it had sunk in that he was dining out with a drakone, but Kaveh got the impression the streamer was also a little on edge about his surroundings. He couldn't imagine why. Remi fit in perfectly with the hip and urbane customers the restaurant catered to.

"It's too bad they don't allow dogs, or I would have brought Lyall." Remi beamed at the server who greeted them and ordered a frightfully expensive bottle of wine before Kaveh could protest. "He was quite annoyed I was going out without him."

"He's a good dog to travel with, then?" Kaveh asked. "Terriers can be very independent-minded."

"That's one way to put it." Remi counted his pet's faults off on his fingers. They were long, slender, and manicured— nothing like Kaveh's callused hands. Everything about Remi was at once elegant and unsettled, as if he might be ready to charm one minute and cause trouble the next. "He hogs the bed, ignores every command I give him, and eats constantly."

"Well, you did choose a terrier, not a French bulldog." Kaveh drew in a breath, unsure why asking Remi personal questions was so difficult. The streamer had certainly not held back with him. "Are those also your least favorite attributes in a romantic partner?"

"Most of my lovers don't stay around long enough to get on my nerves." Remi must have meant the statement in jest. It was hard to imagine someone as attractive and self-confident as Remi being unable to sustain a serious relationship. "Anyway, we're here to practice dating and discuss your list of possible matches. Let's start with what we know so far."

Before Kaveh could gather his thoughts, the server arrived with a wine bottle covered with Italian words Kaveh suspected he wouldn't have understood even if he knew the language. Remi pushed his glass forward. The waiter poured only a splash of wine then waited expectedly.

Remi gave the glass a lazy swirl, sniffed at it, then took a sip. After a pause too long not to be purely for the drama of it all, he announced, "This Nebbiolo is fantastic. You have to try it."

Kaveh thanked the server as he filled his glass and took a sip for courage. It was mouth-puckering dry.

At a nod from Remi, the server left, and Kaveh plunged in. "No one truly understands the Matchmaker, but there are traditional signs and rituals that have continued after the Sundering. My gold bracelet is meant to be an engagement notification. It transforms into a symbol that resonates with the drakone to be paired and does so when the prospective spouse is nearby. I'm fairly sure I know this person, maybe even know them well."

Had Remi noticed the piece of jewelry resembled objects worn by ancient Persian royalty? Kaveh tried to tamp down his anxiety. Even if the vid streamer had been interested enough to research the design, that wouldn't lead Remi to guess that he was sitting across from the only Azdaha on Earth.

During Kaveh's ruminations, Remi had tapped on his smartwatch, frowning at a text. Now he leaned back in his chair, appearing thoughtful. "Do you travel much outside of Tucson? Kat made it sound like you spend all your time working."

Kat. Kaveh repressed a groan. He would have to add him to the list of possibilities as well. His vet assistant was young and close to his large extended family, who would not be pleased with the young man moving to the keep. Not to mention that Kaveh thought of him as a little brother, not a husband.

"Only for professional conferences and not that often." Kaveh reached into his blazer pocket and pulled out the list he had jotted names on while waiting for Remi. There were two columns, labeled MR and MT. He added Kat's name to the first list and handed it over. "I'm certain it's someone currently at the ranch or in the monstertown."

Remi scanned the paper, his eyes intent with interest. They were an unusual shade of dark blue, a contrast to his black hair and olive complexion. Kaveh recalled more than a few conversations when people at the ranch had gushed about Remi's eye color. He hadn't quite understood before now why they found it so striking.

"There are men and women on this list." Remi took another sip of his wine, then typed something out on his watch with rapid-fire precision. "Are any of the monster-town residents on the list part or all Riftworld?"

"Some, yes." Kaveh hesitated. "I put them in order of how well I know them. I think—being demi and all—maybe the Matchmaker has arranged for me to develop a relationship with the person before the process becomes irrevocable."

"Nothing's irrevocable." Remi waved a hand. "Well, a few things, like death. But you don't want to back out of this."

"I can't." Kaveh touched his other pocket, the one that held the gold bracelet, which seemed more and more like a fancy handcuff. "It's my duty to my clan. The engagement gift will transform when I give it to the right person, but I don't want to spring this on someone. I'd rather talk to them one-on-one about what it would mean if they accepted the gift."

"You put Kat at the top of the ranch list." Remi raised his eyebrows. "Can't say I question your taste there."

"Let's try other people first." Kaveh felt rising panic whenever he thought of his young, naïve assistant becoming his husband. "I owe it to Garreth and Chrissie to tell them this is going on, and they're on the list anyway."

"What would you do with Garreth's wife, marry her too?" Remi started laughing as Kaveh gave a reluctant nod. "That's going to be an interesting conversation. I'd love to be a horsefly on the wall when you try to explain all of this to them."

Kaveh winced. "I'd like to keep that one private. But I might want your help with some of the others."

Remi pondered the list again. "How about you come clean about your matrimonial crisis to the ranch owners while I chat up some people in the monstertown? I've already gone there with you once, and people were willing to talk to me."

"How will you know if you've found the right person?" Kaveh asked. "Not everyone in the monstertown on this list will be eager to chat with an outsider about sensitive topics."

"Anyone who lives in the monstertown will know about

the Matchmaker." Remi paused, staring at the entrance to the restaurant. Kaveh turned to see a hulking man with a leather jacket over his shoulder and tattoos covering his arms walk in and glance over at their table.

"I'm the type of person people love to share things with." Remi pulled his attention back to their conversation, acting like he hadn't even noticed the man. "Plus, I'll bring Lyall. Nothing like a cute dog to soften people up." He pushed his chair back and stood up. "I'm going to the restroom, so take a look at the menu and order anything you want. I asked you out, so this date's my treat."

Kaveh meant to argue that point, but Remi gave him a look that indicated he was the dating expert here, and left Kaveh staring in dismay at the menu prices.

Given how long it took Remi to get ready, he wasn't surprised that his dining companion wasn't back until after Kaveh had examined every menu option multiple times. They had natural steak from the ranch, a luxury item even at wholesale prices, and the restaurant had added a significant surcharge on top. Kaveh supported the continuation of the ranching tradition that Moon Star Ranch represented, and the cattle were well cared for, but he wasn't going to have Remi pay that much for him to eat dinner.

Remi finally returned as the waiter was setting down a host of appetizers Kaveh hadn't ordered. Kaveh requested the expensive but not totally outrageous lab-grown steak, as Remi asked for a salad.

"Sorry, I got delayed by a call from one of the sponsors of my trip, so I made sure the staff brought something over to nibble on." Remi pushed over a bowl of blackened peapods. "The mesquite-grilled edamame here is to die for."

"Are you vegan?" Kaveh tried one and had to admit the beans were quite tasty. Then again, he thought everything tasted better after grilling. He wasn't going to convince Remi not to pay for tonight, so he could at least find out his food preferences and plan to repay him in some way.

Remi bit into one of the lettuce wraps, which had a southwestern-style filling of corn, black beans, and adobo sauce. "No, I've just been in a salad sort of mood since I got here."

"I enjoy playing around with my grill and my kitchen." Kaveh gestured to the multiple colorful but tiny plates around them. "Although I usually stick to simpler recipes and larger portions. How about I make you a home-cooked meal? I'm planning to speak to Garreth and Chrissie early tomorrow morning, and afterward we could take Amanita and Ranger and have a picnic lunch before heading into the monstertown together."

Remi laughed. "We haven't even gotten to the main course yet, and you're already hitting on me for a second date. Maybe I don't have much to teach you after all."

KAVEH WALKED over to Remi's cabin the next morning feeling better than he had in months. Telling the truth—or at least most of it—to Garreth and Chrissie relieved a burden of guilt and anxiety that had become such a part of his daily life he'd forgotten what it was like to be in a good mood.

The couple had listened with rapt attention as he explained his drakone background, the Matchmaker, and the likelihood his future spouse was someone he knew. He withheld the details of the bloodthirsty history of the Azdaha, as well as his manifestation of summ, and instead laid out the basic facts of his background.

Xiang Jao had found him in the care of a human family

in Isfahan, Iran, when she and other matriarchs had trav-
eled the post-Sundering world seeking others of their kind
stranded on Earth. Kaveh had been taken in as a foster
child, and the human family had little information about
his past. The matriarch had been able to sense his true
nature but not explain his entirely human appearance. It
was typical for drakones to hold a humanoid form until
adulthood, but no one would normally confuse a juvenile of
Kaveh's species with a human child.

Air drakones rarely attained their aerial forms before
fifty Earth years of age. Rhys, the youngest of the clan except
for Kaveh, had been a prodigy at forty when he soared into
the clouds. Their aquatic cousins, like Ceto, might live a full
century before transforming into their vast serpentine
bodies and diving into the ocean depths. No one knew when
or if Kaveh might be able to achieve an earth drakone alter
form. Even the oldest matriarchs of air and sea knew little of
Azdaha life and culture.

So here he was, he told them, a thirty-year old man
they'd known for years who might someday transform into
a dragon, and who was currently searching for a life partner
selected by an alien process akin to magic.

Garreth thanked him for sharing this with them, and
Chrissie added with a smile that they had suspected their
favorite veterinarian had more in common with his Riftworld patients than he let on. They reached out together
with intertwined hands to touch the gold bracelet, and to
Kaveh's immense relief the object had remained unchanged.

That left a good number of potential matches at both the
ranch and in the monstertown, but he would worry about
that later. Right now, he had a picnic lunch date with Remi
to look forward to.

Last night had been a lot of fun. Remi was a charming

dinner companion, regaling him with entertaining stories about live-streams that had gone disastrously wrong. Kaveh had relaxed enough to tell a few funny anecdotes about his own work, and Remi even pulled their server into the conversation. The young woman was a graduate student in exobiology at a local university, and Kaveh promised to send her an article he was working on about mothcats and their ability to translocate.

He had walked Remi to the door of his cabin and thanked him for a wonderful evening. Only later, as he sorted out his options for a simple but tasty picnic menu for their next fake date, did he realize why Remi drew out that final conversation so long.

He had been waiting for a goodnight kiss.

Kaveh once again wished he was better at picking up on these types of signals. Maybe that had been Remi's idea of a final exam after a night of teaching dating skills.

Maybe it had been more than that.

Kaveh walked up to the cabin, spotting Lyall sitting outside in a pool of shade. The terrier cocked his head as Kaveh lifted his hand to knock on the door.

"He's not even close to ready, is he?" Kaveh could have sworn the dog tried to roll his eyes when he asked the question.

Remi eventually answered the door, his hair sleep mussed and wearing a tight-fitting T-shirt, boxer shorts, and not much else.

After trying and failing to convince Remi he could come back later, Kaveh gave in and entered the cabin with the terrier darting inside with him. He busied himself giving Lyall a package of beef jerky while Remi dressed and performed what he insisted was an abbreviated version of his late, late morning beauty routine.

"The threesome with Garreth and Chrissie is off." Remi summed up and dismissed hours of Kaveh's internal torment in eight words. "And they're cool with you being a dragon. This deserves a celebration. I hope you packed champagne in the saddle bags."

"I brought mint-cucumber water," Kaveh said. "Given that it's not even noon yet. But hopefully the dessert will make up for the lack of alcohol. Plus, you said you were in the mood for salad, and I brought that as well."

"You remembered." Remi beamed at Kaveh as he splashed on a bit of cologne. "I promise I'll try anything else you made. Well, unless it's fried or greasy. Not that I'm picky or anything."

Lyall gave a short bark that sounded like a laugh.

Kaveh finally got Remi out of the cabin half an hour later. They headed out into the saguaros on Ranger and Amanita with Lyall trotting alongside them as Kaveh told him more about the picnic spot.

"It has a view of the old military base with some shade to make it more comfortable for the horses. We used to have our lunch ride end there—wine or beer with cheese and snacks, that sort of thing. But with the rift storms increasing in frequency, I convinced Garreth to keep those rides closer to the ranch."

"What's up with this base that has you worried about a rift storm?" Remi relaxed more in the saddle. He had made progress with his riding in only a few days. It helped that Amanita liked him, even giving Ranger a shove when the gelding tried to lean over and give the vid streamer a nip. "I thought the dragons were the boss of these here parts."

Remi added a ludicrous accent to that last part, and Kaveh couldn't help laughing, despite the topic under discussion. "My drakone clan and its matriarch Xiang Jao are responsible for security in our riftland and in the inter-zone that includes the monstertown and the base. That doesn't mean they govern the various clans who live here. Laws and customs are clan based in the Riftworld, although there are elders, like the guardians, who might be asked to mediate a dispute between clans."

"What kind of mons live in there, then?" Remi pointed at the gray bulk of the abandoned military compound in the distance. "It has a creepy vibe."

"You might be more sensitive to the psychic impact of the species there than a human would be." Kaveh saw Remi stiffen at that phrasing. Did he feel uncomfortable talking about his background even with someone who shared Rift-world blood? Remi had told him he had no idea what clan his birth father had been from and, like Kaveh, had only ever held a purely human form. "Many of the species there avoid sunlight and appreciate the protection the buildings give them to raise their young. One clan, though, has been trapped inside the base by design since the military pulled out. Humans call them phantoms. They're sapient inverte-brates who view all other life forms as a potential food source. They inflicted mass casualties on the troops stationed there."

"About that military pullout." Remi sounded only mildly curious. "How did the military even build the base if it's in a Riftworld interzone? Even basic human tech isn't reliable in an interzone, much less military weapons and electronics."

Kaveh paused a moment before replying. The true answer was that his adoptive clan had expanded the Saguaro Rift and could take over even more territory, a new power that had the potential to dramatically impact human and Riftworld interactions. No other clan had this kind of knowledge, and it needed to remain a secret. He knew little enough about it, as only a few members in the clan understood the Riftworld technology involved. Rhys had once confided to him that a crucial component of the system, an artifact known as the control object, had been placed in the phantoms' territory deep inside the base for safekeeping.

"I'm not sure." That sounded lame even to his ears. "There's a lot about how rifts form and behave no one understands."

Remi seemed satisfied enough with that explanation, and Kaveh spent the remainder of the ride pointing out the desert plant life and explaining how the indigenous cultures of the region used them to survive in the harsh climate.

They reached the picnic spot and tied up the horses. Kaveh had put together the meal last night from pantry staples and the fresh food he had on hand. After putting a tablecloth over the picnic table at the site, he spread out a mix of foods he loved, including a Persian salad with tomatoes and cucumbers, Caramelo tacos with a variety of local salsas, and pan dulce for dessert.

"I can't handle that you're an awesome cook on top of everything else." Remi sat back with a groan half an hour later, after polishing off a good portion of the picnic offerings. He hovered his hand over the last Mexican pastry on the plate, but Lyall stuck his nose in and gulped it down while Remi was trying to decide if he wasn't too full to eat it. "You're smart, sexy, and you can cook Persian-Southwest fusion, if that's even a thing."

Kaveh shifted in his seat, ever uncomfortable with praise. "I'm glad you like it. The restaurant last night was awfully pricey. This is pretty simple stuff."

"But you made it by yourself, for me." Remi waved at the brilliant sunshine and the base silhouetted against the glimmering colors of the rift. "And it's lunch with a view. I get taken out to restaurants all the time. None of my dates has ever set up a romantic picnic on horseback for me."

"I'm doing well with my dating lessons, then?" Kaveh took a sip of the mint-and-cucumber water, trying to cover up his uncertainty about where this pretend date was going. He should be focusing on finding the spouse the Matchmaker had chosen for him, but he wasn't sure he was ready for another fraught conversation with a friend right now. It was easier to sit here and chat with Remi, who understood the Matchmaker and knew Kaveh was a drakone. He hadn't realized talking to someone else with a Riftworld background who lived in the human world would be so freeing.

Remi raised his eyebrows. "A minus."

"Can I raise my grade with an extra credit assignment?" Kaveh truly had no idea how to flirt, but Remi nodded, laughing, so he guessed he had got it right.

"Let's walk off lunch." Remi stood up and stretched, then walked around the table to take Kaveh's hand. He gave his terrier a meaningful look.

Lyall gave a short huff then trotted off to join the horses in the shade.

It was a mild spring day, nothing like the searing heat of summer, but Kaveh felt overly warm all of a sudden. Remi wrapped his slender fingers around his, and the touch felt electric.

They didn't go far, only up an incline to another vantage point that gave them a different view of the rift. There was a boulder with a flat top that made a natural bench of sorts, and they sat down on it, Remi's thigh pressing against Kaveh's.

"It's a pretty spot." Remi angled his head toward the shimmering colors stretching up into the sky, but his eyes never left Kaveh's. A smile played around his lips. "But I'm not sure if it's worth extra credit on your fake dating report card."

"I could kiss you." Kaveh thought that was what Remi wanted, but he didn't want to assume anything.

Remi moved in to press his lips against Kaveh's so fast he misjudged and they bumped noses instead. They both laughed, and Kaveh reached around to put a steadying hand behind Remi's head, pulling him in close.

It ended up rougher than he had planned. It had been a long time since he had touched anyone in a romantic way. He had only ever been with Rhys, who never much liked kissing, even though Kaveh enjoyed it. His former partner had particularly disliked Kaveh being dominant in any way in their lovemaking.

But Remi melted into the kiss. His lips parted, open and inviting, and he moaned into Kaveh's mouth.

Kaveh intertwined his fingers into Remi's hair, enjoying the silky feel of it against his skin. He half pulled the streamer onto his lap, another maneuver that would have made Rhys furious, but Remi only deepened the kiss. Their tongues met, warm and seeking, and Kaveh felt his arousal grow as Remi ground his hips into him.

It had never been this way with Rhys, long and drawn out, with slow and sensuous movements. Remi kissed as if there was nothing more important in the world than the contact between the two of them.

They both needed to breathe at some point though.

Kaveh pulled back a fraction to take in air. "I love the way you kiss."

"Well, you're certainly getting an A in my class." Remi gasped that out before pressing more kisses against Kaveh's neck and jawline. "Do you want to do more? I want to taste you everywhere. I haven't been able to think about anything else."

"I'd like that." Kaveh barely got the words out before Remi slid lower, pulling up Kaveh's shirt and licking down his chest. He wasn't quite sure how Remi got past the combined barriers of his belt buckle, button, and zipper so quickly.

Remi gazed up at him, the pupils of his eyes so wide with arousal his blue eyes appeared almost black. "Do you like oral? I mean, most people do, but I need to be sure."

"Rhys never wanted—" Kaveh wished he could bite back the words. It didn't matter how Rhys had focused so intently on being the dominant partner both physically and emotionally. His intimacy with Remi was what mattered now, not bringing up a relationship that had died years ago. "If you're sure you'd like it."

"I'm positive about two things." Remi leaned forward to drag his tongue over Kaveh's shaft, and all rational thought evaporated from Kaveh's brain. "I'm much better than your ex could even dream of being at this, and I'm already loving it."

He took all of Kaveh at once, and the surge of pleasure from the warm heat of his mouth was overwhelming. Remi hadn't been merely boastful about his talents. The sensations piled up, and all too quickly the pleasure of climax swept over him. He tried to get out an inarticulate warning in case his partner wanted to pull away.

Remi did for a moment, before plunging back down. Kaveh climaxed so hard his vision whited out. The streamer had undone the top of his own jeans as well, so Kaveh reached down to stroke him into a release that followed a few seconds later.

For several moments, Kaveh couldn't do much more

than lay on his back, breathing hard, with Remi resting on top of him. He breathed in the man's faint scent of green grass and shut his eyes against the bright sunshine above them. Colors danced across his eyelids, an aftereffect of what had been the best sex he had ever had, in his admittedly narrow experience.

Then Remi said, "What the hell is the rift doing?"

12

A fter the make-out session and the mind-blowing sex, Remi would have been content to lie in the sun on top of Kaveh for hours. Instead, he had opened his eyes to see the unbelievable sight of the rift shimmering less than thirty meters away.

The damn thing had moved, shifting both the base and the monstertown into the fragment of Riftworld controlled by the drakones.

Kaveh acted surprised but not shocked, which made Remi suspect he knew more than he let on about his clan's ability to control their borders. But Kaveh was concerned enough to ride out immediately to speak to his family.

Remi had assured him he was fine riding alone to the monstertown—even if that now meant traveling inside the rift.

Remi was currently standing in a soccer field near the monstertown's central park which had been set up as a dueling ground for José and Lyall to have a throwdown. He had no idea how he had gone from a romantic picnic date with Kaveh to refereeing a dog fight in a matter of hours.

The townies had been friendly enough when he'd arrived, especially José and Jessie. Everyone had been tight-lipped and uneasy about the rift movement though. Remi made an executive decision to announce Kaveh's Match-maker quest while Lyall did the buddy thing with José. Somehow, things had devolved into him betting on a dog fight between two Riftworld badasses.

Most of the town's inhabitants, children included, had come out to watch and were perched on the field's bleach-ers. Lyall, terrier ears perked up, sat at his feet. The damn dog's tail was wagging, for fuck's sake.

This was a terrible idea.

Remi hadn't seen Lyall fight before, since during the only situation dire enough to require someone to kick ass, his cousin Zale, not Lyall, had been his bodyguard. This wasn't some kind of fight to the death or anything like that, but Lyall couldn't transform into his hellhound alter form without blowing their cover story.

On the other side of the midfield, José bounced around in designer sneakers, talking shit with a few of his buddies while his wife Jessie accepted more bets on the match while swigging beer.

José and Jessie were certainly a well-matched couple, aside from the fact that one was human and the other was a cadejo. In this town, though, that was the norm. Their audi-ence consisted of an eclectic collection of human and Rift-world singles, couples, and a few throuples, along with their mixed children. Everyone wanted to see this show.

At least Kaveh wasn't here—and hopefully wouldn't arrive until this was over. Remi had arrived in the monstertown alone except for Lyall, while Kaveh had trav-eled to the keep, the drakones' fortress inside the Saguaro Rift.

Of course, right now Remi was inside the rift—as was the entire town.

Jessie lifted her beer can to salute Remi then gave her husband a whack on the head to get him to concentrate on the match. Recovering his own focus, Remi did his best cowboy impression and tipped his hat in her direction.

The fight was on.

Jose's lanky body twisted, a contortion of limbs that looked downright painful. A few moments later, a huge black dog stood in his place, jaws open to reveal a wicked set of teeth. The beast stalked forward, an eerie purple light emanating from its eyes.

"I hope you know what you're doing." Remi sucked in a breath. Jose looked a hell of a lot bigger than he had when he and Jessie had come to Kaveh to remove the indenture collar they were using for a little BDSM play.

Lyall had led José to believe he was a benign Riftworld species known as a fairy hound. Like mothcats, some of them chose to keep company with humans, although Remi hadn't met one who mimicked an ordinary Earth dog the way Lyall could. No one had questioned the story, which was good, since even José wasn't dim enough to go up against a hellhound in this ridiculous display of testosterone-filled stupidity.

Lyall gave an unconcerned sniff, as if Remi's concerns were ridiculous.

Remi wasn't afraid for Lyall, of course, only annoyed this was taking so long. Kaveh could come back at any time, and he doubted the conscientious veterinarian would approve. Plus, he had bet a lot on this match, and José needed to lose.

The bet had been for information about who the Matchmaker had chosen as Kaveh's spouse. The dog-lion guardians knew something, but they hadn't wanted money if José won. They wanted information in return, and Remi would have no choice but to answer anything they asked. Wagers were serious business in the Riftworld, and Remi was in that universe now. Between that and worrying Kaveh would be upset about both the fight and the bet, his inner chinchilla was scratching around in his brain, trying to find a way out.

Remi knew that transformation would be disastrous and tried to breathe through his anxiety. There should have been an easier way than this to get information about Kaveh's Mr., Ms., or Mx. Right.

José let out a terrifying growl. Lyall bared his small teeth in a grin back at him. He charged forward, a streak of white, looking comically small compared to the slavering beast José had become.

The fight got rough in short order. José snarled and snapped, using the weight of his body to try and knock the terrier to the ground.

Lyall didn't do much. He was a blur of movement, sure, scooting under Jose's black-furred legs and dodging the cadejo's teeth with less than a whisker to spare. Maybe José might quit out of sheer annoyance, but Lyall wasn't doing anything to end this damn fight. Remi needed him to win so he could figure out if Kaveh's match was in the monstertown.

Then he would...do what, exactly?

Give his father and the Colony an update of course. He should have done it already, when Zale, his half-kraken cousin, had brazenly walked into the restaurant where Remi and Kaveh had been enjoying their first date. Instead, he had lied through his teeth and told Zale to back off, because he still wasn't sure if Kaveh knew anything.

Kaveh's reaction to the startling movement of the rift said he knew a lot.

Remi couldn't let his strange feelings for the man get in the way of doing the job the Colony had sent him to do. Sure, Kaveh was hot, and the sex had been incredible. Not that it shouldn't have been—Kaveh was ace, not a virgin, but still—it had been so different. Pleasurable, yes, but also intimate in a way that Remi hadn't experienced before. He never wanted to cuddle, for fuck's sake, but somehow Kaveh was special in a way that was terrifying.

Remi couldn't afford to think this way. As soon as he knew who the Matchmaker had chosen, he would let Zale know. His cousin would grab the hapless spouse-to-be before the drakones locked both Kaveh and the human into the safety of their keep. Remi and Lyall should be long gone by then.

Unless Arimanius ordered Remi to lure Kaveh's future lover to an easier spot to grab them.

In addition to deceiving Kaveh, Remi would use his abilities to seduce the vet's intended match and then kidnap the unfortunate human for good measure.

Why did this all feel so wrong? Kaveh was only another mark, and there was nothing remarkable about him. Except for his stunning good looks and amazing body. And his smile, which Remi had only seen a few times and wanted to see again, over and over. Then there was his intelligence, skill, and devotion to his work—none of which were qualities Remi had ever admired in the past.

Something was off about his emotional state, clearly. Maybe there was some malfunction with his seductive powers. It was like they had been turned against him, and he was falling for Kaveh and not the other way around.

There was a collective gasp, and Remi jerked his head to see the terrier lying in a heap on the ground. Lyall must have cut it too close and got clipped by the cadejo's lunges. He wasn't moving.

Shit, was he even breathing?

Remi tried to think of something, anything he could do and came up with nothing. His powers didn't work when another overwhelming emotion—in this case, demonic fury —had control of an individual. Running out to physically stop José wouldn't do anything except get himself hurt.

Kaveh. That's who he needed right now. The veterinarian could calm the crowd down and take Lyall away to his clinic and get him all fixed up. He would know what to do and take over, and everything would be okay.

Because Lyall had to be all right.

The cadejo pounced, jumping on the small dog with a howl of glee, and Remi's paralysis broke. He screamed at the huge black dog to stop and charged forward, any flicker of common sense or survival instinct going out the window. All he knew was Lyall—his know-it-all, sarcastic childhood companion and probably the only one in Remi's entire extended family he considered a friend—was hurt and he had to help him.

A hole in reality itself opened up in front of him, a mini-rift lined with dripping lava, smelling of sulfur and crackling with roaring flames.

Remi snapped. His human mind went blank, and his alter form rose to the surface. The chinchilla in him always chose the second option in the fight-or-flight reflex, and Remi hopped out of his pile of clothes in full furry form and ran straight into the hellmouth.

His momentum carried him through the small earth rift.

Remi's normally excellent chinchilla vision blurred, and after a few frantic blinks he realized nothing was wrong with his eyes. A dense fog had descended out of nowhere, so thick he couldn't see more than a handsbreadth in front of him. It made no sense. Fog didn't roll in this fast, especially on a sunny day in Arizona.

The mists parted, and an enormous creature moved toward him. Canine in shape, the monster had balls of flame for eyes and fangs like a saber-toothed tiger.

Remi had thought José was intimidating in his alter form. The nightmare that loomed before him made the cadejo look like a golden retriever puppy. He spun around on all fours and darted away.

He didn't get far.

The beast came after him, making up the distance between them with no effort. A paw pinned Remi to the ground, and all he could smell was sulfur and wet fur.

Then Remi was lifted up in the air, and the part of his brain that wasn't screaming in fear realized he was being held by a pair of hands, not crunched in the slavering jaws of a monster. He gathered enough courage to crack open his eyes.

Lyall, back in his human alter form and stark naked, held him at arm's length, shaking his head. "For fuck's sake, Remi. This was not the time for you to turn cute and cuddly."

An unfamiliar fang necklace around Lyall's neck came to life, slithering around his muscled torso and lower body and encasing the hellhound in new fighting armor. This reptilian living leather was black with a green iridescence on its scales, and various weapons made of bone—knives, daggers, and even a short sword—grew into strategic positions on Lyall's short but powerful frame.

Remi tried to scream at Lyall that this was all his fault, since he had first worried the terrier was dead then fallen into a hellmouth and been chased by Lyall's hellhound alter form. The only creature he had seen more terrifying than that was Ceto, Sea Queen of the Deep.

Unfortunately, Remi was still a chinchilla.

He kicked his legs and let out several angry squeaking noises, followed up with some spitting.

Lyall wasn't impressed. "This is what happens when you suppress your alter form for years. Calm down, take some breaths, and you'll change back."

After some hyperventilation, Remi's panic subsided enough to allow him to transform. It was awkward, painful, and embarrassing. Especially because he was naked, and Lyall was dressed like he had just walked out of a leather bar.

"Let go of me." Remi backed away from Lyall.

Shit, he was actually blushing. That never happened. He spun around in confusion. They weren't on the soccer field but were instead standing in a yard behind a McMansion-style suburban home draped in guardweed.

"What the hell happened?" Remi asked.

"I played a little feint on José to end the fight. You freaked out and showed everyone your cute little chinchilla ass, so I translocated us a few blocks over."

Remi opened his mouth then shut it, swallowing a few times before he could speak again. "You can translocate? I thought only mothcats and hellhound pack leaders could do that."

"I'm *not* a cat." Lyall let out a growl, even though he was in his full human manifestation. "And yes, I can translocate. For obvious reasons, I chose not to share all of my abilities with your father after he tricked me into being his slave."

Remi didn't have a comeback for that, so he lifted his arms up in helpless confusion and came out with, "Where are my clothes?"

"Back at the soccer field, along with the tattered remains of all the lies you've told since you got here." Lyall reached a hand into his living leathers, which opened into a pocket. He first pulled out the servant collar he had convinced Remi to take off him, swore, then retrieved his original living leather necklace. "Put this on. I've got a new one anyway, and it might be a good idea for you to have some protection, since we're about to run for our lives."

Remi took the rawhide cord and fang necklace with a grimace of distaste and shuddered as the dormant Riftworld creature inside it came to life and began encasing his body in a brown version of the BDSM getup Lyall was wearing.

"We're not running anywhere." Remi tugged at his groin, wishing the living leathers weren't so damn tight in the crotch. "Kaveh's coming back soon, and I need to come up with a story to explain everything. Plus figure out who the Matchmaker picked for him."

"Everyone saw you in your alter form." Lyall rounded on him, only a little less threatening now than when he had been in all his awful hellhound glory. "They know you're ratkind, and it's not much of a leap from that to guess the Colony sent you. We did fly in from Boston, after all."

"I can't leave now." Remi wouldn't see Kaveh again if he did that—and why was that the first thought that came to his mind? "I screwed up the Salem job, and I can't mess up this one. I'll think of something."

"No." Lyall folded his arms, his tone final. "Your security is my responsibility, and I'm making the call to pull out. We're inside a drakone riftland right now, and you're not thinking straight. Something about Kaveh has you messed up. If I didn't know there wasn't a romantic bone in your body, I'd think you were falling for him."

"I'm not leaving, and you have to do what I say." Remi gave that statement his best "I'm in charge here" energy, and it came out sounding like a kid demanding ice cream.

"Make me." Lyall didn't budge. Remi had no idea what to do. Arimanius held the ultimate control over the hellhound, not Remi, and he had a sinking feeling that taking the indenture collar off Lyall had been a big mistake.

"Remi?" Jessie's voice rang out through the swirling fog that still encircled them. "José says he can smell you and Lyall. Are the two of you okay?"

Lyall cursed again, this time in a language Remi didn't recognize, and traced one of his lava-red sigils in the air.

He was going to pull them both through another mini-rift.

"Stop," Remi gasped out then lurched forward with both hands around his throat. "Can't. Breathe."

Lyall paused, the half-formed sigil quivering, as if in anticipation. "Come on, Remi. I didn't hit you that hard when I stopped you from running."

Remi fell forward, and Lyall had to grab him to prevent him from falling.

"What's wrong?" Actual fear filled Lyall's voice. Remi clung to him, his fingers sliding down the hellhound's leather armor. He had learned basic pickpocketing skills at his mother's fishnet-covered knee, and he had the indenture collar out of Lyall's pocket and around the hellhound's neck in a matter of seconds.

Lyall's body jerked, and Remi danced backward out of reach as the hellhound reformed, snarling, as a Scottish terrier.

"I'm over here," Remi called out to Jessie as the fog dissipated. She and her cadejo husband, back in his human form, whirled around at the sound of his voice and ran toward him.

"How did the two of you translocate?" Jessie's eyes were bright with curiosity. "And you didn't tell us you were one of the ratkind."

"Lyall's part mothcat." Remi needed to start lying, and he started with that whopper.

The hellhound snapped at his ankle, but the living leathers blocked the bite. Lyall was right, the living leathers did provide excellent protection.

"Also, I'm only half ratkind," Remi said. "As you saw, I can only transform into a petting zoo attraction."

"I thought you smelled tasty when I first met you." José grimaced as his wife elbowed him in the ribs. "What? I'm not saying I *would* eat him when he's a chinchilla. Well, it might be hard to resist chasing him."

"I thought the ratkind transformed into giant rodents." Jessie, despite her party-girl attitude, was far too quick a study for Remi's tastes. Kaveh had told him the cadejo's human wife was a lawyer, specializing in legal representation of Riftworld individuals. "Don't they have their own mafia, as well?"

"So many questions." Remi raised both hands in a gesture of surrender. "I'll answer all of them, I promise, but let's get a drink first."

As Remi had expected, José greeted that suggestion with enthusiasm. "Let's go to the saloon. I'm buying." He beamed down at Lyall. "Hey, nice trick back there. Maybe Remi will take that collar off and you can have a drink too."

That wasn't going to happen anytime soon.

"Lyall loves to lap up scotch from his doggy bowl." Remi

added a touch of compulsion to the couple, and they exchanged a kiss before walking away holding hands, all thoughts of awkward questions gone from their minds. "Lead the way to the bar."

13

K aveh walked into the monstertown's saloon, not sure if he would hug Remi if he found him there or shake him senseless.

The rift's expansion had been alarming, but Rhys's cool arrogance after Kaveh rode all the way to the keep to ask why it happened had been even worse. He told Kaveh that given his match was most likely in the monstertown, a decision had been made to expand their territory to keep the individual safe and allow Kaveh to collect them.

That phrasing and Rhys's refusal to allow Kaveh to discuss this further with the matriarch led to a blow-out argument. Kaveh didn't lose his temper often, but when he did, it took him a long time to simmer down.

The ride back to the monstertown hadn't been enough to take the edge off his anger, but not seeing Amanita tied up at the field shelter had driven any thought of the fight with his ex out of his mind.

It was a short ride from the picnic area to the monstertown, and Remi had been riding on a repoequus—Amanita had fully transformed when they had crossed over the new rift boundary. She not only knew the way to the monster-town, she could intimidate any dangerous Riftworld crea-tures who might have been emboldened by the rift's expansion.

As he stripped the tack off Ranger in record time and pumped fresh water into the trough for the gelding, he told himself there had to be a reasonable explanation that didn't involve a transformed Amanita eating Remi or some monster worse than a repoequus harming both of them.

He cursed himself for not taking Remi to the safety of the monstertown himself and rushed through the gates.

That's when he ran into a group of parents and their kids returning from the soccer field. They hadn't been watching a game, and as he heard various versions of what had tran-spired, his worry turned to annoyance, and finally to dread.

He liked Remi. A lot.

The picnic and what they had done after it had been wonderful, comfortable in a way sex had never been with Rhys. Before he heard the stories about what had happened at the soccer field—what had people been thinking?—his biggest concern had been a nagging feeling of guilt he was being unfaithful to someone whose identity he didn't even know.

Now he worried whether Remi had ever been the person he thought he was.

His entry into the combination bar, coffee shop, and music venue everyone called the saloon didn't go unnoticed. In fact, he became the immediate center of attention, which always made him uncomfortable. He expected the towns-people would be upset and concerned about being subsumed into the drakone riftland without warning, but that wasn't what everyone was asking him about. They were asking about the Matchmaker and his search for true love.

"Kaveh's here!" Remi called out from across the room, and despite everything, Kaveh's heart lightened in his chest. Remi stood safe and sound on the small stage inside the building that featured entertainment ranging from live music to interspecies poetry slams. His clothing had wrinkles and grass stains, but he otherwise looked fine. "There's a whole room full of eligible residents willing to try on your bracelet. I'm calling it speed matrimony."

Remi waved at the restaurant's bartender/barista, a green-haired woman with Riftworld ancestry from an intelligent plant species. She poured out a beer with her twig-like fingers and gestured to Kaveh to come and take it.

He didn't need alcohol now. He needed to talk to Remi.

José bounded over to the bar to grab the drink and brought the sloshing glass over to him. "Congrats on the engagement, dude, with whoever it is. Remi said you'd be cool with a throuple, so if it's Jessie or me we'd be stoked."

"How is Lyall?" Kaveh put ice into his words, and José gave him a sheepish grin. "I heard about the fight."

"He kicked my ass, so he's better than okay." José gestured at one of the tables where Jessie sat with a group of her friends, Snow on her shoulder. Lyall was perched across from her on a chair with an array of bar food and a bottle of scotch in front of him. Not the kind of diet Kaveh recommended for canine species, but from what people had told him, Lyall wasn't a normal dog.

José began a rambling series of excuses about the dog fight.

Kaveh cut him off. "We'll talk about it later."

He ignored the beer José tried to press on him and pushed through a crowd of well-wishers, most of whom were ready to volunteer to become his life partner on the spot. He made his way to the front of the stage and stood with arms folded, glaring up at Remi. For a second, a wholly unfamiliar expression of guilt flickered across the vid streamer's face, before a guileless smile replaced it.

"I need to talk to you in private." Kaveh half expected him to address the saloon again or try to drag him onto the stage, but Remi set down his beer and hopped down. Lyall jumped off his chair and trotted over to Remi's side, sniffing at Kaveh's boots with suspicion.

They all walked out the back, where the saloon's owner had a small garden of plants from both worlds. There was nowhere to sit, but it was the closest place Kaveh could find that gave them privacy.

"Did you find out what happened with the rift?" Remi seemed determined to get his own questions in before he had to answer any of Kaveh's.

"Rhys told me the clan did it deliberately to protect whoever the Matchmaker selected for me." Kaveh didn't want to get into more details before he had a chance to talk to the matriarch. "They've received word that some of the Colony's enforcers are in Tucson."

"What colony?" Remi's air of innocent confusion didn't fool Kaveh for a minute.

"Several people told me you transformed into a rodent alter form during a dog fight between your terrier and José." Kaveh did his best to keep his tone level. The argument with Rhys had been infuriating, but the prospect of finding out that Remi had betrayed him was far worse. "You're one of the ratkind, and you're from Boston. You can't expect me to believe you don't know what the Colony is. The newsfeeds run articles all the time about the rat monster mafia and its leader, Arimanius. I need you to tell me the truth."

Remi glanced over at his dog, who sat about a meter away, sitting stiffly as if at attention. "When I told you I didn't know what Riftworld clan my father was from, I wasn't being entirely honest."

Kaveh didn't say anything, having figured out Remi found silence from him unnerving and often tried to fill it.

"My biological father's one of the ratkind." Remi twisted his fingers together, another sign of nervousness he rarely displayed. Kaveh tried not to think of those same deft fingers undoing his clothing only a few hours earlier. "My mother's always been a free spirit, and she didn't tell me I was part monster until I was a teenager. I didn't want to tell you because I know the drakones and the ratkind...don't get along."

That was an understatement. "Are you one of the Colony's enforcers?"

"I'm not an enforcer of anything except dress codes and happy hour." Remi sighed. "I know this looks bad. Yes, I asked Garreth to set up a meeting with you because I wanted to find out more about the drakones. I thought you might help me convince one to appear on my live-stream."

Kaveh thought back to their first date, when he had let Remi live-stream him at the farmers' market. Remi had convinced a drakone to appear on his show and hadn't even known it was happening.

It was hard to believe that was only a few days ago.

Remi looked at his terrier again, swallowed, then continued. "Lyall's part fairy hound and part mothcat. He's been my companion animal since I was a kid. He prefers his Earth shape, and it's easier for him to maintain it with the collar on. Otherwise, the translocation thing tends to alarm people."

"Lyall's collar is a Riftworld containment device." Kaveh should have recognized it earlier, when Remi had removed it from José's neck. He pointed to Remi's neck, where a single fang hung from a rawhide string. It was hard to imagine a piece of jewelry less suited for Remi's tastes in fashion. "That's living leather armor. And you have a cyberbug in your watch. I don't think there are too many human vid streamers with items like that."

"Lyall has had that collar for years." Remi tugged at the cord around his neck. "This thing was his idea to protect me because we were both worried about going into drakone territory. And I've used Bug to help with my streaming since I was in college."

"You set your dog up in a fight against a cadejo." Kaveh hated the brutality of animal fights, especially ones between part or full-blood Riftworld participants. "You placed bets on him. He could have been hurt."

"José the cadejo had a few beers too many and picked an old-fashioned dog fight with Lyall." Remi shook his head. "They met when I first arrived and became friends. Just ask José. Anyway, the two of them set it up, not me. The bet wasn't for money. It was with the guardians to tell me what they knew about you and the Matchmaker. I was trying to help you."

Kaveh wouldn't have thought the two decorous komainu could be talked into a bet on a dog fight, but Remi certainly knew how to charm people into doing things they never thought they would try.

He was a prime example of that.

Remi continued, the words spilling out too quickly. "At one point I thought Lyall had been injured, and I freaked out. He was faking it to win the match against José. The only thing that got hurt in that match was my pride. I'm not used to being inside a rift, and I changed into my alter form without meaning to."

Lyall beating José in a fight was a surprise, as was the

dog's ability to mimic every detail of a normal Scottish terrier. Kaveh could usually tell if someone from any species had Riftworld blood, and he had treated a number of moth-cats and fairy hounds. He had never heard of a hybrid of the two species, and perhaps that odd background gave Lyall the ability to blend in with Earth animals.

Kaveh let himself relax a little. José might be scatter-brained, but he wouldn't let a true threat to the town enter without notifying Kaveh or the guardians. Part-human Rift-world people like Remi often took mixed animals as pets, and fairy hounds, who could pass for dogs and sometimes talk, were often as friendly to humans as mothcats like Flut-terberry were.

Finding out that Lyall was a fairy hound didn't bother him too much. The species were nowhere near as dangerous as some cadejos who, unlike José, viewed humans as meals instead of marriage partners. Or something truly terrifying, like the Riftworld species known as hellhounds, who often worked as assassins or mercenaries.

Finding out Remi was ratkind was different.

"Did you hurt anyone when you were in your alter form?" Kaveh knew that transformation could be disorient-ing, especially for someone like Remi, who had fully inte-grated himself into the human world.

The ratkind often morphed into supersized rodent humanoids and were known for their violent dispositions. They lived in large groups and had adapted to the human criminal underworld with ease. Even if Remi hadn't meant to cause any harm, he could have panicked. Many people in town, especially those who were Riftworld, were too proud to seek help when they should. He needed to know right away if someone in the town was injured and might need his help.

Remi began laughing, which wasn't at all the reaction Kaveh expected. "Wait, you're worried I attacked someone after I transformed?"

"The ratkind have many dangerous fighters." Kaveh didn't appreciate Remi taking this so lightly. He wished his new friend and now not-so-fake dating partner had told him about being ratkind earlier, but he had to admit Remi was right. His drakone clan would assume the worst if they knew. Maybe Kaveh would have as well.

"Trust me, no one would use 'dangerous' or 'fighter' as an adjective to describe my alter form." Remi shuffled his feet, looking uncomfortable. "I only have a full animal manifestation. Let's leave it at that."

"Many people are frightened of rats, rightly or wrongly." Kaveh tried to make eye contact with Remi, but the man wouldn't meet his eyes. Also, was he blushing?

"My alter form is a chinchilla." Remi buried his head in his hands. "It's so embarrassing, and I did it in front of the whole town. José told me I smelled tasty. Now that we've got that out of the way, can we talk about finding your one true love again?"

Kaveh wasn't sure he heard Remi correctly. Appearing as an Earth animal other than a human wasn't rare among Riftworld people with human blood, although most had alien characteristics, or at least a larger size. The ratkind though—they didn't do small and adorable. On the other hand, despite its rabbit-like appearance, the soft-furred chinchilla *was* in the rodent family.

He held his hands roughly thirty centimeters apart. "You're only this big in your alter form?"

"A *large* chinchilla." Remi sighed. "Okay, not much bigger than Lyall is now. If I'm near a rift, I have abilities I share with the species. I have a craving for salad, as you noticed. I'm fast, and I can jump pretty high. But there isn't anyone in the monstertown, including any random toddler, who couldn't wipe the floor with me."

Kaveh wasn't sure what to do. Remi hadn't been honest with him, but a half human whose only ratkind ability was transforming into a chinchilla wasn't likely to appeal to Arimanius as a prize Colony recruit. Despite the chaos Remi had caused, it didn't sound like anyone had come to harm, and Kaveh had asked him to help with finding his match.

"Are you going to tell Rhys what happened?" Remi blurted out.

For a moment, all Kaveh could think about was the soft press of Remi's lips against his and the warmth of their two bodies melding as they held each other. Rhys had no right to know or care about Kaveh's personal life anymore. The truth about Remi's background, on the other hand, was very much something his family would want to know about.

"I'm inside a drakone riftland, and the only means of transportation I have is a repoequus who's off hunting jackrabbits." Remi drew in a breath, a tremble entering his voice. "I'm scared, Kaveh."

Maybe Remi had lied to him. But Kaveh had withheld a lot from Remi as well. He hadn't told him that out of his entire clan, Kaveh was the drakone Remi should fear the most.

Remi had his chin up, meeting Kaveh's gaze, but it wasn't hard to tell he was truly frightened. It also wasn't unreasonable for him to be afraid. There would be no way to explain to his clan that a half-ratkind reporter from back East wasn't a threat. His clan would assume he worked for the Colony and was a threat to Kaveh's human partner-to-be.

Rhys in particular wouldn't take it well.

"I'm not going to tell my clan anything right now, and I

promise I'll get you safely back to the ranch." Kaveh had made his decision. If he agreed with mistrusting someone based only on their family background, the first person he shouldn't trust was himself. "I need to go inside to find out if I'm going to be marrying someone in the saloon. I'd like to have you by my side if you're still willing to help me."

A relieved smile broke out over Remi's face. "Well, I did win a bet against the komainu to tell me what they knew. Plus, I have people lining up to see if they're your match. I wouldn't be much of a dating coach if I didn't see this through to the end."

A FEW EMOTIONALLY EXHAUSTING hours later, Kaveh had an answer. The Matchmaker had not chosen someone in the monstertown as his partner.

Remi had transformed a dreaded and humiliating process into a party. Everyone was chatting about romance and love, and the number of Kaveh's usually stodgy patients kissing or holding hands shocked him. Recorded music wasn't an option, since they were fully in a fragment of the Riftworld universe, but the more musically talented put together an impromptu live music show, with plenty of slow dances.

No one refused to try on the bracelet or expressed the anxiety Kaveh would have had about the request if he had been in their shoes. As the gold jewelry remained unchanged, his friends and acquaintances laughed and offered up advice, memories, or amusing anecdotes about their love lives. No one seemed to consider the process a personal rejection either.

Remi pushed a beer across the table. "I think you deserve a drink."

"That's everyone, you think?" Kaveh nodded and took a long sip.

"Other than that group, who I'm quite sure aren't in the running." Remi waved to a group of children who had taken advantage of their parents' inattention to run wild. Lyall was in the midst of it all, racing around like he had downed several shots of espresso while Snow flapped around the bar trying to sneak a sip from people's drinks. "No sign of the guardians. I hope they're not going to renege on our wager."

Kaveh leaned back in his chair and watched as a humanoid Riftworld woman moved slowly toward their table. She had leonine features and grayish skin, and there was a sense of absolute stillness about her even while she in was motion, as if she had been made of stone.

Which she had been not that long ago. Kaida, one half of the paired komainu guardians at the gate, had arrived in the saloon in her Earth alter form.

"Kaida and Raion take debts seriously." Kaveh rose to his feet, and a surprised Remi did as well, once he saw who was approaching.

"Good afternoon, Kaida-san." Kaveh gave the komainu a respectful bow. He held the position as Kaida bowed back with agonizing slowness, not straightening until the komainu completed her bow. "As always, I'm grateful for your teaching and guidance."

Remi pulled off a similar bow, shooting Kaveh an impressed look, as if he hadn't expected him to have such a thorough grasp of Japanese etiquette.

Kaida took her seat, and Remi and Kaveh followed suit. The dryad saloon owner swooped in with a cast-iron pot of hot tea and filled three steaming cups before leaving them to their conversation. Kaida and Raion didn't take human form often, but when they did, they enjoyed certain Earth customs, tea being one of them.

"A pleasure to see you as well, Kaveh-san," Kaida replied, before turning with grinding slowness toward Remi. "I am here, however, to resolve the wager your ratkind companion made with my sibling and myself."

"Glad to hear you agree I won." Remi kept his tone light and a smile plastered on his face, but Kaveh could see the tension in his face as the guardian casually identified Remi's Riftworld background.

Kaida stared back at the vid streamer, her expression giving new meaning to stone-faced. She reached out, her speed unbelievable given her glacial movements otherwise, and took both his hands in hers.

Remi sucked in a breath but didn't resist.

She released him a second later, pulling back into her unnatural stillness. "Ah. I see."

"My friend chose an unorthodox method of requesting your wisdom, but please know I asked for his assistance." Kaveh should have realized the guardians would have a far greater ability to identify Riftworld species than he would. He could hardly ask the two komainu to withhold this information from his clan, but he wanted to get Remi to the relative safety of the ranch before Rhys, in particular, found out. "I'm aware of his clan background, as he is of mine."

Kaida raised one wrinkled brow. Kaveh hadn't lied exactly, but the guardians knew he was Azdaha and not another air drakone. Could they also tell he hadn't shared that fact with Remi?

"I'm loving this mysterious wisdom thing you've got going on, but I believe the two of us had a bet." Remi managed to make that outrageously rude interruption sound like a playful tease.

"You want to know who the Matchmaker has chosen as a mate for Kaveh Salehi." Kaida lifted a cup of tea to her lips, the motion taking what seemed like an eternity. She sipped the hot liquid then rested it back on the table. "Kaveh's intended is in the monstertown." She had an odd inflection to her words, as if she was echoing a larger intelligence beyond her own. "And they are not. His match is at the ranch, and yet they are not. Kaveh's love is with him and hopelessly out of his reach."

Remi's smile didn't falter, but his tone grew sharp. "What the fuck kind of answer is that?"

"A truthful one." Kaida rose to her feet, forcing both Kaveh and Remi to do so as well so they could bow their goodbyes. "Farewell to you both. Raion and I will pray for your good fortune. This has been a most illuminating conversation."

14

Remi closed the door to his cabin and collapsed onto the room's small sofa, putting his head between his knees. Spending that much time in a riftland had upset the balance between himself and his inner chinchilla. His nerves were shot, and he simultane- ously wanted to chow down on some sweet hay and run away in an absolute panic.

He lifted his head, searching for Lyall. The dog had darted inside while he and Kaveh were setting up plans to meet for dinner. As much as he wanted to, he couldn't leave the collar on him. He needed Lyall able to transform into his human or hellhound form if Kaveh's terrifying family decided to pay him a call.

Remi didn't believe, deep down, that Kaveh would betray him. He wasn't that kind of guy. Unfortunately for Kaveh, Remi *was* that type of guy.

Kaida, the guardian who spouted mystical nonsense about Kaveh's match, was another story. She could tell the drakone clan about him, but she also could have taken him out in the saloon if she had wanted to. Besides, it had taken a nail-biting hour or more to cross the rift border, and there had been plenty of time for Rhys or one of the other air drakones to swoop down on him if the guardian had told them Remi was ratkind.

Kaveh had stayed by his side right up until he had left Lyall and Remi at the cabin, keeping his promise to see him safely back in the ranch. Meanwhile, Remi had lied to him about everything except wanting to find out who his match was, and that was only so he could use that information against him.

He tried to shake off the oppressive weight of guilt that had been growing throughout the speed matrimony event. Every time someone had touched the bracelet without it transforming, Remi had been thrilled they weren't going to get to be with Kaveh forever and sick over the thought that Kaveh's spouse-to-be was most likely someone at the ranch Remi knew—and liked.

Exhaustion was also eating away at him. He had been able to keep most of the adults in the saloon in a low-level state of mild sexual and romantic arousal, but the effort cost him. Regardless, he needed to get off the couch, take the collar off Lyall, and endure a tongue-lashing from the dog before he collapsed for a brief nap before dinner.

"Lyall, come here." It would be lovely if the stubborn bastard did walk over. That way Remi didn't have to get up, could disengage the collar while horizontal, and then get chewed out while half napping. "I'm sorry about tricking you, okay? Let me take the collar off, and I'll buy out the whole supply of beef jerky in the gift shop for you."

"Kaveh got me the last batch." Lyall didn't sound pissed off at all, which was a surprise.

He also didn't sound like a Scottish terrier.

Remi jerked his head up. Lyall leaned against the wall

near the bathroom in full human form, wearing his skintight living leather armor and more razor-sharp weapons than even a mercenary like him could possibly want.

The indenture collar was draped around his finger.

"You took the collar off yourself." Remi tried to process what happened and failed. "I didn't think you could do that once it was on."

"Not when I'm under an indenture contract, yes." Lyall gave Remi a smile that had far too many teeth in it. "Good thing for me I'm not."

Remi took in the room and tried to calculate his chances of escape. Given he hadn't been able to outrun Lyall on an open stretch of ground with four legs instead of two, he gave that option zero chance of success.

"When did you get out of it?" Remi went with continuing this bizarrely calm conversation, since he couldn't think of any alternatives. Maybe Kaveh could save him from Lyall, if he could get out of the cabin and find him. Then he'd have to explain Lyall was his hellhound bodyguard, assigned by Arimanius, don of the Colony mafia, because Remi was his half-human son. At that point, the only thing Kaveh and Lyall would be fighting over was who got to kill Remi first.

"When you took it off José." Lyall pushed off against the wall and walked closer. He dropped the collar on the coffee table. Remi considered using his powers against him, but that had an even lower chance of working than trying to run away. "You're Arimanius's son, and the tech in the collar is based on bloodlines. It's designed so that you taking it off me wouldn't reverse the contract, but the effort you had to put in to break it off José's neck was enough to do the trick. Then I decided to hang around until the job was finished."

"So you could kill me at the end of it?" Saying it out loud should have made it real, but it didn't feel that way. Just Remi's luck to talk his way out of being ripped apart by angry drakones only to be murdered by his bodyguard.

"Well, you did tell an entire town I was a goddamn mothcat." Lyall let that hang for a moment then gave a long sigh. "No, you little idiot. I stayed because you almost got killed by a drakone last summer when your asshole of a father sent Zale out as the muscle on the job."

"You don't hate me, and you don't want to murder me?" Remi hunched his shoulders as Lyall glowered at him. "I'm not complaining, believe me. I don't understand why."

"I've known you since you were fifteen." Lyall threw up his hands. "When your con artist of a mother sold you to Arimanius after the two of them figured out you had psychic gifts. I'm responsible for you, damn it, but you won't listen to me. Kaveh has been selected by the Matchmaker for a pairing. He won't necessarily fall in love with his match or be happy with the marriage, but he will have an uncontrollable compulsion to protect that person from anyone or anything that's a threat to them. Even though Kaveh likes you, even though the two of you got down and dirty during that picnic, it doesn't matter. He'll kill you to protect her."

"I don't think it's a her." Part of Remi—the sane part—told him not to pick any fights with the terrifying hellhound who had decided not to kill him. The other part of him opened up his mouth and said, "Jeannette's the only likely woman left on the list. My money's on Kat. It has to be him."

Lyall's eyes glowed red, even though he was in his human shape. Remi knew the hellhound found Kat attractive, but he hadn't thought much about it. Kat was seriously cute. Who wouldn't like to bang him?

"I don't know for sure it's Kat." Remi backtracked as fast

as he could. "Kaveh's talking to more friends at the ranch I didn't think were good prospects. He could tell me he's found his one true love when we meet for dinner, and that would be that."

"And then you're going to call Zale and let him threaten Kaveh with killing his match if he doesn't tell them how the drakones can manipulate the rift." Lyall wasn't asking—he was laying out the awful betrayal Remi planned to inflict on Kaveh in brutal clarity.

"No one's going to get hurt. Kat will be leverage against the drakones, that's all." Remi needed to explain to Lyall why he had to do this because if he did, maybe he would start believing it himself. "You saw what they did with your own eyes. They expanded their riftland and took over an entire interzone and all the species in it. If they can do that, they could alter riftlands that don't belong to them. Suppose they use this power to shrink the hellmouth in Oregon where your pack lives?"

Remi didn't know much about Lyall's pack, except that the dog had been exiled. The hellhound made it clear it wasn't a subject he was willing to discuss. Still, Lyall had come from the Mount Hood Rift—or hellmouth, as land rifts were usually called—and the threat to it wasn't farfetched.

"Did you tell Zale you thought it was Kat?" Lyall all but growled out the words.

Shit. Why couldn't Remi have kept his mouth shut about the cute vet assistant? "No, I told him to get out of my damn face and let me do what I do best. Look, it's Thursday night, which is close enough to the weekend for me. If Kaveh hasn't found his match, I'll convince him to ask Kat and Jeannette to go out with us tonight in town. You can come with us or head out to the West Coast to follow your doggy dreams. I'm happy you got out of your contract and even happier you're not planning to take me out before leaving, but I don't have the option of walking away. The Colony is the only family I have."

He hadn't meant that last bit to sound so whiny and needy, but there it was.

Lyall was silent for a long time. Then he shook his head. "I'll hang around until you figure out who the match is, as long as you promise to get the hell out of town once you do. This is going to get ugly fast."

15

K aveh had no idea how Remi talked him into these things.

His clan had incorporated the base and the monstertown into their riftland without discussion or permission, Kaveh still hadn't told the matriarch his Azadah powers had manifested, and the Colony mafia had sent ratkind fighters to Tucson to target Kaveh's future spouse.

It was one hell of a time for him to go to a gay country-western bar with a half-ratkind vid streamer.

He pulled his pickup truck into one of the EV charging spots in the bar's parking lot and glanced over at the ratkind streamer in question.

"It's down to two contestants, Jeannette and Kat." Remi had dressed to casually impress, wearing a crisp linen shirt over tight-fitting pants and yet another new pair of shoes. His wristwatch flashed with iridescence as the cyberbug inside rose up to investigate its new surroundings. "Let's do this."

The two of them got out of the truck and walked to the

entrance, followed closely by Lyall, who had hopped into Kaveh's truck without him noticing.

Kaveh had secretly hoped Remi's double-date plans would fall through. Jeanette had been divorced for a few years now, and with her looks and sunny personality, she had many social options on a Thursday night. Kat, never much of a party person, had an upcoming exam he had been anxious about.

Yet both of them were waiting for Remi and Kaveh at the club entrance, bright smiles on their faces. That made the foursome complete—or fivesome, if you counted the terrier. He had no idea how they would get inside with a dog trailing behind them.

There was a long line to get into the country-western bar, a cover fee the place was charging, and a mysterious list of approved guests. Kaveh liked music, especially country, but the social complexities of this place were too daunting for him to wrap his head around.

None of that mattered. Remi breezed to the front of the line without a word of protest from the crowd, flashed a smile at the club's bouncer, and within a few moments, all five of them—yes, including the Riftworld Scottish terrier—were in.

Remi ushered them through to the outdoor back patio, which had both a bar and a dance floor. Kaveh opted to buy everyone drinks and hold their seats at the bar as Kat, Remi, and Jeannette went off to join the dancing crowd.

The music was loud, the bar packed with bodies, and Kaveh felt out of his element.

He looked down at Lyall, who had found a spot under a bar stool. "Not much of a dancer myself. How about you?"

The dog gave him an incredulous look then settled down on his haunches to survey the room. Kaveh wondered if Lyall could understand him if he tried to communicate by sending mental images to him. Earth animals communicated with each other constantly of course, and many were capable of nonverbal interactions with humans. In the Riftworld, where there was a wide array of diverse species with similar intelligence levels, the human/animal dichotomy made little sense. There were even many intelligent Riftworld species who would be considered part of the plant kingdom on Earth.

He sent out the first mental picture of Remi which came into his mind—the blogger laughing, blue eyes full of mischief and fun.

Lyall's reaction wasn't what he expected. An emotion with no visual component rushed back toward him, all concern and fierce protectiveness. Then the connection slammed shut.

Interesting. Lyall could block telepathic thought like the drakones could. The only other species Kaveh knew who had that level of mental shields were hellhounds. Perhaps the ability came from Lyall's unusual fairy hound and mothcat background.

Lyall glanced up at him, bared his teeth, and then resumed his focus on the dance floor, his tail wagging with the music.

His companions returned shortly after the drinks arrived. They were all flushed from the balmy night and the exertion of dancing. Remi and Kat both accepted cactus fruit margaritas with thanks, while Jeannette grabbed her beer.

Remi pressed closer to Kaveh, sniffing his drink. The contact sent a wave of heat through Kaveh that had nothing to do with the warm weather.

"Does that even have alcohol in it?" Remi asked.

"It's pop." Kaveh chuckled at Remi's blank stare. He had forgotten folks back East called it soda. "I need a clear head tonight."

"I was hoping if you had a few real drinks I could get you to dance with me." Remi sipped at his margarita and did an impressive eyebrow wag.

"What's the deal with you two?" Jeannette leaned against the bar stool and eyed them. "Remi, I'm thrilled you succeeded in getting our Dr. K. here to take some time off work. I heard a rumor about a wedding proposal, and I demand to know all the details."

"I'm so happy for both of you." Kat burst in with that, which wasn't helpful.

Kaveh hadn't wanted to have this discussion this soon in the evening.

Remi looked uncharacteristically flustered after Kat's comment but recovered his poise in seconds. "Kaveh, maybe now is a good time to lay your cards on the table of matrimony."

"Remi and I aren't dating." Kaveh felt Remi hunch beside him, a reaction so slight he wouldn't have noticed it if they hadn't been close. "He's been helping me find someone."

"I have a hard time believing Remi's only your wing-man." Jeannette used her beer bottle to point between them. "The vibe I'm getting from both of you is more like friends with full benefits and a pension."

"I've entered into an arranged engagement." Kaveh found he needed to grip onto something, and Remi's hand, slender and cool, was right next to him. "My family has a matchmaker who's set me up with someone. It's an old tradition and one I respect. Only, in our society, the details can be challenging to work out."

"I thought your family was still in Iran." Kat set his untouched margarita on the bar top. "They sent a matchmaker here to find you someone? Wow, and I thought my great-grandparents were too nosy about my love life. They love to talk about how they were set up by a *miai* service back in the day."

"My family isn't in Iran." Kaveh felt his palms grow sweaty from the tension. Remi didn't let go. "They live past the monstertown, inside the riftland. We call it the keep."

Jeannette didn't make the connection, but Kat did.

"Only drakones live in the keep." His voice trailed off as he swallowed a few times. "Which means you're not human. Why didn't you tell me?"

Kaveh hated to hear the hurt in Kat's voice. It made him feel awful. "I didn't tell anyone for a long time."

"He knows." Kat pointed at Remi, his hand trembling. "You met him a few days ago, but we've been friends for years. You're not talking about some online dating app. You're telling us the Matchmaker curse has been activated. And you invited Jeannette and me out because you think one of us is your match."

"It's not a curse." Kaveh didn't know how the evening had gone so wrong so fast. First the fight with Rhys, then finding out Remi had lied to him. Now everything he had feared about telling Kat was coming true. "I'm not going to force anyone to marry me, but I have to find this person before..."

"Before they escape?" Kat continued for him.

Kaveh reached out to him, trying for physical reassurance and failing.

Kat shook his head and backed away. "I can't handle this right now."

He slipped into the crowd, pushing his way through.

Lyall sprang up, dodging feet and gyrating bodies to follow him.

Both Remi and Jeannette moved to block Kaveh from doing the same.

"Let him cool off." Remi sounded firm. "His thoughts are a mishmash of every bad relationship he's ever had combined with a panic no one will ever think he's good enough for a long-term relationship."

Both Kaveh and Jeannette stared at Remi in surprise.

"You can read minds?" Jeannette asked. "Are you part Riftworld too?"

"Sort of and yes." Remi paused, as if surprised by his own honesty.

"Remi and I have narrowed down the group of people who could be my match." Kaveh tried to focus on Jeannette. Remi had a point. Forcing Kat to confront this now wouldn't do any good. Besides, if Jeanette was his intended, he could focus on apologizing to his assistant for not telling the truth about his background later. "The drakones have enemies, both in the Riftworld and outside of it. I feel terrible surprising you like this."

Jeanette shook her head and laughed. "First off, I've got ten more years and one more marriage under my belt than Kat. I got hitched for love when I was nineteen, and it did *not* work out. Second, you're good looking and rich, if the stories about the drakones are true. And more importantly, you're the kindest man I've ever met. So, buy me a whisky shot and tell me how this match-with-a-monster thing works."

Remi gave a commanding wave of his hand, and a bartender serving two other customers left them and strolled over to take the order.

Jeanette looked pleased with the quick service. She

grabbed the shot glass off the bar top and downed the drink in one gulp. "Is it a true love kiss that reveals your bride- or groom-to-be?"

"No, it's expensive jewelry." Remi motioned for Kaveh to bring out the bracelet, and Kaveh fumbled in his coat pocket and pulled out the amulet.

"Bling works for me." Jeanette reached over and placed the intricate cuff on her wrist.

Kaveh stopped breathing while she hefted her arm up and down.

The object remained unchanged.

"Solid gold, I guess," she said. "Awfully nice, honey, but I think you've got the wrong girl."

He had trouble calming himself even when she handed it back to him. Did this mean Kat was his match? His best friend was furious at him. What was he going to do?

Jeanette gave Kaveh a chaste peck on the cheek and motioned to the dance floor. "I'm going to have some fun and dance, and I strongly recommend the two of you do the same." As she walked away, she winked at the two of them, a smile spreading across her face. "Don't worry, Dr. K. I've got a good feeling your Mr. Right will come around."

Obviously she meant Kat and was trying to reassure him. Kaveh sagged against the bar, relief warring with despair. "I couldn't have handled that any worse."

"I think Jeanette took it pretty well." Remi tugged at Kaveh's arm. "Giving Kat some time to let this sink in is the right move. By the way, you're still number one on my dance card, and I'm not going to let you forget it."

Remi yanked him to the dance floor, ignoring what seemed to Kaveh to be all too blatant stares from men around them. Then he stopped, and the two of them faced each other.

The DJ decided to slow things down at that point, playing an older country song Kaveh knew well. Remi made a brief effort to complain about it then pressed himself against Kaveh.

It felt good to hold someone.

It felt good to hold Remi.

Kaveh knew some line dances, but he had never slow danced with anyone. The couples around them were swaying together or making out, and he didn't feel self-conscious. Instead, he slipped his arm around Remi's waist, enjoying the gentle friction their bodies made against one another. He could catch the scent of cactus fruit on Remi's lips, and that made him want to kiss them.

He pulled away a fraction, looking down at Remi's face. The pupils of his blue eyes were wide, and his breath had sped up.

"May I kiss you?" Kaveh asked and had to brace himself as Remi's lips crashed into his own.

Kaveh kissed him back. The warm sweetness of his mouth was intoxicating, and arousal flared. He deepened the kiss, his tongue sliding in. It might have been the stress of the past few days or the inhibition of being in a crowd where many were doing the same thing, but he felt none of his usual reservations about expressing physical affection in public.

Remi pulled back for air, his lips swollen and his eyes dark with desire. "You're amazing." He hesitated then went on, the words coming out in a rush. "Come back to my cabin with me. Please. One night won't matter, and you're not married yet."

The temptation, once the offer was there, was over-whelming. Not only for the physical pleasure but the opportunity to be close to Remi and see him unguarded, without the walls he built up to keep everyone out.

There was so much pressure on Kaveh now that he felt ready to explode. He had handled the situation with Kat poorly, and worse yet, it was now likely his young friend was his assigned spouse. The only action that would make his clan draw back the rift to its original position was Kaveh taking him to the safety of the keep. He felt sick at the thought of forcing Kat to do that. Maybe waiting until morning to talk to him again was best.

And until the bracelet changed shape, Kaveh was still a free man.

Remi mistook his silence for a negative response. "I'm sorry. I know you're still angry about me lying to you, which you have every right to be."

Kaveh stopped him from saying more with a kiss. "Going to your cabin is exactly what I need right now."

16

I t took about thirty minutes to get back to the ranch, but for Remi it seemed like an eternity. Kaveh had first made sure Jeannette was fine with taking a robotaxi back to her place and then had taken one more look around for Kat before the two of them got into the pickup and drove away.

Remi kept his hands off Kaveh during the drive with great difficulty. He focused on reassuring Kaveh that Kat was perfectly safe and would have cooled off by tomorrow, all while telling himself that Lyall would keep the vet assistant safe.

It was a measure of Kaveh's distraction that he didn't remember they had left Lyall behind until they were at the cabin door, and Remi had to stop him from heading back to the bar.

Thankfully, his watch buzzed with a text from Kat. As upset as the vet assistant was, he still wanted to make sure Remi knew his "terrier" was safe.

"See, I told you Lyall had to be with Kat." Remi showed Kaveh the text then fumbled for the metal key to his room, desire and longing making him clumsy. "He left when Kat did, and Lyall's awfully good at tracking people down."

As a hellhound, that usually meant following the trail of someone he wanted to assassinate. But Lyall liked Kat, and Remi was sure everything would be fine as long as the dog was watching over him.

They stepped inside Remi's room, which had both working electricity and the soft glow of shroom lights. Some odd effect of that terrifying drakone-controlled rift moving closer to the ranch, no doubt.

That was fine too. Romantic, even.

Remi had one more night in a world where he and Kaveh could be friends, lovers, even a couple.

Tomorrow, Kaveh would talk to Kat and give him the bracelet, which would turn into something cute and adorable, and they would kiss and make up. Tomorrow, Zale and the other Colony enforcers would try to use the Match-maker's choice against the drakones, and Kaveh would realize what a lying piece of shit Remi was. Tomorrow, Remi would leave and never see Kaveh again, or Lyall, and he would be back in Boston.

Alone.

That was fine too. It had to be. Because there wasn't any other way this would end.

"Can we talk about what you like?" Kaveh had taken off his hat, and he was still holding Remi's hand. It felt like a proposal, formal but emotionally intense. "Or what you don't like."

Remi stepped in close and threw his arms around him because he couldn't remember the last time someone had taken the time to ask him that question. "I like most things, and if I don't, I'll tell you."

"Rhys and I are both drakones, so we didn't worry much

about protection," Kaveh began then paused as Remi reached over to open the nightstand drawer next to the bed and showed him the contents.

"I'm a hypochondriac, so I test myself for Riftworld and Earth pathogens monthly, and as you can see, I've got plenty of condoms and lube." Remi paused because maybe he was assuming too much. "We don't have to go that far, if you'd rather not."

"I'd like to go as far as you want me to." Kaveh pulled Remi into another kiss, with that single-minded intensity he had.

It was as if nothing else in the world mattered—except for Remi.

The kissing grew frantic, as Remi tried to savor the tangle of lips and tongues so he could remember every taste, every sensation.

Then the two of them were on the bed, with Kaveh straddling him. There were far too many clothes in the way, and they both tried to help each other get naked at the same time, which led to a little fumbling and a lot of laughter.

Kaveh's body was everything Remi had been fantasizing about and more. He had the rugged upper body of a man who worked with his hands every day, and his thighs looked like they could bend an iron rod.

Speaking of rods, Kaveh's cock was nothing short of magnificent, large and thick. They were both already aroused, but there was so much skin to explore they ended up spending time kissing and touching each other all over. It was slow in all the right ways, and Remi found himself desperate for more at the same time as he wanted this soft lovemaking to go on forever.

"You have a riftmark." Kaveh ran his fingers, rough and callused and so, so arousing, over the small design etched onto Remi's right hip bone. "It looks like a neuron—a nerve cell."

"I think it was supposed to be a tree." Remi pulled Kaveh's face up for another kiss then began to grind against him.

He didn't want Kaveh to focus on the mark or think about it himself. Remi had received the riftmark—a type of Riftworld tattoo—from his father when he turned fifteen and became a full member of the Colony. It signified both Remi's psychic abilities and his loyalty to his large and larcenous family, and neither of those mattered right now. They were part of tomorrow, which was going to be awful, and not part of right now, which was glorious.

"You said we could go as far as I wanted." Remi shifted his hips again, pleased at the low moan this elicited from Kaveh. "I want you inside me."

"We can do that." Kaveh reached out for the bedside table and located the condom and lube with flattering urgency.

"You also said Rhys only liked things his way." Remi let his head fall back onto the pillow, admiring Kaveh's deft, quick movements with the supplies. There were advantages to a medical education he had never considered. "Have you ever topped before?"

"No, but I think I can figure it out." Kaveh slid his fingers up the sensitive skin on Remi's inner thigh and went higher, pushing with firm but gentle strokes.

Kaveh was certainly a fast learner. Remi bucked his hips up, the pleasure threatening to unravel any coherent thoughts in his mind. Kaveh slid his fingers out, and Remi hooked his legs over Kaveh's broad shoulders. The vet lined himself up and entered him, the stinging burn turning into white-hot shocks of sheer bliss as the two of them moved together in a rhythm so natural and perfect it was as easy as breathing.

Remi climaxed first, from the friction of Kaveh above him alone, and the vet came a few seconds later, his weight collapsing down. It felt so good to feel Kaveh above him, a comforting, solid presence.

It felt like safety.

It felt like love.

Remi tried to squirm out from underneath Kaveh, suddenly desperate to get away from these crazy thoughts and feelings. One night was what he had asked for, and Kaveh had given it to him, in both a literal and figurative sense. Wanting anything more than that was only going to make tomorrow even worse.

Kaveh pressed his hand against his chest to hold him down, a possessive move that shouldn't have been so arousing, especially since Remi had just had the best orgasm of his life. "Let me take care of you."

Those words were so unexpected, so surprising to hear from anyone's lips, let alone one of Remi's sexual partners, that he could do little more than nod and let his head loll back. A wave of pleasant languor swept over him, part afterglow and part fatigue, and the surge of panic receded.

Through half-open eyes, he saw Kaveh dispose of the condom and slip into the bathroom. He returned a minute later with a warm facecloth and washed both of them up before rearranging himself and Remi so they were lying face-to-face.

"Pretty good for my first time on top?" Kaveh gave him a grin that was saucy and close to wicked. Remi wanted so much to see more of this side of him.

"A plus-plus on your final dating exam." Remi pulled the

blanket over both of them, his body cooling off after the exertion of their lovemaking.

Kaveh's expression grew more serious, and he reached out to stroke the side of Remi's face. "I'd rather it wasn't so final."

The conversation shouldn't be going in this direction. If this had been one of Remi's usual encounters, he would have come up with some clever turn of phrase or witty remark to get things back on the casual sex track. Hell, if one of his usual flings had brought up this topic, Remi would have had his clothes on and been slipping out the door by now, even if it was his room.

"I have to leave tomorrow anyway." Remi should have been pulling away but instead found himself pressing closer to the warmth of Kaveh's body. "My sponsors have another site they want me to check out."

It was a lazy, unsophisticated lie, totally not up to Remi's standards.

Kaveh kept stroking Remi's face, his fingers gliding over the faint stubble on Remi's cheeks. "You'll miss the Friday rodeo, then."

He'd miss more than that when he left, but Lyall was right. Remi needed to get out before it all went down. But that still left tonight, and there were hours until morning.

He opened his mouth to ask Kaveh to stay with him, but the vet's body went rigid, and the softness of his gaze when he looked at Remi hardened into a scowl.

"Three of my clan are here." Kaveh rolled off the bed and began to throw on his clothes.

Remi jerked back, surprised at the sudden change in his demeanor.

"They never come this far from the rift," Kaveh said. "Something's wrong, and I think it's better you stay inside."

Before Remi could think of something to say or ask Kaveh how he knew all of this, Kaveh had pulled on his boots and swung the door open, closing it behind him with a click of finality.

Remi did not, of course, stay in his room.

He threw on an all-black ensemble and sneakers in case hiding and running might be involved. Opening the door didn't seem discreet, so after peeking out of the room's windows, he lifted the one that didn't open over a cactus and crawled out.

He could barely make out an indistinct conversation from around the corner of the building. Remi grimaced then focused on transforming partly into his alter form. His chinchilla ears picked up what his human ones couldn't, and he edged along the wall toward the conversation. It was being held in the drakone language, which Remi could follow without much difficulty.

"I don't care if you find my tone and manner abrasive." A male voice, deep and all too familiar. It was Rhys, Kaveh's ex-lover and all-around asshole. "The reputation and safety of the clan is what matters here, not the sensibilities of a human who should be grateful for the opportunity to join our clan."

Patronizing prick. Remi leaned forward, straining to hear more. He had started eavesdropping in the middle of the argument, but he guessed the ungrateful human they were discussing was Kat.

If Kaveh's family thought the cute wrangler wasn't deferential enough for them, they would lose their shit over Remi's attitude.

"Rhys is no diplomat." This from an older female. "But he has a point. We can't be seen as unable to protect the human the Matchmaker chose for you. This is for your sake, Kaveh. Rhys cares for you, as we all do."

Remi took a few hesitant steps to the edge of the shadows. He could make out three individuals silhouetted in the glow of shroom lamps mounted on some of the taller cacti. The ranch was feeling the effects of the expanded rift, even without a rift storm.

Kaveh's outline would have been recognizable even without his cowboy hat. A second, larger individual had a reptilian quality to his shape and had to be Rhys. The third stood a head taller than the others, red-and-gold scales gleaming like a torch in the dim light.

That had to be Xiang Jao, Matriarch of the Saguaro Rift clan.

Remi pressed back into the darkness, his heart pounding. Even in humanoid form, she would be unbelievably dangerous.

"We ran the Colony enforcers out of the human city." Xiang Jao's words sent a chill through Remi. Zale wasn't his favorite relative for a lot of reasons, but he didn't want to see him hurt or killed. Not to mention that, since Lyall had escaped his contract, Zale was the only one around who could protect him. "Your intended must be taken into our safekeeping, and you should rejoin the family in the keep until the situation has stabilized."

"Kat doesn't want this to happen." Kaveh sounded ragged, more distraught than Remi had ever imagined he could sound. "I haven't even confirmed the match with the amulet."

"Let me collect him, then." Rhys spoke again, talking over Kaveh's immediate objections. "If he isn't your match, an apology and a generous gift should assuage any of the human's complaints. If the amulet transforms, then he's your husband, and you can order him to remain in the keep."

"I'm not going to let you touch him." Kaveh didn't sound distraught anymore. He sounded furious, and Remi felt another pang of envy. Kaveh would do anything to protect his friend and now almost-fiancé, of course. Adorable, clueless Kat, who had stormed away from a gorgeous man who only wanted to protect him and keep him safe from the bad guys.

Namely, Remi and his family.

Rhys shoved Kaveh in the chest, and things went south quickly.

Kaveh spat out a string of words, utterly unfamiliar to Remi, who prided himself on his Riftworld language skills. Green flames leaped up around Kaveh—shit, was he on fire?

Remi couldn't stand here and do nothing. He started forward, prepared to rush out and put out the flames if necessary.

A rubbery, muscular shape wrapped around his chest. Remi would have screamed if a large hand hadn't clamped over his mouth. He spent frantic and useless moments trying to thrash free before he recognized the tentacle holding him fast.

Zale.

Arizona was one hell of a dry place for a half kraken, but his brutish cousin often partially transformed to add a pair of tentacles to his human shape.

Remi stopped struggling, instead trying to catch the rest of the conversation. His ears still worked, even if his mouth didn't.

"This is how you repay us, when we took you in and saved you?" Rhys's emotions boiled out in his words. Shock, fury, and an emotion Remi knew all too well—fear.

"We'll discuss this when you're calmer." Xiang Jao's tone was icy, and a moment later her red-and-gold full drakone shape snaked upward into the sky, growing larger as she gained elevation. A smaller gray version joined her, the two swimming through the night sky as if it were a vast ocean.

The flames around Kaveh died away. He put a hand to his forehead as if wondering what he had just done, then reached into his pocket. Light glinted off the gold surface of the bracelet as he walked toward the main building of the ranch, his body rigid with tension.

Remi sagged in relief. Kaveh wasn't hurt, only capable of some kind of drakone fire magic that had impressed even the matriarch.

Then Remi remembered his cousin was still manhandling him.

He jerked his head back, slammed it into Zale's nose, then followed it up by stomping on the half kraken's instep.

"Shit." Zale released his hold, the tentacle whipping back and off Remi. He kept his voice down to an angry hiss, even though Kaveh was now out of earshot. "What are you doing? I was trying to rescue you."

"Why are you here?" Remi spun to face him.

His cousin was a full head taller than him and currently wearing a leather jacket and an outfit that screamed illegal motorcycle gang. He loomed over Remi with his pale skin, overly muscled upper body, and long brown hair that was currently writhing like a pack of unruly eels.

"Let me repeat the part about saving your ass." Zale gestured at Kaveh. "Did you miss the fireworks? That green flame trick is called summ, and you don't want to be anywhere near it. Kaveh Salehi is the Azdaha drakone Xiang Jao took into their clan. Even she's afraid of him."

Remi's first thought was that this was ridiculous. Kaveh

was at least part drakone, yes, but he couldn't be the canni-balistic monster dragon Lyall had warned him about. Kaveh was honest and caring and—nice. And he was the kind of guy who wouldn't even find that last part embarrassing.

Then another, furious thought followed. He couldn't believe Kaveh hadn't told him. Sure, he had mentioned he had joined the clan at young age, but he had left out the part about being a terrifying earth drakone with poisonous flames as a weapon.

He had lied to Remi. Lied to everyone, in fact, because Xiang Jao's and Rhys's reaction had been one of both fear and surprise. Of course, Remi had been far more deceitful, but that was beside the point.

Kaveh wasn't supposed to be the one who kept dark secrets. That was Remi's job.

His silence while he tried to process all of this annoyed Zale, who had the attention span of a minnow. "Let's go. I got an awesome Harley for this job, and you can ride on the back."

"I can't leave now." Remi found himself making the same argument to Zale he had made to Lyall. "Kaveh's under the Matchmaker curse. I've spent the past few days trying to help him figure out who he's matched with. He has a drakone amulet that will change shape when his future spouse touches it."

"We know who it is." Zale snorted. "Lyall told us. It's that Asian kid who works here. Plus, we already have him. We've had a tail on you the whole time here. The Don insisted on it. The Pouch Twins grabbed Kaveh's future hubby after he left that bar in Tucson."

Zale's words sent a chill through Remi. The twins were two of the Colony's most violent enforcers. They could transform into massive humanoid versions of giant African pouch rats, although their nickname came from their tendency to steal anything that wasn't bolted down.

"What do you mean, Lyall told you?" Remi had been the one who let Lyall know Kat was the match, but he had hoped the hellhound would keep an eye on the vet assistant, not turn him over to Colony enforcers.

It didn't make sense. Lyall wasn't under the indenture contract anymore. He could have left at any time, leaving Remi's half-chewed body behind if he felt like it. If he hadn't wanted revenge on Remi—which to be fair, wouldn't be unreasonable—why would he go after Kat? He liked the vet assistant. A lot. He couldn't hide something like that from Remi's psychic ability, even with the mental shields he had. The hellhound could have simply left. Instead, he had stayed, gone with them to the club, then turned Kat over to the Pouch Twins.

An awful thought crystallized in his mind. Lyall hadn't been able to get out of his indentured servitude for years. Arimanius was very good at keeping his claws in someone once he got a hold of them. Remi could testify to that. Maybe Lyall had lied about tricking Remi into breaking the indenture contract. Instead, the hellhound's sudden freedom could have come from making a different, better bargain with the head of the family.

Lyall had set things up so Remi would distract Kaveh while he delivered Kat into the hands of the Colony—and Remi's father had given him his freedom for it.

"The twins told me they grabbed the kid first, but Lyall showed up and said the Don gave him new orders. The hellhound has the hostage now." Zale waved in the direction of the new line of the rift. "The snakes have pushed out their territory somehow, so maybe the plans changed. I don't know what the fucking dog is doing, but it's not like he can lie to us. We own him."

The Colony didn't own Lyall anymore. Was the hell-hound going to threaten to hurt Kat in order to force Kaveh to give him the information about technology that could move rifts? Somehow, he had never thought of Lyall being that cold-blooded. It was the sort of plan Remi's father would have come up with. Then he remembered he had convinced Lyall to stay by warning him the drakones could use their new power over rifts to come after Lyall's pack on Mount Hood. Seen in that light, Lyall might be thinking of this as a way to protect his family.

To sum up, this whole shitshow was Remi's fault, and Kat might die a horrible death because of him. Then Kaveh would hate him even more.

"Where are the Pouch Twins?" If he found the twins, they might know where Lyall and Kat were.

A plan began to form in Remi's mind.

A stupid, poorly thought out, downright suicidal plan.

"Mabel and Fable told me they were going to the monstertown first. Someone told them there was expensive shit in Kaveh's clinic there, and you know how the twins are when they think they can score some loot." Zale let out an exasperated breath. Talking about operational details bored him. He liked to bust heads, not plot complicated strategy. "Anyway, you're done here, little cousin. After what happened in Salem, the Don will put me in eight cement sneakers if I don't get you out of here in one piece. Get going, or I'll carry you to the bike."

"I get to ride on a Harley. That's awesome." Remi plastered on his best fake smile. He could cling, cursing, to his cousin's back as they drove out of town, deal with his father's fury that he hadn't followed the game plan, and leave Moon Star Ranch behind forever.

Or he could try something spectacularly dangerous and likely get killed in the process.

He sucked in a deep breath, focused on his inner self, and transformed.

As Zale spun in a circle trying to figure out where the hell his cousin had gone, Remi raced away on four paws, leaving his clothes behind.

17

Remi transformed back as he approached the stables. As awful as the creepy living armor was, he had to admit that it was preferable to nudity, especially since he was planning to ride to the monstertown.

He ran into Javier, who thought Remi's all-leather outfit was hysterically funny—until Remi hit him with the full force of his compulsion. He exerted his powers, convincing the man that saddling an unstable horse known for her violent tendencies so Remi could take a midnight ride was a reasonable idea. Then he asked the wrangler to strip off his clothes and hand them over, which proved not at all difficult.

Of course, if he knew how to saddle Amanita, he could have saved himself time and energy. Kaveh would be happy to teach him how to do it.

No, Kaveh wasn't going to teach him about horses, and Remi wasn't going to be Kaveh's dating instructor anymore either. If he could get up enough courage to free Kat and survive the experience, the best he could hope for was getting away without seeing Kaveh's revulsion when he understood the depth of Remi's betrayal.

Twenty minutes later, he sat on Amanita, who had been let out of the stall and tacked up by a compliant Javier. Remi hadn't done any nighttime riding, but after a mental exchange with Amanita that included images of Kat holding assorted horse treats, he felt confident the half repoequus would get him to the monstertown safely.

Anything after that wouldn't be safe at all.

As he rode, he tried to put together a plan in his head. A SWOT analysis, perhaps. That was corporate and impersonal. It didn't include emotions, like worry over what had happened to Kat, dread over what Arimanius might do to Remi for disobeying orders, or his hopeless longing for more time with Kaveh. He kept thinking of the warm afterglow of lying next to one another, sated, happy and together in a way he had never felt before.

No, no, back to cold-blooded business plans.

S was for strengths. He still had a few of those. Once he crossed the rift boundary, he would be riding on a half-alien horse with poison fangs. The Pouch Twins wouldn't expect him in the monstertown, so he had the element of surprise.

Weaknesses. Well, he had a lot of those. To start with, he had no idea if Kat was in the monstertown or how to free him if he was. Mabel and Fable knew all about Remi's psychic powers, and it wasn't like he could go head-to-head with Lyall and live to tell the tale.

Opportunities? If he could rescue Kat, there were people in the monstertown who could protect the vet assistant, like the guardians. Remi could hightail it out of there and come up with some bullshit story that blamed everything on Lyall. Since the hellhound must have plans to return to his home-sweet-hellmouth in Oregon, he would make the perfect scapegoat. Kat and Kaveh would live unhappily ever after, and Remi would go back to his lonely Boston brownstone and try to forget Kaveh even existed.

Threats. Remi didn't want to think about those. There were too many of them. Lyall and/or the Pouch Twins could figure out what he was doing and eat him (Lyall) or seriously maim him (the twins). Zale had more brawn than brains, but he could figure out that Remi had headed to the monstertown and was bound to come after him soon.

Then there was the biggest threat of all—Remi's feelings toward Kaveh. He didn't want to leave and never see him again. But it wasn't like he could tell the vet the truth. At best, he would hate Remi for lying to him or, at worst, turn him over to his drakone family.

Between the full moon and his enhanced night vision this close to the rift, the trip wasn't difficult, only slow. He was sure Amanita could go faster, but whether that was safe for the repoequus and whether he could stay on her back at a canter weren't questions he could answer.

He paused as he approached the entrance to the monstertown. Both guardians sat motionless at the entrance as before. In the distance, the indistinct bulk of the abandoned base was barely visible in the low light.

Remi pulled on the reins, and Amanita stopped. She tossed her now-horned head as he dismounted, and he staggered as images flooded his brain. A giant jellyfish mon drifted through the air, its glowing body floating through metal doors ripped off their hinges then passing through debris-strewn corridors. The skeletal remains of a dead soldier lay rotting against a wall, and the monster sent a questing tentacle toward the corpse. It moved on at a languid pace, its translucent frills giving it the appearance of a possessed bridal veil.

"Why are you doing this?" Remi fell to his knees, the horror and fear reverberating through his brain and wiping out any possible lustful counterattack to Amanita's assault.

The images faded, and Amanita regarded him with her beetle-black eyes before tilting her graceful neck in the direction of the base.

Not an attack, a warning.

"That's a phantom, then." He stood up, his legs shaky. "There's one of them inside in the base trying to get out?"

The repoequus gave an angry huff, and Remi was inundated with images of dozens of the floating ghost brides from hell swarming through the half-destroyed remains of a building interior.

He held up a hand to forestall any more information from Amanita. "Lots of monster jellies at the base. Do not stop to take the tour. Got it."

Her form rippled, and her tack disappeared, somehow incorporated into her scaly hide. She tossed her head and trotted off into the saguaros.

"Enjoy the jackrabbits." Remi gave her a quick salute and took off on foot to the monstertown entrance.

He bowed to both of the lions, who gave no sign they were anything except solid stone. The gate swung open for him, and he walked down Main Street. Nothing seemed out of the ordinary, if that word could be used to describe the town on any occasion. Shroom lights lit up the streets, but most of the inhabitants were inside, perhaps deciding that might be safer given that their interzone community had become part of a riftland.

Now that he was here, he felt more uncertain about his plan. He needed allies, but there wasn't anyone he could trust. He could try to track down José and Jessie, but he couldn't explain why he needed their help without telling

them who he was. His plan depended on plausible denia-
bility of any connection to the Colony.

Remi headed to Kaveh's office first, since Zale had
mentioned the Pouch Twins wanted to rob it. It was closed
of course, the windows dark.

Except for a quick flash of light, winking out as soon as
he spotted it.

The twins were up to their usual larcenous ways. Remi
approached the building with caution. He considered and
then rejected the front entrance and instead skulked
around, prepared to break in through the back door. It was
already open, the window smashed, and the door unlocked.
Fast and sloppy—this job had the Pouch Twins' grubby
paws all over it.

Once inside, it wasn't hard to figure out where the
burglars were. Loud screeches came from the aviary, and the
glow of shroom lamps lit up the partially open door to the
room. Remi crept down the hallway, trying to make as little
noise as possible. He was within a meter of the door when a
voice rang out behind him.

"Put your hands up or I'll shoot."

Remi froze then lifted both arms into the air. His heart
pounding in fear, he turned around to face a familiar
lumbering creature close to twice his size. A pinkish face too
small for the body below it was twisted into a confused
expression, and a hairy, paw-like hand was pointing a
banana in Remi's direction.

Well, there was a reason Fable was considered the brawn
and not the brains of the Pouch Twins.

"What are you doing here?" Fable jabbed the fruit at
Remi then considered it for a long moment, as if unsure why
it wasn't his gun. Of course, since the monstertown was now
in the riftland, a gun was nothing more than an exciting

choice for a paperweight. "Zale was supposed to get you out of town."

Remi let his hands fall to his side and started talking. "Change in plans. Orders from the Don. I need to take Kat— the hostage, I mean— straight to Arimanius."

"Huh." Fable scratched at one ear. "The Don is here? He never comes on jobs, but I guess he's got a real problem with the drakones."

"That is why it's operationally critical I take possession of our target and move him to the alternate location." Remi glanced at the door to the aviary. "Is Kat in there?"

"No cats, only birds." Fable peeled the banana and began to eat it. "Mabel thinks we could sell them and make some money, but I think we should make off with some of the doc's medical equipment instead."

Remi took a breath. The problem with tricking the twins was that the best cons relied on the marks themselves buying into the lie, adding their own fantasies and thoughts to the original bait. Fable and Mabel had been accused of many things, but overthinking and creativity weren't among them.

"Kat Nakamura is the hostage," Remi said. "Kaveh Salehi's Matchmaker-chosen partner."

"Oh, you mean the kid." Fable shook his head. "We did snatch him, but Lyall showed up and said he was taking him to the military base to be eaten by the phantoms."

Remi stopped himself from blurting out a shocked *What?* in Fable's face before the door behind him opened wider, spilling light into the corridor.

"Stop fucking around with whoever you caught and kill him." Mabel stood silhouetted in the door frame. She wasn't much smaller than her twin brother, but unlike him, she held a large bowie knife in her hand, which *would* work in a riftland. "Oh, it's little Remi. Come on in here and help with these cages."

She gestured for them to enter and disappeared inside. Fable clapped a hairy arm over Remi's shoulder, and he had little choice but to play along.

The aviary was trashed, and Remi had to hide his fury at the twins for messing up all of his hard work. That reaction wouldn't fit with the lies he was currently telling, and the twins wouldn't believe Remi had done any actual manual labor in the first place. He hardly believed it himself.

Empty cages gaped open, except for one enclosure where all three of the phoenixes were shoved in together. The fire birds fluttered their wings, squawking in distress. Remi looked around, worried something had happened to Snow.

"Bad guys, bad guys." Snow's voice came from over his head, and Remi looked up to see the cockatoo perched on a top shelf.

"That one won't shut up." Mabel pulled another knife, one of the weighted throwing blades she was so talented at using.

Remi lunged forward to block her from hurting the bird.

He succeeded in knocking the knife sideways, and the blade hit one of the windows with significant force, leaving a star-shaped crack. Any relief he might have felt fled when Mabel grabbed his throat with her free paw, hoisting him up off the floor.

His vision began to go black around the edges, and he kicked at her uselessly.

Fable came over and yanked at her arm. She dropped Remi onto the floor and began to argue with her brother.

"Don't choke him. He has to tell us the new plan." Fable

jabbed the remnants of the banana in Mabel's face until she grabbed the peel and hurled it on the floor.

"Lyall said there was a new plan too when he took that skinny guy we were supposed to kidnap." Mabel had multiple knives, and Remi didn't even have a piece of fruit to defend himself with. She tended to have a quicker temper and a more suspicious mind than her brother. "What's this about a new-new plan?"

Remi propped himself up on his elbow and forced himself to make words come out of his raw and bruised throat. "The white bird is worth a fucking fortune. You'll get more money for him than all of the fire birds put together."

The twins stopped their posturing and turned toward him, the mention of money getting their undivided attention. Remi crawled to his feet, posed in front of Snow, and made a dramatic flourish in the bird's direction.

"This is a rare mix of a sulphur-crested cockatoo from Mossy Nipple Bend in Australia and a copper-banded Rift-world phoenix." Remi followed that spiel with a telepathic outreach to Snow. He rarely tried using his psychic abilities on animals, but it had worked with Amanita, so he sent images of vintage music videos to the bird. "Snow here can shatter security glass with one squawk and send fireballs to take out security guards. Everyone is going to want this bird, trust me."

Snow puffed his chest at the compliments and began sashaying along the windowsill to the beat of one of the videos, adding the lyrics with a squawk. "Money, money, money."

"It sings too." Fable regarded Snow with new appreciation. "Good job, Remi. Now climb up there and bring it to us."

"And make it snappy." Mabel pointed to the cages strewn

over the floor. "Put that parrot in one of these, and let's get going. I'm talking to the Don before I agree to another secret plan."

Remi had no desire to deal with his father right now. The type of bullshit he was spouting at the twins wouldn't fool Arimanius for a second, and he needed to figure out what Lyall had done with Kat.

"Let me find the most secure enclosure for him." Remi bent over the cage crammed with alarmed phoenixes, using his body to block the twins from seeing what he was doing. "Snow's trickier than he looks."

Snow, who always wanted to be the life of the party, launched into another rendition, this time an old hip-hop classic. That gave Remi a few precious seconds to set things up. He stumbled over things, acting as awkward as he could, then pushed a collection of empty boxes and cages against the wall and climbed up toward Snow.

The bird kept singing, a manic gleam in his black eyes. Overstimulation. Remi recognized all the signs of an impending cockatoo meltdown.

"Please." Remi held out his arm toward the bird. "I need your help right now."

Snow raised a claw in invitation then backed away as Remi got closer. He moved his head in a rhythmic motion as if encouraging Remi to join him.

Not encouraging.

Demanding.

The makeshift ladder underneath Remi wobbled dangerously. It was hardly the best platform to show off his dance moves.

"What's taking so long?" Mabel wasn't known for her patience. "Get the damn bird down here or I'll throw something and knock it out."

Remi imitated the bird's horizontal head bob, swaying from side to side. He snapped his fingers and added a few moves with his hips. Fable, who had more patience than his sister, at least when humiliation was involved, burst into laughter. Remi ignored him, focusing on the parrot. Snow danced closer, trying to imitate Remi's movements. The animal lifted one claw again, this time preparing to hop onto Remi's arm.

The junk underneath Remi's feet shifted again. Then the entire pile gave way, and he crashed to the floor.

Several things happened at once. Snow squawked in alarm and sprang into the air. The noise sent the phoenixes into a frenzy, and they scrambled out of the cage door Remi had unlocked, shrieks and sparks flying everywhere.

Remi ended up sprawled out on the floor, landing on his head, which hurt like hell.

Fable shouted and scrambled to chase the firebirds. His foot caught on the banana peel, and in a perfect and unintentional act of physical comedy, he went crashing into a collection of storage containers.

Remi scrambled to his feet, but Mabel still had her big knife and was pointing it at him.

"You did that on purpose." Her finger tightened on the hilt, her eyes narrowed and furious. She was going to kill him over this, and his father probably wouldn't do anything more than dock her pay for a few weeks.

Snow landed on Mabel's left arm and cooed. She lifted her arm, and the bird took the opportunity to scramble to her shoulder. Had the Pouch Twin not been threatening him with a deadly weapon, Remi would have warned her to keep the cockatoo away from her head and neck.

Since she did, though, Remi shut his mouth and

watched as Snow darted out with his beak and took off part of a hairy earlobe.

Mabel screamed and dropped the knife. The firebirds didn't take that well at all. Balls of flame roared over the room, all at about chest level. Remi curled into a fetal position on the floor as Mabel and Fable swore and yelped then raced out of the room.

Remi didn't uncover his eyes until the back door to the medical building slammed shut. Blood covered his palm. His blood. He must have hit his head harder than he thought. Then he coughed because the phoenixes had set fire to the room. Of course they had. That was how his luck had been lately. His vision swam, and he struggled to remain conscious. He was going to die of smoke inhalation if he stayed here.

Snow landed on his chest and, after a moment's consideration, gave him a hard bite on the shoulder. Remi groaned and lifted his head. The room began to fade to black, and he rested it back down again.

"You should leave." Remi gestured to the smoke now billowing around them. "No one's coming back to save me."

Snow cocked his head and said one word. "Kaveh."

18

Kaveh only rode out to the monstertown on Ranger because he didn't know what else to do. Kat hadn't answered his phone or responded with any new texts. With rift effects spreading past the ranch and into the city, that could be because cell service was poor—or it could be something else. Garreth was still working in his office when Kaveh came in, but the ranch owner hadn't heard from Kat either.

He suspected his assistant didn't want to talk to him, but the confrontation with Rhys and Xiang Jao had convinced Kaveh he had to tell Kat everything. He didn't want to have his friend trapped between mafia enforcers from the Colony and Rhys's contemptuous view of humans, but that was the reality of the current situation.

Another reality was that his summ powers had manifested at the worst possible time. He had hoped to talk to the matriarch alone and share this development with her, but Rhys had made him absolutely furious. Kaveh didn't want to think about what would have happened if the summ had hit

Rhys. He didn't want this awful inheritance from the parents he had never known.

What he did want was to go back to Remi's cabin and crawl into bed next to him.

But he couldn't.

Remi was leaving tomorrow morning, and he understood Kaveh had obligations and duties that had to take priority. Besides, with the way Rhys was acting, the ranch wasn't safe for Remi. Kaveh was grateful he had kept Remi's ratkind background a secret from his drakone relatives.

After spending an hour brooding over the events of the evening, he had concluded that asking the guardians for their advice would be the wisest course of action. He needed to talk to someone objective about all of this.

Well, maybe not all of it.

Having sex with Remi wasn't something he could bring up with two lion dogs. It also wouldn't be appropriate to share the depth of his feelings about Remi with them—or anyone. Kaveh had already damaged his friendship with Kat, likely beyond repair, because of his duty to his clan. He couldn't add on the betrayal of falling in love with Remi right before he was forced to marry Kat.

Was he falling in love with Remi?

Kaveh tried to push that thought out of his mind and focus on the problems the guardians might be able to advise him on. His furious display with the matriarch and Rhys had only made the situation worse. He hadn't told his family he had developed the poisonous fire ability Azdahas were notorious for, partly because of the unspoken unease he had always felt about his birth clan. The Azdaha clan had warred against and even hunted other drakones for millennia. His ancestors had done the same to humans, back thousands of years ago when a rift in ancient Persia had opened long enough to establish serpent dragons as the embodiment of evil and chaos.

Guilt over his background had hung over him since he was old enough to understand that Xiang Jao had taken him after the Sundering even though he was the child of her worst enemies. His birth parents were no more than a dim memory, but he felt their ominous presence hovering over him even now when his anger over the argument with the matriarch and Rhys still boiled under the surface.

Threatening his clan members with his toxic fire had been wrong. As frustrating as his clan's dismissal of Kat's feelings was, he couldn't blame them for wanting the young vet assistant under their protection. The Colony had sent their people into Tucson, and as angry as he was with Rhys, he was glad his ex had driven them away. The mafia-like Colony had recently attacked Ceto's human husband in the waters off Massachusetts, and Kat could become a target.

Lost in his thoughts, he only realized something was wrong as he drew closer to the monstertown's gates. Both guardians were missing, and at least one of them should have been protecting the town against threats from the outside.

Unless there was a threat *inside* the town.

Kaveh urged Ranger into a canter then slowed as a large bird flapped toward him, sparks rising above its wings. A moment later, Snow landed on his arm.

"Bad guys, bad guys." Snow cocked his head. It could have been Kaveh's imagination, but the ever-mischievous bird seemed more solemn than usual.

He had no idea how the bird had escaped and why it would have taken flight into the desert at night. He tried to soothe the parrot by stroking his head, but Snow squawked and tried to nip his hand.

"Little rat." Snow ruffled his feathers, as if frustrated, and the meaning hit Kaveh all at once.

Something had happened to Remi.

Kaveh galloped toward the entrance, Snow flying along beside him. As he drew closer, he saw a dog-like shape on top of the town's outer wall, near the barred and shut front gates. José sat on the top of the barrier, using his cadejo night vision to scan the surrounding desert. As the most formidable Riftworld individual in the town other than the guardians, it would make sense he had taken up the guard position.

Spotting Kaveh, José launched himself off the wall, dropping over six meters into a graceful crouch. He transformed into human form and swung one of the gates open.

"I'm glad you're here." José pointed up the street, and with a sinking feeling, Kaveh realized the smoke was coming from his office building. "Two of the ratkind trashed your clinic. The phoenixes set the place on fire trying to escape."

"Is anyone hurt?" Kaveh was breathing hard, and not from the ride. Maybe he had misunderstood Snow and Remi was safe and sound back at the ranch.

"Remi." José winced at Kaveh's expression and rushed out the rest of the story. "We pulled him out, but he's got a bad cut on his head and with all that smoke..."

Kaveh didn't stop to hear more. He swung off Ranger and handed the reins to José before breaking into a run toward his clinic.

Smoke billowed out from a shattered window. The phoenixes soared overhead, screeching with their alien metallic cries as sparks showered down from their wings.

Raion sat underneath the birds, as immobile as when he and his sister Kaida guarded the front gates. Dust swirled up around him, extinguishing the sparks from the fire birds. A small crowd of town residents were nearby, hovering over someone on the ground.

Jessie jumped up as Kaveh approached, waving him closer with frantic hand movements. "He has a head injury and smoke inhalation, I think."

She pointed to Kaveh's medical backpack, resting on the ground next to more supplies salvaged from the clinic. Jessie had a law degree, not a medical one, but worked as an EMT and volunteered at Kaveh's clinic. Her wild fashion sense often led to outsiders dismissing her as flighty, but she was as solid as a rock during a crisis.

Kaveh crouched down, and Remi gave him a wan smile then coughed.

"Tonight's gone downhill since I saw you last," Remi said.

He squeezed Remi's hand and forced himself to concentrate on a quick trauma assessment. After ruling out a neck injury, Kaveh got to work. He cleaned and stapled the laceration on Remi's scalp, then did a more detailed assessment with a living crystal bioadapted to provide feedback on individuals with Riftworld physiology. Thankfully, nothing more serious showed up.

Other than the cut and a mild concussion, Remi wasn't badly hurt. Jessie had been right to question smoke inhalation, but a short time later, Remi was propped up on the ground, breathing normally and eating a cheese snack bar provided by one of the Goat Sisters.

"Snow is my hero." Remi waved the snack bar at the bird, who fluffed his feathers in pride. "He flew out to get help. Raion rescued me before I became barbecue, and he put out the fire."

Jessie and the others filled Kaveh in on the attack, with

Remi adding in rather nonsensical details that didn't shed much light on what had happened. He also didn't make much sense when Kaveh asked him why he was here in the monstertown, mumbling about needing some nighttime video for his wrap-up stream tomorrow. Despite the man's brave front, Kaveh was worried Remi had lingering post-concussive effects.

One thing was clear—this had been a ratkind attack. Maybe Remi had been in the wrong place at the worst time, or maybe his association with Kaveh had made him a target. He needed to get the man somewhere safe.

"I think you're okay to travel." The best option was to have Jessie bring Remi back in the town ambulance, which was a modified horse-drawn carriage. Once they were past the new rift boundary, they could call a city ambulance, and Remi would get a full hospital evaluation. "We'll get you back to the ranch. I've got to check out the damage and make sure the ratkind who did this don't attack anyone else."

"No, I want to go with you." Remi stood up, wobbled, then pressed close to Kaveh, dropping his voice to a whisper. "I need to talk to you. In private."

Kaveh put an arm around Remi's waist and waved off several well-wishers. They walked a short distance away, Kaveh's sense of unease growing.

"It's about Kat." Remi ran his fingers through his hair then grimaced as he touched his scalp wound. "I'm starting to remember now. I overheard the two burglars talking about a hostage and the military base."

The Colony had abducted Kat.

Cold, sick dread filled Kaveh. He couldn't think of a better place than the base for them to hold him. The barrier keeping the phantoms inside the inner core relied on complex drakone technology the matriarch herself had put into place. He knew little about it, except that it was forbidden for any of the clan to enter the facility. That could disrupt the cordon and risk the release of the ferocious invertebrates.

"Thank you." Kaveh clasped Remi's shoulder and was surprised when the man flinched. He pulled away, upset at himself for losing focus. Remi was injured and manhandling him was inexcusable. "I'm sorry. You've been through too much tonight. I'll get Jessie to bring you back, and I'll inform my clan. We'll save Kat."

"This can't wait." Remi twisted his hands together, his face pale. "The information is time sensitive. I mean, we need to go up there now. I can help. The person who's holding Kat—he'll listen to me."

Kaveh raised his hands in a soothing movement and was about to insist Remi lay back down and rest when a voice grumbled behind him, rough as gravel.

"My apologies, Kaveh-san, for the interruption."

Kaveh turned to see that Raion had taken on his humanoid alter form, which he did only when he needed to communicate more complex information to anyone not a komainu. Jessie stood by his side, her eyes wide.

"Kaida has contacted me." Raion bobbed his stone head. "The sparkleflies have detected an issue at the base. The cordon around the phantoms has weakened."

Sparkleflies were Riftworld insects capable of conscious thought as a mass hive mind, and they lived in the abandoned base. They served as an early warning system for threats from there, and the guardians could communicate with them.

This wasn't good.

If a rift storm broke out, enhancing the phantoms'

power, they could break free and attack the monstertown. At least they couldn't cross the rift boundary and threaten the ranch. They couldn't modify their Riftworld bodies enough to become a threat outside the riftland.

"Has Kaida-san notified the matriarch?" Kaveh tried to push down the fear rising in his chest. If the phantoms escaped into the outer part of the base, Kat and whoever held him captive there would die terrible deaths. The ratkind had played a dangerous game, and now everyone could lose.

Raion gave a somber nod. "Kaida must now return here to protect the town by my side, and no one in the keep can enter the base without destroying the rest of the barrier."

"Can I enter?" Kaveh asked. Raion and Kaida were the only ones outside of his clan who knew about his true background as an Azdaha. Maybe one good thing could come from his birth family's bloodthirsty history. His birth clan was so different from the aerial drakones that it might be possible for Kaveh to go inside and not disrupt the containment system for phantoms.

"Possibly." Raion's stone face reassembled into a frown. "You are young, Kaveh, and have not transformed yet into your drakone alter form. It would be a great risk."

"I can go inside the base." Remi swayed, grabbing Kaveh's arm to steady himself. "It's not like I can mess up any dragon whatchamacallits, and I'm sure the rat people will listen to me if their lives depend on it."

Raion looked skeptical.

Kaveh shook his head. "Go with Jessie. You need a hospital."

"If those monster jellies are out there, Jessie and I might not be safe traveling to the ranch." Remi tightened his hold on Kaveh. "At least let me go out to the gates with you. I came here on Amanita, and you need all the help you can get."

Kaveh hadn't considered how Remi had gotten from his cabin and the bed they had recently shared to the monster-town. Amanita knew the way of course, but how had Remi taken her out here? None of the wranglers would have allowed a guest out at night on any horse, much less the repoequus.

Remi let go of his arm and walked toward the monster-town gates, his gait still wobbly, and Kaveh pushed aside those questions. He gave as swift a bow to Raion as etiquette would allow and caught up with Remi, linking their arms.

When they arrived at the entrance, Remi peered through the metal gates as Kaveh gave José a brief rundown on the worsening situation. That devolved into an argument about the cadejo joining him at the base. The phantoms were a drakone responsibility, and Kaveh wanted José to stay right where he was. Besides, Amanita was the quickest way for him to get to the military facility, and the half repoequus wouldn't tolerate the cadejo anywhere near her.

"Amanita's on her way." Remi nudged José, interrupting the discussion. "You could sniff out Lyall if he was anywhere close, right?"

Kaveh had forgotten Kat had texted Remi that the terrier was with him. He prayed the ratkind hadn't injured or killed the fairy hound.

"Sure I could. Got a great nose." José answered Remi's question without stopping the argument. He pushed his finger into Kaveh's chest. In anyone else, Kaveh would have taken it as unacceptable aggression, but from José it was more like an overexcited puppy jumping up on him. "You need backup out there. I'll stay downwind from the repoequus."

"You need to stay here and protect the town and your wife." Kaveh tossed that in. It was a low blow, but the bond to protect Jessie was too powerful for the cadejo to ignore.

"Okay, fine, but I don't see why Remi gets to go with you and I have to stay here." José made a face at the gate that couldn't be described as anything other than a pout.

"He's not going with me." Kaveh turned back, but Remi wasn't leaning on the gate anymore. He was on the other side of it, seated on Amanita. She was in her repoequus alter form, with the addition of a saddle and full tack, all in pearl-white scaled leather. She bared her fangs, hissing in José's direction.

"Sorry, but this is something I have to do myself." Remi gripped the reins and gasped as the repoequus launched into a gallop.

19

Remi had seen the wranglers and other guests riding their horses at a quick pace. He had even been obliged to take a riding test during which the horse bounced him around on the saddle before building up to a decent speed for about a minute.

None of that had given him an inkling of what riding Amanita at a full gallop would feel like. She raced into the night, her mind unhelpfully sending images to Remi of him falling off and cracking his head open. Remi pushed back with more horse porn, and the mare went faster, her giddy sense of freedom downright infectious.

The emotional swing from terror to exhilaration was distracting enough that he ignored the significance of the spitting moisture against his face until a green flash illuminated the desert around him.

A rift storm was coming.

Remi could feel it now, the power of it tugging at his alter form. Given that he was riding an animal who would pounce and eat him if he transformed, he gave his inner chinchilla a firm lecture about shutting up and staying in the background.

He pulled up several meters from the outer perimeter of the military base, a fence topped with barbed wire, broken up by empty guard houses. The growing storm had blocked out any moonlight, and the looming walls of the structure were only intermittently lit up by flashes of green in the sky.

Sliding off Amanita, he patted her on the neck. She tossed her head and the saddle and reins disappeared into her scaly hide. He expected her to flood his mind again with pictures of the terrifying jellies, but she sent an image of Kaveh at him.

A warning? Or maybe a suggestion?

Remi sighed. "I know going in by myself is stupid. But this is all my fault, and I have to try to get Lyall to listen to me."

If that didn't work, he could try to psychically push Lyall into feeling aroused by the vet assistant, which might make him hesitant to hurt Kat. Lyall's mental shields were good, but Remi had played this trick on him once before with success. His abilities were strongest when sexual attraction already existed.

Amanita didn't seem impressed with his logic. She ignored him and began snuffling around, probably hoping to find something small and furry to eat.

Remi walked over to the closest guard station, pulling a small shroom light out of his pocket. Its bluish glow was brighter with the increased power from the storm, and it gave him enough light to walk without falling over the debris scattered around. He stepped over the shattered remains of the raised gate that had let in vehicle traffic, his sneakers crunching over the broken glass that had once protected soldiers in the guard shack. The shroom lights also emitted ultraviolet light, and he hastily moved the beam away from what had to be old blood stains.

The base hadn't switched hands without casualties, most of them on the human side. Remi had skimmed over background history on the base while prepping for this job. He had even considered shooting a vid or two at night here to play on the spooky monster reputation the place had.

As the ominous reality of the place sank in, Remi put that thought on the Terrible Idea shelf. If he got out of this mess, he was going to do an entire stream on Flutterberry, the spoiled mothcat.

Something clattered across the ground, and he shivered. If that was a scorpion, it was an awfully big one. The sound came from his right, and he had to make a quick decision on how to begin his search.

Remi turned left. Circling the main building seemed to be a reasonable option. Heading away from the scuttling noises appealed to him.

His light picked out the rusting remains of army vehicles and weapons tossed away during flight. A pocket of shadow in the building wall attracted his attention. It was a hole about two or three meters in diameter, too regular in outline to be caused by a remote explosion.

He was gathering his courage to go inside the dark scary opening when the screaming started.

Startled, he pressed himself against the wall as a horde of clacking insectoid Riftworld animals poured out of the opening. They were each close to a meter in length, with shells studded with debris and a shape that approximated that of a scorpion. He hadn't been that off with his hearing, then. They were a Riftworld species he had never seen before and hopefully would never see again.

Something had frightened the creatures, whatever they

were. Trash scorpions seemed a good enough name, and
Remi wanted to follow them in flight.

But another scream rang out, and he made his decision.

He was going in.

Despite the shroom light, the room he stepped into was
so dark he couldn't make out much except for bulky forms
that could be furniture—or monsters about to kill him. He
partially transformed, the improved low-light vision and
hearing from his altered eyes and ears offset by a spike of
panic. Chinchillas didn't do heroics.

He ignored a growing certainty this was the worst decision he had ever made and forced his legs to move. His
surroundings were clearer now, the terrifying shapes
resolving into overturned cubicle desks. Part of the ceiling
had collapsed in one corner, and a door leading out to a
corridor had been torn off its hinges.

The screams had come from that direction.

A purplish glow provided more light in the corridor. It
came from masses of phosphorescent fungi that coated the
walls and dripped down from the ceiling.

Remi picked up his pace, now hearing a snuffling noise.
As faint as it was, it was enough to guide him down a
branching corridor. Another cry ripped out, agonized and
despairing, and he couldn't stop himself from peering
around the corner. He stared, trying to take in what he was
seeing.

Bubbles of water drifted up from the floor to the ceiling,
a dizzying reversal of gravity. Soft white light diffused
through the liquid curtain, turning the spheres of water into
glowing orbs.

It was beautiful, as was the creature trapped behind the
display. Translucent white and close to Remi's height if it
stood instead of floating in the air, the creature swayed in a

gentle rhythm. Delicate, frilled tendrils gestured to him, calling him to come closer and help free the poor thing. It was lovely and kind, and he would have everything he wanted if only he let it out.

"No fucking way, bitch." Remi said that part out loud.

It was a phantom, trying to lure him to his death. Remi pushed the phantom's psychic assault out of his mind and followed it up with a mental image of a sea turtle gobbling down jellyfish. Not exactly a sexy thought so his counter assault didn't have much impact on the murderous inverte-brate, but the creature pulled the plug on its psychic version of a siren song.

Colors flashed over the phantom's skin, not a language exactly, but Remi had always excelled at interspecies communication.

This food is not as stupid as the big one.

With a sinking feeling, Remi took a closer look. The phantom floated over a crumpled shape on the floor. He took in a hulking tattooed arm then and a thick leg. Finally, he caught a glimpse of a face, set into a frozen expression of dazed fascination.

The phantom had Zale, and that didn't bode well for the half kraken's continued survival. His cousin must have put two of his accessory tentacle-brains together and figured out Remi wanted to find Kat for his own purposes.

Remi had no idea what to do. The inverse waterfall must prevent the phantoms from getting out but *not* stop them from luring prey in with their psychic abilities. He couldn't fight a monster that had incapacitated one of the Colony's best fighters. Maybe Lyall could do something, but Remi hadn't found any sign of the hellhound, or Kat.

He needed to follow Amanita's advice. Kaveh would be here soon, even if he couldn't enter the base proper without releasing the barrier that prevented the murder jellies from breaking free. Remi could retreat to the guard post, meet Kaveh there, and come clean.

The thought of admitting his treachery to Kaveh made him want to vomit. It might be better to stay here with the phantom.

No, that was a good way to get killed.

Remi made his decision and stepped back, but he was brought up short by a forearm across his throat.

"You little traitor." Those words and Mabel's voice sent a chill of panic into Remi. The pressure against his throat barely let him take in a breath, and she held something sharp against his left flank that had to be the knife she was planning to sink into his kidney. "That stunt with the bird, telling us the Don sent you—all lies. No sign of Lyall or the hostage here either."

"Zale told us you sucker punched him and ran off." Fable loomed over him now, a metal-tipped baseball bat instead of a banana in his hand. One of his caterpillar-like eyebrows had been singed off by the fire birds, giving his already unpleasant features added asymmetry. "Now that jellyfish thing's got him. It's your fault."

"I came here to see if Lyall was following orders." Remi wheezed out the words, which weren't exactly a lie. "Maybe the hellhound pulled a fast one on us both. Look, Zale's in trouble. Don't you want to help him?"

"That overgrown jellyfish is going to eat someone." Mabel snarled the words into his ear. "I'd rather it was you than Zale or the two of us. Go in and get him out, or I'll gut you right here."

Neither of those options sounded appealing.

Remi was desperate enough to try a partial truth. "Kaveh Salehi is the Saguaro Rift clan's Azdaha, an immensely powerful earth dragon. Let me go, and I'll talk Kaveh into helping Zale. That way no one gets eaten."

"Go in there now or you're dead." Mabel released his neck and shoved him forward.

Remi ended up sprawled in front of the water curtain, staring up at the swaying tendrils of the phantom. Colors flashed across its glittering, bell-shaped head, giving him an impression of smug satisfaction on the phantom's part.

"Zale, wake up." Remi tried to reach out with his powers to his cousin, but all that did was cause Zale to groan and mumble, "You're beautiful," in the phantom's direction.

Tasty little rat, working with our snake enemies. The phantom's colors flashed with fury and a need for vengeance. An image popped into Remi's brain, a glowing, elongated oval that pulsed with light. *They used our own flesh to trap us here, tortured us with hunger, and stole our power to expand their lands. One by one, we were forced to eat our own kind to survive. Now we are free and will devour all of you.*

Remi didn't have the mental bandwidth to handle the confusing mix of images, emotions, and nonverbal information coming from the phantom. All he knew was that he was going to die soon, along with Zale, if he didn't come up with a plan. He reached out a shaking hand toward the bubbles. They were widely spaced apart and his hands could pass through them easily. More emotions flashed across the phantom's translucent skin—anticipation, triumph, and an aching hunger.

Remi transformed and darted inside the barrier. It was insanely difficult. His chinchilla side was now dominant, so part of his brain was screaming *run, stupid, run* while another part was dodging tentacles that crackled with electrical energy. He found an exposed forearm and bit Zale as hard as he could.

The half kraken cursed then gazed up at the phantom and gulped. He pulled his knees up and launched himself through the bubble cage as the furious phantom flashed dismay and surprise and sent a bolt of electricity toward him. Zale flattened himself on the floor and the discharge hit Fable in the chest.

There was screaming and chaos, which made it an excellent time for Remi to listen to his rodent brain and run. He leaped forward then felt his body jerk to a halt.

The phantom had a tentacle wrapped around one of his hind legs. He could feel an electrical charge building in the viscous appendage that held him fast. Ozone hung in the air, and his thick fur stood on end as the phantom prepared to electrocute him.

Something else wrapped around his stomach, and he thought for a second that the phantom had coiled another jelly-like appendage around him, so he'd be twice as dead.

Then his body felt like it was being pulled apart in two different directions, an agonizing pain that ended with him flying through the air as Zale yanked him free with one of his own tentacles.

Remi transformed back, gasping, and the living leather crawled over him, covering up the angry red marks on his abdomen and chest.

"We need to get the fuck out of here." Zale pulled him upright, and the two of them staggered toward the exit.

Remi couldn't agree more. He forced his rubbery legs to work, and they bolted out the door moments before a second, more explosive bolt of electricity hit.

They broke into a run down the corridor. A light glowed ahead, and as they drew closer, Remi could see Mabel dragging Fable into the destroyed cubicle farm, holding a shroom torch in one hand. She stood over her twin, her face a mask of fury. She began shouting at Zale, as Remi knelt down beside Fable and put two fingers on the Pouch Twin's neck, hoping desperately to feel a pulse.

"You did this! You killed him!" Mable shoved Zale out of the way and grabbed at Remi, her claws sliding off the reptilian armor he now wore.

Zale swung out two more tentacles and jerked Remi toward him.

Seriously, living leathers were the best. He would never make fun of Lyall's fashion sense again.

"Try to touch him again, and I'll cut you." Zale held a knife in his hand the size of a machete, and Mable growled but held herself back.

A groan broke the building tension.

They all stared down at Fable, who was clearly not dead.

"This job sucks." Fable tried to push himself up and failed. He reached up a hand, and his sister helped him up. Fable shook a massive, clawed fist in Remi's face then swayed on his feet. "And it's all that little brat's fault."

Remi needed to get away from the three of them and find Kaveh. Lyall and Kat weren't here, and the phantoms wouldn't be for much longer, since it sounded like something had already damaged whatever strange Riftworld tech had kept them captive. Everything was spiraling out of control, and he didn't want Kaveh to catch him chatting with three Colony enforcers.

He opened his mouth to make some sort of argument that would convince them to let him leave, but before a word left his lips, Mabel slammed her fist into his abdomen, and his vision went black.

20

Kaveh swung off his panting, terrified, horse knowing he had no choice but to leave Ranger alone in what was now a hostile riftland during a major storm.

After Remi had charged off on Amanita, Kaveh had been forced to ride Ranger to the base. The bay gelding didn't like the brutal pace Kaveh had set to catch up and stop Remi from whatever foolish heroics he was planning. His horse liked the worsening rift storm even less.

He stroked Ranger's neck, petting him and telling the horse he would be back soon. The gelding had been trained to be ground tied, but leaving him and traveling on foot was a risk Kaveh had to take.

Remi would be at the base by now, facing down ratkind criminals and kidnappers at best and deadly phantoms at worst. It wasn't like Remi turning into a chinchilla would help him if one of the floating invertebrates attacked.

Kaveh headed out into the spitting rain and unsettling energy of the storm, following the remains of a main road that had been built over twenty years ago to carry military equipment and personnel to the base. In his rush to cover the distance remaining on foot, Kaveh didn't notice the tell-tale flickering blue lights before the swarm circled around him.

Strange and beautiful all at once, the mass of small, alien organisms shifted from an amorphous mass to an array of tesseract-like shapes.

Sparkleflies.

The Riftworld insects had given Kaida an early warning about the weakening of the restraints on the phantoms. He had never heard of them interacting with a drakone. They must have sought Kaveh out to give him crucial information, but he wasn't sure he could communicate with them. The fact they had left the compound was odd enough, and he didn't think their appearance in his path was an accident.

He tried to calm himself, open his thoughts, and invite their form of telepathy into his mind. That wasn't easy. Panic over what could have happened to Remi during the time it had taken him to get here threatened to overwhelm the concentration he needed.

A few descended, swirling around him in lazy pulses of blue. He forced himself to focus and sent out telepathic images of both Kat and Remi.

The buzzing of the sparkleflies intensified, and the combined intelligence of thousands of the insects sent back an answer, but to only one of his unspoken questions. The images of the recent past they provided were bewildering— and horrifying. Kaveh could see Kat in his mind as his assistant rode up to the base on Pogo, appearing unhurt, if anxious. A hulking canine as large as a grizzly loped along next to him, eyes glowing a dull red.

A hellhound.

Infamous for working as assassins or mercenaries, the

hellhound clans loathed the drakones and had no business coming close to the Saguaro Riftland, much less inside it. Yet one of them had accompanied Kat and his horse, with little reaction from either one of them. His vet assistant could have been intimidated into cooperation, but Pogo would not have responded that calmly if one of the notorious canine predators was truly in its Riftworld form. It was more likely Kaveh was seeing the scene as the sparkleflies had, their vision able to pierce the superb cloaking ability hellhounds were known for.

The next set of images was even more confusing.

Kat stood inside the gates of the base, watching as the hellhound prowled toward the main building but making no attempt to flee. More images unwound from a different perspective and possibly a different time period. First was a sphere of energy exploding upward from the base, a massive power surge that left the physical components of the building untouched. This had to be another example of the sparkleflies' ability to see things drakones couldn't.

He was watching the destruction of the containment that kept the phantoms inside.

The next scene did nothing to calm his fears. The view shifted to an interior sealed door with acid eating away at the metal framework and the first pale appendage extending out of a smoking hole where the lock had been.

Kaveh's heart thudded with panic at the visions, but he concentrated, sending images again of Kat and Remi to the sparkleflies.

Nothing came for several moments. Then another visual sequence played out in his mind, of the hellhound emerging out of a round opening in the outer wall of the base. In the next image, Kat kicked a frightened Pogo into a gallop and raced off with the hellhound by his side.

Finally, the telepathic connection showed Remi. He held a shroom lamp in one hand, sending light into the same gaping hole the hellhound had exited from. He stood still for a moment, as if hearing something, then bent over and stepped inside and away from the sparkleflies' vision.

Kaveh ran the remaining distance to the front gates of the base, unsure if he should worry more about Remi facing down a horde of phantoms or a hellhound brazen enough to enter a drakone riftland and kidnap a human.

There was no sign of Remi on the outskirts of the complex, where Kaveh could enter without fear he would disrupt the wards placed to contain the phantoms.

If the vision the sparkleflies had provided was accurate though, he was too late. The phantoms had already escaped.

His legs burning and gasping for breath, he held up the shroom lamp he had brought and spotted Amanita inside the base's outer fence, feeding on a javelina she had killed. The remains of the pig-like creature lay strewn around her hooves. Amanita lifted her head, her mouth smeared with blood, and regarded him with large eyes that flashed blue in the light of his lamp. He approached her with a good deal of caution, but she allowed him to stroke her now-scaly snout. An image of a frightened and abandoned Ranger came into his mind, and he projected it toward her. She shook her head and snorted then trotted away in the direction Kaveh had come. He sent up a quick prayer she would find his horse and protect him.

Remi had left the repoequus waiting for him out here and must still be inside. Kaveh wasn't sure if that was good or bad news. He circled around the building, trying to match the location from the sparkleflies' images, then came to a halt when he heard harsh shouting.

His light illuminated a now familiar circular opening in

the wall. A soft glow came from within, likely from other phosphorescent light sources.

The arguing voices grew louder.

Phantoms didn't communicate with spoken languages. If Remi was inside, someone else was with him, and it didn't sound like a friendly conversation. Other than the multipurpose knife tool he carried with him at all times, Kaveh's only weapon was his summ, which he didn't want to use even if he could figure out how to call it up.

Then he heard Remi cry out in pain, and Kaveh stopped caring about who or what he might be facing. He charged in, and the summ responded to his fury by flooding into his hands.

Inside the room, he took in the scene. Remi stood hunched over and gasping, surrounded by three hulking ratkind. Two were massive humanoid rodents, with clawed hands and rodent-like heads on top of their large frames.

The male had a large club at his waist, and the female was waving a knife at Remi in a threatening manner. Kaveh couldn't tell if the third man, a tattooed biker type who held an even larger knife and had tentacles sprouting from his back, was an unusual ratkind hybrid or outside muscle they had brought in.

The flames in Kaveh's hands roared into a fireball without any thought on his part, arcing mere centimeters above the heads of the tallest ratkind before dissipating onto the far wall.

The Colony enforcers crouched in fear then turned to face him.

"The ratkind have no right to trespass on drakone rift-land." Kaveh stood with both hands raised and emerald fire licking up both of his arms. Rage burned inside him as well, a fury that these criminals had dared to touch Remi. "Move a muscle, and I'll kill you where you stand."

That was a bluff.

He couldn't use his awful power when they had Remi as a shield and was unsure if he could control the flames now that the summ had manifested again. His anger was fueling the poisonous fire, creating an inner tension that urged him to take the lives of the three criminals who had invaded drakone territory, likely colluded with the hellhound who had abducted Kat, and now were threatening Remi.

"I'm here for him." Kaveh gestured at Remi and focused on the man's face, pale with terror, hoping to reassure him he would rescue him from the three dangerous criminals. "Hand him over to me, and you can leave our riftland with your lives and nothing else."

"Fine," chorused the two rodent-like ones.

At the same time, the biker/cephalopod wound a tentacle around Remi's waist and shouted, "No fucking way."

The female snarled, yanked Remi out of the biker's suckered grasp, and threw him toward Kaveh.

It happened so fast that Kaveh had Remi in his arms even as his mind panicked, sure his unnatural flames would kill the man he had grown to care about so much. But the summ vanished back into his body, leaving Remi shaking but unhurt. He was dressed in his living leathers, and perhaps the protective organism had prevented any injury.

Kaveh would never have been able to forgive himself if the lack of control over his awful new power had killed Remi.

The three Colony enforcers took advantage of his surprise and bolted, darting out of the punched-out section of wall. The female went first, with the limping male close behind her. The tentacled biker hesitated as he followed them, shooting a last glance back at Remi, perhaps to threaten him one more time.

Kaveh breathed a sigh of relief. The three goons had been scared off and Remi was safe. Releasing his grip around Remi, Kaveh gently turned him around. He had to make sure Remi was okay then get him out of here. The base was far too dangerous.

"Please, Kaveh." Remi had never sounded so small and miserable. "Don't hurt me."

Kaveh pulled back from him, gut clenching. Of course Remi would think the worst. Now he had seen the real Kaveh, the child of monsters who could call up a deadly weapon in his hands. He could have told Remi the truth, but instead had lied, telling him he was as human as anyone else despite his drakone blood. He hadn't shared the blood-thirsty history of his birth clan, or the new, awful power he could barely control.

"I'd never hurt you." Kaveh swallowed hard, despair and guilt making him choke out the words. "There are things I should have told you about my background and about the flames, but I didn't know how to bring it up or make you understand."

"I'll find Kat, I promise." Remi acted as if he hadn't heard anything Kaveh said, words pouring out of him. "He's not here, and the twins and Zale don't have him. I'm sure he's okay. I can find Lyall and fix this."

Remi talking about his dog at a time like this didn't make much sense, and that wasn't much of a surprise. He had suffered a concussion and smoke inhalation, been assaulted by ratkind goons, and then come close to being killed with summ.

Kaveh hated that Remi thought he needed to beg not to

be killed or prove himself by trying to help Kat when he wasn't the one responsible for all of this. "When I saw the ratkind threatening you I was furious, and my control slipped. The power I have is called summ, and it's unique to my parents' clan. The Azdaha. That's what I am."

Remi stared back at him, not saying anything.

He must have been stunned by Kaveh's admission. Remi knew a lot about the Riftworld for someone who had grown up in Earth society. Species like phantoms and hellhounds —all of whom presented a threat to humans—were the type of rift people who frightened and fascinated humans. If Remi knew the earth drakones were more dangerous than even those infamous clans, learning the man he had made love to only hours earlier was an Azdaha must have been a shock.

Kaveh needed to clarify the situation's seriousness without panicking Remi further. Then he had to get him to safety. If Remi never wanted to see Kaveh again after this, that would be what Kaveh deserved. "I know who has Kat, and there's nothing else you can do to help him right now. He left the base sometime earlier tonight on Pogo."

Remi still didn't respond.

"Lyall wasn't with him," Kaveh added. "But I'm sure your dog is fine and back at the ranch." He had deep concerns the fairy hound wasn't okay at all, with a hellhound and ratkind criminals on the loose, but he didn't want to share that right now.

"Kat wasn't with Lyall?" Remi finally spoke, his voice frantic, and Kaveh cursed himself for bringing the topic of the terrier up at all. "Wait, how do you know all of this?"

"There's a hive of sparkleflies who live in the base, and they communicated with me right before I found you." Kaveh glanced around the room, nervous the ratkind might return or, worse, the phantoms he had seen escaping the base might find them. He needed Remi to understand and cooperate, and he wasn't doing a good job of explaining the situation. "They're Riftworld insects, a mass hive mind, that the guardians convinced to work here as an early warning system. They don't think about time the way we do and sometimes show possible futures instead of reality."

"I know what they are." Remi took a step back, putting more distance between them. The small gesture shouldn't have hurt so much, but it did. "They can transmit visual images of what they see like Bug, only telepathically, instead of with a human-tech interface. What did they see?"

"Kat was with a Riftworld species known as a hellhound." Kaveh waited for more of a reaction from Remi—fear or horror—but Remi took that information almost too calmly. "They're traditional enemies of the drakones and exceptionally dangerous. I think this one removed something from the base, an object that was keeping the phantoms confined here."

Remi gave a slow nod then said in a hesitant tone, "Not that it's a good thing, but if Kat's with a hellhound, at least he'll have some protection from the phantoms that have escaped."

Kaveh's last hope the information from the sparkleflies was more of a warning than reality faded. "You saw a phantom?"

"One of them had Zale—that's the guy with the tentacles—and I was trying to convince the other two to tell me what they did with Kat." Remi tapped on the living leathers, and the organism shifted to allow him to peel back the armor from his right leg. His skin was red and raised, with marks from a phantom's tentacle, which was capable of delivering a killing electric charge to its prey. At Kaveh's expression of horror, Remi added, "I got away, but the phantom was angry and sent me a mental image of something that looks like a glowing dildo. Is that what you think was stolen?"

Rhys had described the control object, which Kaveh knew only as a critical component of his clan's ability to confine the phantoms to the base, as an elongated egg. Remi had to be talking about the same item.

If the cordon had been weakened and only a few of the phantoms had escaped, the current crisis was manageable. But if the hellhound had taken the control object, there would be nothing stopping the phantoms from rampaging all over the expanded riftland. Even worse, the hellhound could bring the control object back to their pack, where it could be used against Kaveh's clan.

This was a nightmare.

"You need to get back to the ranch on Amanita." Kaveh hated the thought of letting Remi out of his sight, but there were no good options left.

The ride to the ranch would be at night, through what was now a riftland. Remi might encounter any number of dangerous species, not to mention the Colony enforcers and the hellhound. The only place more dangerous was deep inside the base, where Kaveh had to go. Remi had confirmed what the sparkleflies had shown him—at least some of the phantoms had made it out of the core. Kaveh's presence in the base could no longer make anything worse, and he had to know what had happened.

"If the control object is missing," Kaveh said, "whoever stole it could use it against my family. I have to find out if it's still here. The phantoms are a species incapable of surviving outside a riftland. They might be able to make limited excursions during this rift storm, but the ranch is outside the rift barrier. Hunker down in your cabin, and you should be safe."

"You can't go looking for those murder jellies." Remi looked longingly at the exit through the wall then back at him. "It's too dangerous. Besides, your clan put the monster-town in danger. Shouldn't they be the ones to clean this mess up?"

Remi had a point, but given Rhys's dismissive attitude toward the monstertown, which the matriarch and the clan elders must have supported, Kaveh needed to handle this himself.

He put an arm on Remi's shoulder, relieved the streamer didn't jerk away, and moved him toward the exit. "I'll be fine. Get to the ranch, and I'll come as soon as I can. Amanita should be able to scare off anything that tries to attack you."

They stepped outside, and Kaveh was relieved to see no sign of anything more dangerous than the repoequus, who walked out of the darkness to give Remi a concerned sniff. Ranger stepped up beside her, alive and well, and for once not annoyed by the vid streamer.

Amanita had come through.

Kaveh helped Remi mount the repoequus and gave his hand a squeeze. "Everything's going to be fine. I'll find out what I can here, and when I get back, I'll find Kat."

Remi opened his mouth then shut it again. He kept his fingers gripped around Kaveh's. "We need to talk. About everything."

A flash of green lightning lit up the swirling clouds above and a low rumble resounded like an angry creature's growl through the air. The storm had worsened, and it would be hours before it passed.

"We'll talk, I promise." Kaveh gave Amanita's flank a firm

pat to get her moving. "Get across the rift barrier as soon as you can."

21

Remi rode through the rift storm, at once desperate to get away and aching to turn Amanita around, tell Kaveh everything, and beg him not to go farther into the base.

He tried to stop thinking about what a total piece of shit he was and focus on not falling off Amanita. They were riding through a hellscape. The gloom around him was punctuated by flashes of green energy streaking down the sky, lighting up the saguaros one minute then plunging the landscape into darkness the next. It was raining in earnest now, soaking his hair and dripping into his eyes. The power in the storm tugged at his ratkind side, threatening to transform him into his alter form. Fortunately, his chinchilla side was quite satisfied with the plan of running toward safety, and he and Amanita pounded forward.

Another flash of ethereal light from the clouds lit up the tall palm trees that marked the ranch. It was close, maybe another ten or fifteen minutes at Amanita's current speed. Something was odd about the view though, and it took Remi far longer than it should have for him to figure out why. They hadn't passed through the rift yet. There was no sign of it stretching before him, with the ranch where it should be, on the other side of the damn thing.

That could only mean that the drakone clan had expanded their territory again, this time swallowing up the ranch.

Remi hadn't known what he would do when he got back. The obvious option was to run away as fast as he could, find Zale, and get out of town. He was fine with leaving the Pouch Twins behind to face whatever Kaveh and the other drakones wanted to do with them, but his tentacled cousin had at least tried to save Remi's life. If any other job had gone this badly, he would have counted himself both lucky and talented that he had conned his mark one last time and escaped with his life.

Instead, the sick pit of guilt sucking at his insides had only grown worse. Kaveh could be killed by the phantoms and all because Lyall had apparently decided to steal this fucking control object and kidnap Kaveh's fiancé as a bonus.

That last part still didn't make sense to him. Remi deserved Lyall's vengeance a lot more than the charming and clueless Kat.

In any event, the game had changed. The ranch was in the riftland, vulnerable to attack by many mons and especially the phantoms. The humans there couldn't use shotguns against them or even call for help from the city. Remi wouldn't have any transportation to get out of the riftland. Amanita's mental images were now focused on her young colt, and it wasn't like he could ride into Tucson on a repoequus and try to get to the airport.

The ranch was locked down when he arrived. Shroom lights were on in the main building, and there was enough light in the stables for him to bring Amanita inside.

Her colt came barreling up, sending awful images of terrifying mons rampaging across the desert and devouring various versions of Remi.

"Great to see you too," Remi told him and dismounted from Amanita.

The saddle and reins she could form from her flesh disappeared again, and she nuzzled her colt. Around her, the other horses in the barn seemed on edge, close to spooked, even to Remi's untrained eye.

"Keep an eye on the others, okay?" Remi risked a quick scratch behind Amanita's horns then headed for his room.

He walked to the cabin at a brisk pace—not panicking, only moving with prudent speed. Fortunately, he had stashed his key behind a barrel cactus, because during his transformation into chinchilla form in the base, he had lost everything but his living leathers.

Remi slipped inside and shut and locked the door. In place of the now defunct electric light fixtures, a soft glow came from the Riftworld fungi in hanging lamps. He paced around the room, noticing that the guardweed had gone from dried-out vines to a writhing silver-and-green organism, creeping along the walls and wooden supports under the ceiling. One tendril dropped down, two leaves opening up like a questioning mouth. Remi backed up, and the plant pursed its green lips in disdain before retracting up to the ceiling. The ranch's defenses didn't think much of him as a dangerous Riftworld interloper.

He decided to keep the living leathers on rather than convert them back to a tacky necklace. The reptilian armor had been awfully useful tonight. His watch, with Bug inside, was still on the bedside table. He tucked it inside a pocket that opened up in his skintight armor, hoping that meant he could keep Bug with him even if he had to transform again.

A low rumble resounded from the door. Remi whirled around, his chest tightening with fear. This was a terrible time for Lyall not to be here.

The door shook, and Remi scanned the room for a weapon he could use to defend himself. A closet full of semi-automatic rifles would have been useless even if he knew how to shoot. Most Riftworld people transformed into their alter forms for battle, but he didn't think a few strong kicks from a chinchilla were going to do anything to the snarling beast about to break into his room.

He spotted a wine bottle on the sideboard, a nice Chianti he had picked up, thinking he would share it with Kaveh. Grabbing it by the neck, he crept up to the door, which was vibrating with the force of whatever was trying to burst through. His mouth felt like sandpaper, and it was all he could do to hold onto his human form. The rodent brain inside him wanted to be as far away from the entrance as possible, but Remi wasn't going to win any sort of fair fight. The only chance he had was to use the bottle to cave in the skull of the monster outside.

The lock gave way and the door crashed open. Something huge and snarling charged into the room, and Remi swung the wine bottle at it with all his strength.

The bottle missed the monster, shattering against the door frame and sending expensive Italian wine everywhere. The guardweed vines that had been twining around the ceiling dropped down and attacked the beast, encircling its limbs and neck and yanking it upright.

And Kat Nakamura ran into the room, arms outstretched.

"Stop it! Stop hurting him." Kat yanked at the vines, and they retracted, dropping their victim on the floor.

Lyall transformed back into his human form, dressed in

his own black living leathers and splattered in wine. "What the fuck was that, Remi?"

Kat let out a distressed squeak. Remi, who now held a broken bottle with jagged glass fragments like a barroom brawler, lowered it with some reluctance. It took all of his self-control not to stab the hellhound.

Lyall had scared the hell out of him.

"Don't freak out." Kat grabbed a pillow from the couch and began blotting wine off the hellhound. "Lyall's not here to hurt you, even though he told me all about you and I think you're an awful person."

Remi glanced from Lyall to Kat, furious. The hellhound had shown Kat his true form, told him Remi was ratkind, and related a whole sob story about his indenture.

There had to have been an easier way to get Kat into bed.

"I know you're working with those giant rats who wanted to kidnap me." Kat put his hands on his hips and did his best to give Remi a hard glare. He was even more attractive when furious. "And Lyall is such a good dog"—Kat paused then recovered— "I mean, such a wonderful rift person, that he still came here to help you."

"And almost got my head bashed in as thanks." Lyall rose to his feet and licked some wine off his arm. "It's a good thing you didn't try that trick with my bottle of whiskey."

Remi was a lot better at manipulation and lying than braining monsters in the head with a bottle, so he reached out toward Kat with his powers and went for helpless and pathetic, rather than handsome and sexy.

"I can't believe my adorable puppy is an alien mon." Remi dropped the shattered bottle for emphasis and swayed on his feet as if he might swoon.

Kat only rolled his eyes.

Damn it. Kat wasn't a drakone or a hellhound with incredible mental shields. Why wasn't this working?

Lyall, who had walked across the room for the sole purpose of grabbing one of Remi's favorite T-shirts, used it to dry the rest of the wine off. Kat dropped his gaze to Lyall's tight-fitting leather pants and blushed. Remi expected Lyall to smirk at that, but the hellhound gave the veterinary assistant a goofy smile back.

Great. Lyall complained nonstop about humans, and now he had a crush on one. One that was obviously reciprocated, since Remi's ability to manipulate sexual thoughts didn't work well on anyone already smitten with someone else.

"Okay, fine. I'm a terrible ratkind person, and I lied to you." Remi hated when he had to tell a mark the truth. "But at least I didn't steal some magic dildo and let killer jellyfish loose to run amok."

Remi gave Lyall his best you're-guilty-as-hell look.

"Neither did I," Lyall shot back. "I went into that military-industrial camp of horrors to find out why the rift has gone wild and the phantoms got loose. We're in the midst of a superstorm, the monster jellies are out, and without the control object, the rift could expand far enough to make all of Tucson a feeding ground for them. You're the master thief, Remi, you tell us where it is."

"I saw an image of it when one of the phantoms tried to eat me, and that's all I know." Remi threw up his hands. "And don't blame Zale or the Pouch Twins because they came close to being eaten by the jellies before Kaveh tried to fry them with summ."

Lyall raised an eyebrow in surprise.

"Yes, Kaveh is the Azdaha." Remi found a towel to mop the wine off himself. The world might be ending, but he still had standards. "Feel free to gloat about being right about that."

"Is he okay?" Kat looked stricken. "I feel bad about yelling at him, but Kaveh should have told me he was an alien dragon a long time ago. Anyway, I need to talk to him about this Matchmaker thing. I'm *not* okay with it."

Kat and Lyall exchanged glances.

Ugh. This was not the type of love triangle Remi enjoyed being in the middle of. Lyall hadn't kidnapped Kat, but he had managed to infatuate the vet assistant—all while running around with four legs and a bad attitude.

"Kaveh thought Zale and the twins were trying to hurt me—which was true, at least for Mabel and Fable—and then he sent me back here so I could be safe." Fuck, it sounded even more awful when Remi said it out loud. "He went back into the base to see if the control object was still in there."

"Kaveh doesn't know the truth, or he wouldn't have tried to help you." Kat's words weren't helping Remi's crushing feelings of guilt any.

Damn, over twenty years without a conscience, and this was the second job in six months Remi's fledgling sense of morality had messed him up.

"Kaveh always thinks about everyone else and not himself." Kat's voice broke with those words. "He trusted you, Remi, and you lied to him."

There wasn't anything to say to that. Remi was such a horrible person even Kat couldn't find anything good to say about him.

Lyall cracked his neck and sighed. "I can't translocate for a while, but I could take a run back to the base and check."

"No, we need to stay in the cabins." Kat sounded down-right bossy about it. "That's the rule during any rift storm, and this one will go on for a while. Kaveh knows more about dangerous mons than anyone else here. The defenses in both the main building and all of the guest housing should stop anything."

A scream rang out, high-pitched and sounding as if it had come from someone young, like a child.

Remi jumped. "What the hell was that?"

"The phantoms." Lyall sounded grim. "They're here."

22

Kaveh raced across the desert, leaving the abandoned military base behind. He was asking even more of Ranger, who was exhausted by all of the riding Kaveh had done tonight. The horse had waited in the outer perimeter for his return. That was good news.

The loss of the control object, on the other hand, was an awful development. He had caught only glimpses of a few phantoms still trapped behind remnants of the disrupted cordon, and there had been no sign of the egg-like device that should be secured in the core of the military complex. Phantoms were now loose within the riftland, and even though the monstertown had strong defenders, there were too many potential meals there for the ravenous invertebrates not to attack. Kaveh had to go there first, even though Remi should now be at the ranch and Kat was still missing.

Kat, who had ridden away with a hellhound after Kaveh revealed he was a drakone, something he should have told his assistant years ago. Maybe Remi was right and the hellhound would keep Kat safe, perhaps to use him as a bargaining chip against Kaveh and his clan.

Kaveh would leave Ranger in the town to rest, update the guardians, and ask them to notify his clan of the developments. There were other horses in the monstertown, and once he checked that Remi was safely in his cabin, he could resume the search for Kat.

He paused at the top of a rise, his eyes straining through the gloom. The monstertown was lit up with a host of Riftworld light-producing tech. There was no sign of any phantoms or evidence the walls were breached. Beyond it should be the new boundary of the rift, which would appear as a glowing wall stretching up into the night sky, even in darkness.

Only it didn't.

The riftland had expanded again, and Kaveh had a sinking certainty the next interzone it had gobbled up included Moon Star Ranch. The phantoms fed on anything and anyone they could catch and, worse yet, had enough intelligence to identify the two major sources of food in the immediate area—the monstertown and the ranch. They were more than smart enough to choose the softer target.

The monstertown had the guardians, who could communicate remotely with the matriarch. Moon Star Ranch wouldn't be able to hold off an entire swarm of phantoms, and his clan had no obligation to defend the humans there.

And Remi was at the ranch, where Kaveh had told him to stay put in his cabin, thinking he'd be safe.

Kaveh made his decision and turned Ranger around.

Fear gripping his chest, he tried not to picture the worst. The ranch would be in lockdown from the storm, and with any luck, Remi would be inside his room or the main building, all of which had Riftworld protections Kaveh had set up himself.

His return to the ranch, pushing Ranger to the very limits of his endurance, felt like an eternity. He rode up to the outer buildings, seeing no one. The horses tied in the temporary stable were spooked, nostrils flaring and whinnying in fear as they stomped their hooves. No wranglers were in sight, which was how it should be, but the horses were far too vulnerable if the phantoms attacked.

He dismounted, taking a few precious moments to lift the tack off Ranger. An angry hiss sounded behind him, and he whirled around, his hands raised to repel an attack. Amanita stood before him with her monstrous colt by her side. The young repoequus's blood-red scales gleamed in the dim glow of hanging shroom lights, now providing the only illumination as alien clouds swirled overhead and dusk faded into night.

Amanita launched a psychic assault of information at him, and Kaveh lowered his mental shields to let the images in. She showed him a nightmare of phantoms floating through the ranch grounds, ghostly white tentacles twitching as the invertebrates swam through the air like water.

Kaveh focused on the repoequus, projecting every image of protection he could think of as he flung his hands out to indicate the stable. Amanita tilted her head in a questioning manner. He gestured to Ranger, who was panting, eyes wide with terror and exhaustion, then at the other horses. Despite Amanita's alien blood, she had formed a bond with the big gelding. After another moment of consideration, Amanita came forward and rubbed against Ranger's neck, then pushed him toward the minimal shelter the open-air stable provided. Her colt followed, giving a soft whinny.

Kaveh sent a silent prayer up to several gods sacred to his adopted clan that Amanita and her colt would be able to hold off a phantom attack on the full-blood horses and jogged toward the cabins.

It didn't take long for him to spot a phantom.

One floated in front of a cabin door, questing tentacles pulling at the wooden frame. All of the guest houses had guardweed inside them, but they wouldn't hold back a determined phantom indefinitely. He raised his hands to hurl summ at the monster, but the floating invertebrate sensed his presence and floated away from the door.

Electric currents jumped from one part of its skin to another, and the monster sent a lightning-like bolt directly at him. His reflexes were quick enough to dodge the blow, and when he raised both hands, his summ sizzled out to strike the invertebrate, a surge of poison and fire fused together.

The phantom made a horrible noise, high-pitched and inhuman, and fluttered its now smoking and damaged tentacles. It lurched forward, the eerie and graceful drifting now a crippled stagger, and dropped to the ground in a viscous heap.

The creature would have attacked the guests in the cabin if Kaveh hadn't intervened, and he knew it. That didn't make him feel any better about using his hated talent to kill an intelligent being.

Kaveh went to the door of the cabin and shouted for the people inside to stay put and keep the door shut. Without waiting for an answer, he hastened down the corridor between the cabins, searching for more floating invaders.

The ranch buildings were all locked down, and Amanita was protecting the horses. So far, he had seen only one phantom and no evidence of anyone injured or killed. Perhaps Amanita's visions had been more warning than reality and the majority of the jellyfish-like monsters were elsewhere in the riftland, hopefully facing down the rage of his entire clan. They were deadly creatures, but he had driven one away and could probably handle a small number of them with his summ.

A terrifying snarl ripped through the night air, and Kaveh broke into a dead run toward the sound. The ranch dogs didn't sound like that. The hellhound was here, and now he had to stop both it and any stray phantoms on the ranch. He didn't have far to run. The noise emanated from the camp's petting zoo, and when Kaveh got a good look, he stopped dead in his tracks.

There were two terrified children inside the petting zoo, surrounded by over a dozen phantoms—far more than Kaveh could hope to overcome.

Standing in front of the kids to protect them, bare-headed and holding a small furry animal in his arms, was Kat.

The gated enclosure that held the species Kaveh called his Riftworld animal ambassadors was lit up with the electric glow of the invertebrate monsters, all floating less than a meter above the ground. There was something odd about their movements. Instead of surging together to breach the guardweed Kaveh had planted, they were tangling their tentacles together, moving in a rhythmic fashion with one another.

Realization struck him. He was observing phantom mating behavior. Although the creatures weren't well understood even by other Riftworld peoples, Kaveh was fairly certain they didn't stop a hunting assault to have sex with one another. Something—or someone—had used a psychic attack to distract them from their assault on the petting zoo.

Strengthened by the rift storm, the strangling vines Kaveh planted around the ranch wove through the petting zoo's fence, darting out tendrils that struck any phantom tentacles that came close enough. The guardweed wasn't powerful enough to hold back this many of the invertebrate attackers, but it had done good work. A few of the phantoms lay on the ground tangled in knots of plant matter, their unnatural glow fading.

One intruder floated away from the attempt of two others to engage it in a three-way coupling and attacked the fence, tentacles crackling with electricity as it burned the writhing vines.

Kaveh raised his hands to hurl summ at it, but a massive shape raced out of the shadows, pouncing on the translucent monster and taking it down in a swirl of matted fur and razor-sharp teeth. The hellhound tossed a severed tentacle to one side, spitting out jelly-like flesh with a disgusted snort.

It spotted Kaveh and froze with a growl of warning, hunching backward with its ears flattened against its head.

Kaveh stepped forward, trying to decide whether to attack or negotiate. The hellhound was one of the largest he had ever seen, and they were ferocious fighters who despised drakones. Worse yet, he had no idea how long the phantoms would be distracted by their unnatural mating behavior. If they all swarmed at once, they would kill both him and the demonic dog. He wouldn't be able to fight off this many at once.

Kat spotted him and gave a yelp of alarm. "Kaveh, are you okay? Your hands are on fire."

"Just protect the children and stay back." Kaveh took another step toward the hellhound.

His assistant's next words brought him up short. "The giant dog is Lyall. I know that sounds crazy, but he's a Rift-world person and he's trying to help us."

Kaveh hesitated and dropped his hands—and the hell-hound lunged for him. His reflexes were fast, but the dog monster was faster.

It leaped into the air, missing him entirely, and landed with a wet splat behind him.

Kaveh whirled around to find the dog tussling with a phantom on the ground, the invertebrate's gelatinous flesh stained pink from wounds on the hellhound's huge body. Kaveh grabbed at the phantom's head, summ scorching out from his fingers and searing the creature's oversized cere-brum into smoking jelly.

Lyall backed away and watched him with eyes glowing like coals, wary but not hostile.

Kaveh tried to project calm and a lack of threat. Hell-hounds were famously ill-tempered but as intelligent as he was, and the beast had taken out a phantom that would have had its paralyzing tentacles around Kaveh before he even knew what was happening.

The dog swung its gaze at the fence and gave a sharp bark.

Kaveh risked a look back and saw a trio of the phantoms floating into the fence, electricity sparking around the enclosure.

The children screamed again.

Kat stepped forward, brandishing the furry animal in his hands with both arms extended in a remarkable replica of a famous scene from a Disney movie. He was holding a large chinchilla, which was odd, since Kaveh had placed the zoo's only rescue chinchilla, a Riftworld hybrid, with a nice family in the monstertown three months ago.

It couldn't be...

But it was.

This was Remi in his alter form, and he was using a

psychic assault against the invertebrate attackers. He hadn't told Kaveh about that ability.

The chinchilla kicked its legs furiously. The phantoms stopped their assault and began to stroke each other with their glistening appendages.

"Kaveh." The hellhound was gone, and in its place stood a young man with silver hair, dressed in tight-fitting living leathers. The armor was popular with the Riftworld mercenaries when they were in humanoid form.

Kaveh realized with a sinking feeling that he had seen a similar version quite recently. On Remi.

"Remi can't keep this goddamn jellyfish orgy going much longer," Lyall said. "Light up as many of the fuckers up as you can, and I'll do the rest."

Kaveh didn't process Lyall's words right away. Then the full impact of them hit him. Remi had known his cute Scottish terrier was a hellhound. And he had lied through his teeth about it.

A fairy hound and mothcat hybrid—how had he fallen for that?

In retrospect, it was obvious. The most powerful hellhounds could create mini-hellmouths and translocate through them, and all of them could disguise their form, taking on the shape of an Earth canine with ease. Remi had even told Kaveh that his "fairy hound" had recommended he obtain living leathers. All the evidence had been there, but Kaveh hadn't put it together because he wouldn't have thought Remi capable of that level of deceit.

That meant the argument inside the base with the three ratkind—no, the *four* ratkind, Remi among them—had been between a group of Colony enforcers and the ratkind spy they had sent in ahead of time.

Fury replaced shock, and he was about to demand more

information when Remi's psychic assault faltered and the floating monsters attacked. A group surged toward the fence, their focus again on killing and eating. Electricity crackled over their translucent bodies, and as Kat staggered back, Remi wriggled free and dropped to the ground.

Kaveh sent two balls of swirling green fire toward the mass of invertebrates, and Lyall raced forward and leaped, transforming into his hellhound alter form in midair as he set upon the phantoms. The two of them fought in tandem, Kaveh sending out flames that channeled the floating monsters into Lyall's snapping jaws.

It was an effective tactic. But the phantom's delicate-appearing bodies were surprisingly resilient, and there were far too many of them. Kaveh and Lyall were soon forced into standing with their backs to the fence. The guardweed was dead or dying, and exhaustion was taking a toll. Kaveh's poisonous green flames were the most effective, but he didn't have the stamina to continue using it.

Lyall was panting, his savage attacks slowed by fatigue. He drew closer to Kaveh, snapping at any glowing tentacles that came close but unable to take the fight directly to the monsters.

They would all die here.

The phantoms would use their paralyzing power to immobilize Kaveh and Lyall then move in for the easier targets of Kat, Remi, and the children. In the best-case scenario, the beasts would be hungry enough to finish off their prey. In the worst, their bodies would be dragged back to the phantoms' lair, conscious but unable to move as they were fed on by the nymph larvae of immature phantoms.

One of the invertebrates sent out a jolt of electric power, and Kaveh shoved Lyall aside, the crackling ball of blue barely missing them and hitting the fence instead. The last guardweed vine shriveled, and then the limited protection it had provided was gone.

Something small and furry raced by Kaveh's feet, and he spotted Remi's chinchilla form dodging and weaving between the phantom's trailing appendages.

Despite everything, Kaveh hoped Remi would make it out of this alive. It was becoming clear that none of the rest of them would. He dragged Lyall into the yard of the petting zoo, joining Kat in putting the two crying children in the center of their three bodies.

Sensing victory, the phantoms massed together for one final push.

Kaveh called up a weak crackle of summ and braced himself for the end.

An awful, alien shriek broke through the hum of the phantoms' electric hunger. Amanita's colt appeared out of the darkness, and even Kaveh winced as horrific images and emotions of fear and torment poured out of the baby repoequus. Kat let out a gasp and fell to his knees, and the two children shrieked in terror.

The new psychic attack enraged the phantoms, who turned from their frontal assault on the petting zoo to move toward the colt, their tentacles twitching with electric power.

The colt bolted away, and Amanita struck.

Back in human form, Remi clung to her back as she charged into the group of invertebrates, who had bunched close together as they prepared to go after Amanita's foal.

The effect resembled a bowling ball hitting a pile of balloons. The phantoms bounced around in the air, many reeling from bites delivered by Amanita's venomous fangs. Her poison hit the jellyfish-like creatures hard, paralyzing their tendrils and causing them to drop into glowing white mounds on the ground.

The surviving phantoms flowed away through the air, leaving their fallen where they lay. Off to look for easier prey, Kaveh guessed.

A burst of wind swirled through the piled-up bodies of the dead or dying phantoms, hurling them in multiple directions. The gusts caused Amanita to stagger to one side and Remi to fall off.

Kaveh ran forward, his earlier fury replaced by fear that Remi was injured. The streamer climbed to his feet when Kaveh reached his side, and without thinking, Kaveh drew Remi in toward him.

He was still holding onto him when Rhys descended from the storm clouds above, his sinuous aerial alter form creating eddies and bursts of wind before he regained his humanoid shape and landed in front of them.

"That"—Rhys pointed at Remi, his lip curling in disgust —"is a ratkind spy. You've been taken for a fool, brother."

Two other air drakones dropped down from above and transformed. Tarasque, Xiang Jao's first husband, and the matriarch herself, red-and-gold scales glittering in the dimming light from the dying phantoms around them.

"Great, the flying snakes finally decided to make an appearance." Lyall's words dripped with scorn as he limped over to stand on Remi's left. "Were the three of you waiting for the phantoms to eat their way through the humans at the ranch before you showed up? This disaster is your fault."

Rhys bristled with anger, never a good sign. He had a vicious temper when provoked. "That creature is the rat's hellhound bodyguard. They are both enemies on our lands and deserve to be treated as such."

Kaveh found his voice.

"Remi and Lyall were protecting the humans here." As angry as Kaveh was about Remi's falsehoods, the man could have left them all to die. Instead, Remi had risked his life to find Amanita and her colt and convince them to help. "I knew about Remi's background. Not every one of the ratkind means us harm."

"He's Arimanius's son." Xiang Jao's voice cut through Rhys's splutter of outrage. "Isn't that true, Mr. Gatti?"

Remi straightened then addressed her fluently in the air drakone language, rather than English. "His half-human one, yes."

Kaveh dropped the arm he had around Remi's shoulder. Even after the revelation that Lyall was a hellhound, some part of Kaveh had wanted to believe that Remi had been caught up in the Colony's plot by accident or through pressure on their part.

Instead, he was the closest they had to a crown prince.

"Remigio Gatti is also the ratkind involved in the attack on Ceto's human husband." Xiang Jao caught Kaveh's gaze and held it. "Do you still want to protect him now that you know he targeted your Matchmaker-chosen human as well?"

"Ceto's 'human' has a name." Remi's knees were trembling, which Kaveh could tell only because he hadn't moved far from Remi's side, as horrified as he was by these revelations. Remi's voice didn't reflect the fear Kaveh could tell he was hiding. "It's Jal, by the way. And the other human you're referring to is called Kat. Nice, short names. Maybe you should try using them."

"How do you know this?" Kaveh wanted this all to be a mistake, not a devastating betrayal that kept getting worse by the minute.

"Ceto told me." Xiang Jao came closer to all three of them. In a way, there was more tension in the air now than when the phantoms had been attacking. "Remi has a powerful psychic seduction ability, which he used to manipulate Ceto's human, much as he has manipulated you and your intended spouse."

Xiang Jao gestured behind them at Kat, and Kaveh turned to check on him. He had stayed in the enclosure, one arm around each child. He flushed at her words, confirming every damning fact.

"I'm surprised Ceto let you live." The matriarch gave Remi an assessing look. "She's not known to be forgiving when her possessions are threatened."

"*Jal* convinced her to let me go." Remi added more of a bite to his words, which Kaveh didn't think was wise. "Or as you put it, her human possession."

Kaveh thought back to all the times he had noticed other people's fascination with Remi, which he had chalked up to Remi's attractiveness and charm. There was also the odd behavior of people in the monstertown's saloon when Remi had convinced everyone to try out the Matchmaker bracelet. All of the couples dancing, lovers kissing—none of that had been real. It had been mental manipulation on Remi's part. It was no wonder Amanita had taken a liking to him. He used a psychic assault against others as she did, only focusing on lust, not fear.

Kaveh's mental shields protected him against those types of attacks, so Remi had been forced to fall back on more traditional methods of seduction—gaining Kaveh's trust by helping in the clinic and telling funny stories over dinner. Then there had been the picnic and the one night Remi wanted to spend in bed with Kaveh.

All part of the plan.

Nothing Kaveh had felt about the man over the past week had been real at all.

"If you know so much about the Colony, you must have heard my father trapped a hellhound under an indenture contract." Remi avoided looking at Lyall as he spoke. "Lyall came to drakone territory only because I forced him to. And he kept Kat safe when my cousins tried to kidnap him. He's free from that contract now. Let him leave. He didn't come up with this plan. I did."

"Now the little rat wants to order about the matriarch of our clan." Rhys had stayed quiet longer than Kaveh expected, probably because the older Tarasque had put a large, green-scaled hand on his shoulder. Now Rhys's temper flared out, even nastier than usual. "They both deserve to die, along with that foul repoequus and her spawn. Kaveh's match needs to be taken to the keep immediately, whether he consents or not."

Both children burst into tears and howls of protest, the girl yelling at Rhys not to hurt the demon unicorn baby and the boy shouting loudly that his father was a lawyer and would sue them. Kat managed to shush the two then stepped forward.

"I'm not going anywhere." Kat turned to Kaveh, eyes blazing in anger. Kat never got angry, even when he should. "Kaveh, I'm sorry, but even if that bracelet changes when I touch it, I don't feel that way about you. Also, I'm not going to stand by while your relatives murder Remi and Lyall, not to mention Amanita and her colt. They saved me and the kids and you as well."

The matriarch gave Kat an exasperated look, but Rhys went further. He shoved forward and yanked at Kat's arm.

Lyall must have been as exhausted as Kaveh felt after the battle, but he moved with lightning speed. He had ripped

Rhys's hand off Kat and put himself between the vet assistant and the angry drakone before Rhys had a chance to react.

"Get your claws off him and leave Remi alone, or I'll rip you into so many pieces even the phantoms won't want to eat what's left." Lyall's eyes glowed with the fires of a hellmouth.

Kaveh saw the situation crumbling into a blood bath if he didn't do something. He stepped forward and physically pushed Lyall and Rhys apart, flaring out summ with both hands for emphasis.

Even Xiang Jao took a step back, and silence fell over the group.

"That's enough." Kaveh drew the fire back into his hands, hoping his clan would view it as a sign of control over the summ, rather than the limited power he had left after the battle with the phantoms. "No one is harming anyone unless they go through me first. I'm not forcing Kat to come to the keep or even to try on the bracelet to confirm he's my match. It's not what he wants, and I respect that. What's important is that there are still phantoms out there and they are our clan's responsibility. The humans here are in danger because the ranch was absorbed into our riftland without permission from its inhabitants."

"The control object is gone," Xiang Jao said. "The Colony sent Remi to steal it, and this precipitated the crisis with the phantoms. He and his hellhound have been inside the base. The sparkleflies observed this."

"The phantoms broke out of the inner core before I arrived." Remi wasn't lying about that, Kaveh knew. Remi had gone there to find Kat and had met up with the three ratkind there. Had their kidnapping plan gone awry when Lyall decided to help Kat? "One of them almost ate me and my cousins. I went in there to find Kat, not your glowing dildo thing."

"Well, I went in there to steal it." Lyall didn't sound at all remorseful. "But it was gone by then, and Remi doesn't have it. If he did, I would have slapped him upside the head, taken it from him, and destroyed it. I don't want to see that technology in Arimanius's greasy paws any more than I want the drakones to have it."

"Lyall's telling the truth." Kat's voice was shaky but firm. "He went in to check, and it was gone. Then he made sure I got safely back to the ranch."

Kaveh wasn't good at picking up on romantic vibes between people—in fact, he was awful at it—but Lyall's and Kat's body language was obvious enough even he could tell there was a mutual attraction. He felt nothing but relief that Kat had rejected their Matchmaker pairing, but Kat falling for a hellhound? Even given all the bad-boy types Kat had dated, Lyall was on a whole other level of dangerous.

But the hellhound had protected Kat from the ratkind and stayed to fight by Kaveh's side.

Kaveh owed him.

"Kat, if you agree, I'd like to ask Lyall to stay with you and the children until the threat has passed."

An expression of pleased surprise flashed on Lyall's face, and Kat's relieved smile left little doubt he was in favor of the plan. Maybe Lyall would be a better type of bad-boy boyfriend, or perhaps this infatuation would be short-lived. Either way, it was for Kat to decide, not Kaveh.

Lyall looked over at Remi then back at Kaveh. The hellhound must have known he wouldn't stand a chance against four drakones, but he wasn't the type of guy who would back down from a promise to defend someone he cared about.

Kaveh respected that type of loyalty.

"I give you my word no harm will come to Remi." Kaveh put his hand on Remi's arm, and this time the streamer did flinch. "He can return to his cabin, and I'll set the guard-weed to keep him inside. In the morning, Javier can take him into town using the horse-drawn carriage if the rift boundary hasn't returned to normal."

"You're the youngest of our clan and in no position to make these types of decisions." Rhys sounded choked with anger and fury, likely due to Kaveh defying him. This was a blow to his ego, and Kaveh's ex-lover didn't take those well.

"And I am the head of the clan." Xiang Jao's tone brooked no further argument, and Rhys bowed his head even as his eyes flashed with anger. "If the hellhound was compelled to come here and has no further ties to the Colony, I have no issue with him leaving our lands when the security of everyone has been assured. The rift expansion has become unstable, and it may take some time to reverse it. As for Arimanius's son, it appears you, Kaveh, have been most injured by his actions. If you're content with letting the ratkind spy return to his father, I will not stand in your way."

Remi had been staring at the ground during that speech, but when she finished, he gave a sullen nod.

Kaveh pointed toward Remi's cabin. "I'll take you there now. You and I need to talk."

23

R emi stood outside the door to his cabin, silent and miserable, and waited for Rhys to come out. The asshole had insisted on searching his room for dangerous Colony weapons before allowing Kaveh to lock Remi up inside it. The drakone returned and did little more than grunt in Kaveh's direction before leaving the two of them alone.

Kaveh still said nothing.

Remi hated the silence. He'd rather have Kaveh scream at him or tell him what a lying piece of shit he was or maybe even hit him.

Of course, if Kaveh lost control of his summ for a moment, he could kill Remi with a touch. That was what Remi had thought would happen when Mabel had shoved him forward as Kaveh's hands were blazing with green fire.

Remi should have died in Kaveh's arms. He certainly had done enough to deserve it.

Instead, Kaveh had believed Remi's lies over and over then made sure Remi got back to the ranch safe while he risked his own life trying to help everyone but himself.

At least now Kaveh knew the truth.

Remi was a manipulative serial liar who twisted love and desire into a tool he could use to control people, and that was all he ever would be.

They walked through the damaged cabin door, which Rhys had left gaping open, and Kaveh finally spoke. "Was there anything we did together this week that meant something to you?"

Maybe silence was better than this.

"I was doing my job." Remi hated the way he sounded, sullen and whiny. "The Colony's the only family I have. I'm not a fighter, and I can't intimidate underworld enforcers. What I can do is make almost anyone want me, for a little while, and that's a valuable enough skill for Arimanius to keep me around."

"You're not answering my question." Kaveh waved a hand at the strands of guardweed, and the vines swarmed over the door, closing it behind them.

"Why does it matter?" Remi walked over to sit on the bed. The covers were rumpled from their lovemaking, but the sheets were cool to the touch, the warmth of Kaveh and his own body together long gone. "I came here to find out the secret of how you control the rift. My clan and yours are enemies, and spying is what enemies do."

"Stealing, lying, using your ability to make people like and trust you—that's what you call a good day's work?" Kaveh leaned against the wall. He didn't act angry, although Remi knew he was hurt and furious. He sounded like he wanted to understand Remi, maybe so he'd never make this sort of mistake again. "You said you didn't take the control object, but you came here, lied to me, and manipulated everyone around you so you could steal our knowledge about altering the rift boundary. That's what the control object does, and that's why your father wants it."

"If the control object can manipulate the rift, why did your clan put it in the base with the phantoms?" Remi stopped, information he had been too frightened and over-whelmed to analyze coming together in his mind.

The Saguaro Rift drakone clan should have locked up the control object in their keep. Instead, they had put it inside the base, where Kaveh had said no members of his clan could enter without damaging the cordon keeping the phantoms captive. Maybe the deadly invertebrates had been used as involuntary watchdogs for the object, but that seemed risky. The jellies could have learned how to use it themselves. Now it had been stolen, and the phantoms were rampaging throughout the riftland. The two things had to be related.

Kaveh shook his head. "I don't know, but that's not what's important right now. We're talking about why you think using your psychic ability on unsuspecting people is acceptable."

"Is imprisoning an entire clan inside the base and starving them into cannibalism to expand your territory acceptable?" Remi thought back to his strange nonverbal exchange with the phantom at the base and the raw fury pouring from the creature's mind. Now things were making sense, and it was even more awful than he had thought. "The control object had to be near the phantoms because it fed off them, forcing them to devour one another to stay alive."

Kaveh stiffened. "That's not possible."

"The phantom who tried to kill me told me so." Remi had been so busy wallowing in guilt that he hadn't recog-nized the truth when it had been flashed into his mind.

The phantom's imprisonment was the secret to the drakones' ability to expand and contract their riftland.

It was a neat trick—slowly drain the life from beings with the same object that kept them prisoner. Maybe this new Riftworld tech could be expanded to species other than the phantoms. Remi's lie about the drakones using it against their hellhound enemies had more truth to it than he had known. And the hellhounds weren't the only clan the drakones might come after.

The Colony could be next.

"I don't think for a minute Rhys would hesitate to torture and confine my family the same way he and your clan did to the phantoms." Remi was quite sure of that.

"The phantoms are dangerous." Kaveh sounded defensive now. "As you pointed out, one came close to killing you and three of your clan's enforcers. The base is an entire ecosystem, and the phantoms have plenty of natural prey inside there."

"They did until you began to expand your riftland." Remi now understood the basics of the technology, and the images and emotions the phantom had thrown at him fit into a disturbing picture. "As your territory grew bigger, theirs grew smaller. They starved, stopped reproducing, and eventually began eating one another. If the control object hadn't been taken, letting them loose, eventually all of them would have died. Then your clan would need to imprison another 'dangerous species' to take their place. That's what your control object does. It gained power every time the phantoms were forced to eat one of their own kind to survive."

Kaveh drew in his breath. "That's a serious accusation." He hesitated then continued. "I'll admit I don't know much about how the control object altered the rift boundary, but I can't believe the matriarch and my clan would be part of something like that."

"Then they're conning you the same way I did." Remi felt awful saying it, and the hurt in Kaveh's eyes was enough to make him feel ill.

It didn't matter. Kaveh hated Remi now and always would, and whatever emotions Remi felt toward him needed to be stamped out. He wanted this to be over and for Kaveh to leave him in his little prison of a cabin. Then he could be miserable and guilty alone, and tomorrow, he would go back to Boston.

Remi had discovered the drakones' secret, for the all the good it did. It wasn't like he could do anything about the control object and the awful threat it posed. All he could do was run back to Father, like the pathetic half-human loser he was.

He reached for something else to say to drive Kaveh away. "Why don't you go check on Kat? Maybe if the bracelet changes, he'll get over his crush on Lyall."

Kaveh straightened, as if deciding there was no point in talking to Remi anymore, and walked toward the door. He patted his coat pocket as he did. It was a movement Remi had seen before, a semi-conscious tic. Kaveh needed to assure himself the gold amulet that would tell him when he had met his Matchmaker-approved true love was still there.

"Remi." Kaveh stopped before he reached the door, and his voice was cold and frightening. "Give it back to me. Now."

"You think I stole the Matchmaker bracelet?" Remi was incredulous and furious.

Granted, he could have lifted the object easily—he had great pickpocketing skills—but why would he have bothered? The amulet was only a tool to make it easier for the drakones to identify the Matchmaker's choice. If he stole it, nothing would change. Kat would still be the only person Kaveh was meant to be with, and since the vet would never force anyone to marry him, he would have to settle for making sure Kat was safe.

Lucky Kat. Even though he had rejected Kaveh before the vet had even proposed, he would still have someone powerful and kind to make sure he was okay.

Remi stood and held up his hands. He was still covered in the skintight living leathers, the creature's flattened body hugging every curve of muscle, every angle of his body. "I don't have it, but by all means feel me up a few times to make sure. You seemed to enjoy that earlier."

That was petty and cruel, but Kaveh thinking Remi was even a worse person than he actually was hurt. A lot.

Kaveh turned to face him, his face darkening with anger. Remi should have been terrified he had pushed things too far. The man had several excellent reasons to beat him senseless or kill him, and Remi shouldn't have given him yet another one.

He was too angry at himself to care.

"What's on your wrist?" Kaveh's tone changed, from fury to something that sounded like fear.

Remi glanced at the familiar watch he wore and tapped the face of it in irritation. "It's my Rolex. Which, just so you know, I bought with money I earned and didn't steal."

Kaveh's face paled. He took a few quick strides forward and grabbed Remi's left hand, holding it up so the light from the shroom lamps glinted off the gold timepiece.

It looked exactly like Remi's Rolex—except it was gold, not platinum.

And it was here, instead of in his brownstone in Boston where he had left it.

Remi snatched his hand away from Kaveh and fumbled at the clasp. No, this couldn't be happening. He had already lied to Kaveh, betrayed his trust, and put the vet's best friend in danger.

The Matchmaker couldn't have picked him for Kaveh as the final part of a cruel joke.

He managed to get it off his wrist, noticing the added detail of paired griffins on either side of the watch face. That and the type of metal were the only differences from his real Rolex. Apparently, the fucking Matchmaker had a sense of humor.

"Take it." He shoved it at Kaveh. "I don't want it. This isn't my fault. Everything else is. But not this."

"You know it's not going to change back." Kaveh took the watch from him, his eyes not leaving Remi's face. "I should have realized you were the one earlier when the guardian spoke to us. I was looking in the wrong places, at the wrong people."

"I *am* the wrong person." Remi backed away.

The room felt small and claustrophobic. Like a luxurious prison, which was where he'd been spending the rest of his life if this didn't end now. He'd be added to a hoard inside the keep, another pretty plaything in a pile of treasure.

"I'm the ratkind spy who lied to you, seduced you, and worked with my cousins to steal your clan's secrets," Remi said. "I'm the worst fiancé you could possibly imagine, and that's why we both need to forget this ever happened."

"Please." Kaveh spoke slowly, as if Remi was a frightened animal he needed to calm so he could treat it.

That wasn't too far from the truth. Remi's inner chinchilla was threatening to break out again, and tonight had been awful and humiliating enough without that happening.

"I want you to be safe," Kaveh said. "That's the promise I made to Lyall, and it's what the Matchmaker connection is about. Arimanius sent his enforcers after Kat when it seemed he was my match because he knew he could use that person as a bargaining chip against me and my clan. What do you think he's going to do when he finds out it's you?"

"My father's not going to know anything about it." Remi's mind was churning, one part thinking about how he could get away from Kaveh and another part reeling in shock that this had happened. "I have a lot of practice lying to him. I'll be gone tomorrow, and you can make up a story to tell your family."

"I don't want to lie about this." Kaveh had to stop sounding reasonable and caring. It was making Remi feel even more awful.

"You lied about being an Azdaha, the Saguaro Rift clan's secret weapon." Remi was uncomfortably warm all of a sudden, the living leather armor too tight and the walls too close. "You even lied to your clan about being able to call up summ. I think you'll be able to handle it."

Kaveh bit his lip, and Remi could tell his words had hit like a slap. He had to do this, had to push Kaveh away. There was no way a kind, honorable man like Kaveh should end up with someone like Remi.

"Will you at least consider letting me keep you safe?" Kaveh stepped closer to him, and Remi's body reacted, part of him wanting nothing more than to fling himself into Kaveh's arms.

"No." Remi had to be firm, had to make Kaveh leave. "Even if I wanted to stay with you, which I don't, I'm not going to let myself be locked away in a drakone fortress like a shiny trinket you found. Your clan hates me, they hate the Colony, and the feeling is mutual. I hate your family, and I hate you." His voice broke.

There was silence again between them, with Remi digging his fingernails into his palms to stop himself from crying. Kaveh simply stood there, his face somber.

"I'll respect your wishes." Kaveh pushed the fake Rolex into his pocket and walked to the door. He turned for one last look at Remi. "Please take care of yourself. I'm...very sorry. About everything."

And then he was gone, and Remi fell onto the bed and tried to tell himself this hadn't been the worst mistake of his life.

24

Remi waited until dawn, too wired up and distraught to catch even a few hours of sleep. As the morning sun lightened the sky outside the windows, there was a knock on the door.

He approached the door warily, and the guardweed tumbled down to stop him from going any farther.

"Remi, it's Javier. It's safe to come out, so I'm going to open your door, okay?"

Remi felt the dull pain of disappointment as he recognized the rideshare driver's voice. Of course it wasn't Kaveh. Remi had told him to get lost in as nasty a way as possible.

The door opened, and the guardweed rebounded upward like released springs to reveal Javier. He had a large knife on his belt, a crossbow in one hand, and a quiver of arrows on his back. He was ludicrously over-armed if he had come to be Remi's jailer.

"How are you doing?" Javier sounded concerned.

Remi realized Kaveh had lied—or at least not told the ranch staff the truth about Remi's background and actions. The weapons were for any dangerous mons hanging about, and Javier didn't know Remi was one of those.

"I heard you were with the group that got attacked by the jellies," Javier said. "Thank God everyone's all right."

"I'm fine." Remi went to grab his suitcase, trying to ignore the pink animal carrier in the corner. He didn't want to think about never seeing Lyall again, which was as ridiculous as pining over Kaveh.

He and Javier walked toward the ranch entrance, with Javier relating stories of how the ranch had hunkered down when the combined effects of becoming part of a riftland and the storm had hit.

"Kaveh told us the rift should move back in a few hours." Javier pointed to an open carriage with two horses in harness.

The animals looked rather smug as they stood next to expensive pickup trucks that had been rendered useless. A familiar white bird with a yellow crest sat on one of the horses. Snow had gotten loose again. At least one creature at the ranch would be sorry to see Remi leave. Too bad he didn't have any Brazil nuts on him.

Remi had more or less stared at the ground as he walked, going over and over his last argument with Kaveh, but as he looked at the carriage, he realized something about the landscape didn't make sense. He scanned the horizon, confused, then spotted the shimmering barrier far off in the distance.

Last night was a blur, granted, but the rift's boundary had been only a kilometer or so outside the ranch proper. Now it was much farther out—and a lot more humans were living with the natural laws of the Riftworld.

"The drakone riftland has taken over the city." Remi felt uneasy.

Rhys had talked about expanding the riftland to protect
Kaveh's intended, but whatever Kaveh had told his clan, he
must have let them know there was no need to keep their
lands expanded now. Could something have gone wrong
with the control object that drained power from the phantoms? There was still no explanation for how it had disappeared. Remi didn't have it, and Lyall and Kaveh had
searched for it without success at the base.

"Maybe it'll take more time." Javier was using a soothing
voice, as if he didn't want Remi to panic. Or maybe he
wanted to reassure himself as well. "Kaveh said it would be
better by the morning, and he's a man of his word."

Remi wanted to snap back and say that wasn't true. But
if he were to compare untruths, his lies had been a lot more
damaging.

"Is the airport affected?" Remi asked, before realizing
that without cellphone service or internet Javier and the
ranch staff knew as little as he did about what was going on
in Tucson. "I have a flight I need to catch."

"Kaveh said you had a family emergency and needed to
leave." Javier looked abashed. "Sorry, didn't mean to pry. But
we can take a ride out in the emergency storm lane on the
highway and get an idea of what's going on. So far, the only
news has come from Flutterberry. She popped into the main
building last night with Snow tagging along. It was good to
hear my family's safe, but she couldn't tell us much about
what was going on in the city."

Remi lifted his luggage into the buggy and sat as Javier
picked up the reins and called out to the horses. The
carriage had modern springs and comfortable seats, technology that wasn't impacted by being inside a fragment of
the Riftworld. The ride was bumpier than a car and a lot
slower, but Remi was too miserable to care. He closed his

eyes, not wanting to see Moon Star Ranch grow smaller as they rode farther away. Javier did his best to keep up a cheerful chatter about Snow's frequent misdeeds, and the bird himself snuggled against Remi, as if he wanted to give him comfort.

Snow didn't try to bite even once, as much as Remi deserved it.

Javier swore in surprise. Remi's eyes opened, and he snapped his head up. A huge shape twisted through the air above, descending in a vortex resembling a scaled tornado.

Panic gripped Remi's throat. A drakone was coming right at them, and it wasn't Kaveh.

It was Rhys.

Remi made a quick decision and shouted at the driver to stop. He hopped out of the buggy as Snow flapped up into the air, giving squawks of alarm.

"Javier," Remi said, "get out of here."

He glanced around for a place to run or hide, but they were on a two-lane highway that had no traffic and no cover other than some scrawny undergrowth.

Rhys landed with a thump in front of Remi, transforming into his alter form as he did. One look at the drakone's expression told Remi he had come to do more than yell at him.

"I don't have the control object." Remi rushed the words out, sensing even before they left his lips that his protests were meaningless.

Rhys smiled, and there was nothing friendly about it. "I know you don't have it."

Then he lunged forward. Remi took the only option left to him and transformed.

He darted between Rhys's legs then ran as fast as his four legs could carry him. There must be some ground cover or maybe even an abandoned burrow. The wind started then, a furious blast that sent him sprawling and left him gasping in a heap.

Remi heard Javier shout at the horses and the creak of wheels as the buggy took off down the highway. The wrangler knew better than to take on a drakone, and Remi could only hope the man would seek out Kaveh as soon as he returned to the ranch.

Whether Kaveh would care about what Rhys did to Remi was another question.

In the meantime, the only thing Remi could do was try not to be killed.

He suppressed the urge to run and instead went limp, lying unmoving in the dust. The heavy tramp of Rhys's reptilian feet sent vibrations through the ground as he approached.

The footsteps stopped all too close to him. He could hear the drakone's raspy breaths and guessed that Rhys was standing over him, trying to figure out if the blast had broken Remi's neck.

A foot prodded him. When Remi still didn't move, Rhys gave a grunt.

Cracking one eye open a fraction, Remi saw the drakone bending over him, his clawed hand reaching out to grab him.

Remi bit Rhys as hard as he could.

Chinchilla bites weren't particularly powerful, but Rhys wasn't expecting it and jerked back in surprise.

That gave Remi enough time to scramble a few feet away and transform. The living leathers wound around his human body, and thanks to the Riftworld influence, he had added abilities when it came to chinchilla tricks like hopping, jumping, and kicking.

He used that last talent to put his armored foot into Rhys's groin. As the drakone doubled over, Remi landed another kick to his head.

Then he ran.

The only shelter in sight was the rusted remains of an abandoned gas station too close to the rift to be worth the expense of converting it to an electric charging station.

Maybe if he had hit Rhys's balls hard enough, he would have enough time to reach the crumbling structure, transform back, and disappear into an opening too small for Rhys to get at him.

He never made it.

The massive serpentine body of Rhys's aerial drakone form descended down, a blast of wind sending Remi flying through the air toward a pile of brush and rocks.

Remi hit hard, his face protected by a chitinous shield that appeared as the living armor reared up like a cobra hood over his head. The armor prevented the impact from smashing his bones, but he was left winded and dazed, sprawled out on the ground as Rhys towered over him. The drakone held a leather-and-metal band in one hand.

Remi recognized Lyall's collar a second before Rhys snapped it around his neck.

His body twisted and writhed, the living leather armor transforming into a thin string around his neck as he returned to rodent form. He was suspended in the air as Rhys held him up for inspection.

The drakone's eyes glittered with malice. "This way, you'll be nothing more than a heap of rat bones in the desert."

25

K aveh wasn't in the mood for a visit from a mothcat. But Flutterberry could pop in any time she felt like it, so her arrival to the monstertown via one of her mini-portals was hardly a surprise.

Snow perched on the fur on her back wasn't as expected but perhaps even less welcome. Not that Kaveh didn't have a soft spot for the mischievous half parrot, but he did tend to cause chaos wherever he flew.

Kaveh didn't need any more chaos after last night.

Snow cocked his head, his usual swaggering air no longer in evidence.

"Little rat," the bird said.

He sounded sad, or perhaps that was Kaveh projecting. Maybe Snow only liked to say the phrase, or perhaps he did associate the words with Remi and knew he was gone. Either way, Kaveh didn't want a reminder of the terrible mess he had made of everything. The Matchmaker truly was a curse and not the near-divine intelligence the drakones thought it was.

"I'm sorry, Flutterberry," Kaveh said. "I've got a lot on my hands right now, and it might be best if you stayed near your human companions."

Having a lot on his hands was an understatement. After his awful parting with Remi, he and Tarasque had scoured the ranch grounds for lurking phantoms, while Rhys flew off to consult with the elders on how to draw back the boundaries of the rift. The matriarch, for her part, had gone to the main building to make a rare apology to Garreth and the other humans at the ranch.

There hadn't been any time to confront her about Remi's accusations that the clan had knowingly tortured and imprisoned the phantoms using the control object.

At least, that was what Kaveh had told himself.

Kaveh had allowed Tarasque to wind-walk him back to the monstertown, where he had treated injuries from several town residents caused by fighting off the phantoms. Fortunately, none were serious, although José had suffered a significant electrical burn to his hind leg. The cadejo was resting at home now, with Jessie hovering over him.

At least the frantic work and lack of sleep had distracted him from thinking about Remi. Kaveh felt hollowed out and emotionally empty. Remi's betrayal had been awful, but watching the panic and fear in the man's eyes when he realized he had been the Matchmaker's choice all along was crushing.

Remi was terrified of him and for good reason.

Kaveh wasn't the conscientious veterinarian and teacher he pretended to be. Remi saw him as he truly was—an Azdaha killing machine who could force the person selected for him by the Matchmaker to come to the keep and never let him go. Kaveh was a killer now. He had used his summ to take the lives of multiple sapient creatures. The fact he had done so to protect the lives of others didn't make the memory of it less sickening.

"My servants are in no danger." Orange-and-russet colors shimmered over Flutterberry's wings, colors Kaveh knew indicated indignation and annoyance, although he couldn't parse the more complex nuances of the mothcat's chromatophoric language. "I translocated them farther away, and it was wise I did, since most of the city is now riftland."

Kaveh stared at her. The monstertown was still without any functioning advanced human technology, but he thought that was because it had taken longer for Rhys and the others to pull the rift boundary back to its original position. But the matriarch had promised that the ranch would be outside the riftland by morning.

Tucson itself shouldn't have been affected at all.

"Is that why you're here, to tell me that there's a problem with drakone control of the rift?" Flutterberry was intelligent and found humans amusing, but sallying forth to defend the citizenry of Tucson wasn't a mothcat thing to do.

"The problem isn't with the drakone control of the rift but rather what some of you are doing with that power." After that pointed remark, Flutterberry turned her graceful neck back to give Snow a long-suffering glare. "I'm quite exhausted making all these portals, but the bird insisted. Something about the pretty ratkind male you were so friendly with."

Kaveh had asked Javier to take Remi to the airport in the morning, too angry and hurt to do it himself. Had Remi decided not to leave immediately and continue the Colony's plot of stealing the control object? That didn't make much sense. The ratkind didn't take stupid risks. Run away and live to steal another day was one of their mottos.

Maybe Remi had tried to leave, and someone had stopped him.

No, that couldn't have happened. Rhys's boiling anger and argument that both Lyall and Remi should be killed wouldn't have led him to the drastic step of disobeying the matriarch.

Unless he hadn't disobeyed her but followed her instructions.

Kaveh's mouth went dry. He tried to keep calm and see if he could get more information from the parrot hybrid. "Snow, what's wrong with Remi?"

"Little rat," Snow repeated in his singsong voice.

The bird grew frustrated at Kaveh's lack of understanding and fluffed his feathers with theatrical flourish, sparks showering over Flutterberry, who gave a yowl of pain. The half parrot flapped over to Kaveh's arm, tiny embers floating around him.

He spoke again, the words chilling, and his voice a perfect replica of Rhys's gruff tones.

"You'll be nothing more than a heap of rat bones in the desert."

KAVEH WOULDN'T HAVE HAD a chance to get to Remi without Amanita. The repoequus hadn't returned to her equine form after she and her colt had defended the Earth horses from the phantoms. The two of them were hunting jackrabbits in the saguaro forest close to the monstertown, and Flutterberry was able to locate them and communicate Kaveh's desperate need for transportation with surprising speed. The mothcat hadn't even asked for presents before doing so, which was a first. He resolved to buy her whatever she wanted for the favor.

He asked the Goat Sisters to take an urgent message to the guardians and—the gods help him, Lyall the hellhound—then swung into the saddle with Snow on his shoulder. They were riding too fast for the half parrot to fly, but the bird was able to give Amanita a mental image of Remi's last location.

Amanita raced off through the desert, and Kaveh hoped the interspecies communication between the two Earth-Riftworld hybrids was sufficient to allow her to take him to Remi.

He had to get there before it was too late. Precious time had elapsed since Snow had overheard Rhys's threat. How much time, the context of the interaction, and whether the matriarch had sanctioned Rhys going after Remi—there were too many unanswered questions.

Kaveh didn't want to believe that Rhys, his former lover and family member, would ignore the oath Kaveh had given to Lyall and attack Remi. He also didn't want to face the possibility that Xiang Jao, more of a mother to him than the drakone who had birthed him, had sanctioned this.

He cursed himself for withholding the information that Remi was the Matchmaker's choice from his family. That would have given Remi immunity from the violence the drakones meted out to enemies like the ratkind. It also meant the clan would view Remi's freedom and choice in the matter as irrelevant. They had been appalled their aquatic cousin Ceto had been paired with a human marine exobiologist whose life work was about understanding Rift-world peoples. His clan would be far more horrified to learn Kaveh's intended husband was a half-human Colony spy with a psychic ability to seduce anyone without the mental shields to block him.

Amanita slowed, her breaths coming in harsh pants. At

first, Kaveh was worried he had pushed the mare too far, too hard. She had more stamina than an Earth horse, but they had taken a punishing pace through the heat to get this far. Then he saw they were near the highway, close to an abandoned fuel station.

The repoequus halted, her sides heaving with exertion. Snow took flight, sparks flying from his feathers as he winged his way toward a rusted heap of buildings.

Kaveh dismounted, checking for his utility knife at his belt. It was absurd. Rhys had manifested his aerial form earlier than any other air drakone in living memory. His ex could manipulate the wind to his command, and his aerial form was enormous compared to Kaveh's human shape. The only weapon Kaveh could wield successfully against Rhys was his summ.

It was an awful thought. The touch of Kaveh's poisonous fire would kill Rhys, and using it would be murder.

A darker part of him took satisfaction in that.

Remi was his. How dare Rhys try to harm or even touch him? If his ex had hurt Remi or worse—had killed him— Kaveh would drench the ground with his blood.

No.

Kaveh forced his breathing to slow, trying to push those violent fantasies from his mind. He wasn't a mindless monster filled with bloodlust from his Azdaha birth and fanatical jealousy from the effects of the Matchmaker.

He would first ascertain if Remi was okay and then talk to Rhys. Despite his ex's anger about the Colony plot, he had to respect Kaveh's point that the situation was complex, and cooler heads needed to prevail. Then he would get answers, both from Rhys and Xiang Jao, about the control object.

His rapid steps took him close to the decaying remains of the gas station, a leftover from the age of internal combustion engines when the use of energy sources had sped the Earth's environment into its current cycle of weather instability and desertification.

He spotted Rhys, in his human alter form, focusing on a saguaro cactus in front of him.

Kaveh approached, taking care to make his steps slow, careful, and above all, silent. There was no sign of Remi, but there was something bizarre about Rhys being alone in the ruins of an old gas station. He tried to make sense of the scene. Something was attached to the cactus, a mass of fur and blood against the prickly green of the plant.

Realization struck, and blind fury overwhelmed him. It wiped out any rational thought and replaced it with nothing but a need for vengeance.

He hit Rhys hard, driving his shoulder into the larger drakone's form.

Rhys didn't react fast enough, and Kaveh landed on top of him. His outstretched hand found a nearby rock, and he used it to smash his ex in the face.

Kaveh climbed to his feet, every fiber of him wanting to call up the poisonous fire that would end Rhys's life.

He forced himself to control that impulse and rushed over to the saguaro. There was an animal strung up against the thorns, larger than the Earth chinchillas Kaveh treated. The species was a fragile prey creature, with delicate bones that could be easily broken. A bloodstained rawhide string encircled the animal's neck, a small tooth hanging from it. A collar, too tight and oddly familiar, was in place above it.

Remi opened his blue, limpid eyes and stared up at Kaveh.

He was alive.

Relief and renewed fury coursed through Kaveh's veins.

Remi had lived long enough for Kaveh to get here only because Rhys had decided to slowly torture him to death.

The string was the living leather armor, and the collar was the device that had held José in his cadejo form. Green fire flickered over Kaveh's thumb and forefinger. A sudden certainty that his summ couldn't harm his matched partner swept over him, and Kaveh pulled his utility knife out and pinched the blade until it glowed green. Protecting Remi's delicate neck with one finger, he cut through the constricting band, leaving the string of the living leathers in place.

The collar sizzled away into a viscous slime that fell to the ground. Remi morphed into his human form, naked and bleeding, and as Kaveh carefully lowered him to the ground, the living armor activated and spread out to protect and cover Remi's bruised and battered skin.

A few meters away, Rhys staggered to his feet, staring at Kaveh in a mix of shock and anger.

Kaveh took another moment to check that Remi had a decent pulse at his wrist and regular respiration before standing up to confront his former lover.

"You sadistic bastard." Kaveh's fists were curled by his sides. He was afraid if he relaxed them, the fire burning inside of him would explode out and immolate everything in his path. "Tell me the truth. Was this your idea, or did the clan give you permission to attack someone granted safe passage out of our lands?"

"I did what you should have done." Rhys held himself stiffly, a trickle of blood running down his left temple from the rock's impact.

The air around them was hot and motionless, without even a trace of a breeze. Rhys's ability to impact the air around him wasn't unusual for an air drakone, but his talent for using it as a weapon was. There was a reason even older members of the clan deferred to him on matters of security. Rhys had adopted some of the dress and mannerisms of the Welsh warriors of the past, and this habit often went beyond affectation to worship of all things martial.

"He tricked and humiliated you," Rhys growled. "You've come into some of your Azdaha powers, for better or worse. At least use them against this filthy enemy."

Kaveh pulled the amulet out of his pocket, the watch's gold surface flashing in the glare of the noon sun overhead. "Remi has been selected by the Matchmaker for me. This transformed when he touched it. I don't care what he did or who he works for. He's mine to protect, and you had no right to assault him."

Rhys froze, his eyes fixed on the watch. "That's not possible. The Matchmaker wouldn't select one of the ratkind to marry into our clan. It's unnatural, an abomination."

"Don't worry." Remi drew himself up to a standing position, and Kaveh reached out to steady him. The streamer spat out blood at Rhys's feet. "I have no intention of becoming your fucking brother-in-law."

Earth chinchillas might be fragile, but human-ratkind hybrids like Remi had impressive resilience. Remi also had a terrible problem with authority figures, but Kaveh could hardly fault him for that.

"How did the rift move to encompass the city?" Kaveh felt a growing suspicion that Rhys had done more than attack Remi. "The matriarch promised the ranch would be in its usual interzone by morning. Instead, our riftland has spread over a vast human city and put thousands in danger."

"Our enemies stole the control object." Rhys responded too quickly, as if he had an answer planned out. "Your beloved Colony spy came here with one of our hellhound enemies. They would love to use our own creation against us."

"You're a shitty liar." Remi sounded hoarse, but his voice grew stronger as he continued. "Lyall would have destroyed it if he found it. Pissing off both the Saguaro Rift drakone clan and the Colony would be his idea of a good time."

"And you're an excellent liar." Rhys spread his hands and laughed. "You've done nothing but deceive and manipulate everyone around you."

There was blood visible on his hands, crusted under the claws at the tips of his humanoid fingers.

Remi's blood.

Kaveh took another step forward, the need to punish Rhys for what he had done pounding in his ears. "I don't care about your opinion. Remi was under my protection when you attacked him. You didn't know then that he was my match. Now you do. I'll kill you to keep him safe, Rhys, and since you were chosen by the Matchmaker yourself, I know you understand why."

"You're a child." Rhys sent a dust devil spinning toward them, a reminder of his power.

Kaveh moved forward to block it from hitting Remi, but it left the two of them coughing and briefly blinded.

"A child with a dangerous trick, yes, but that's all you have," Rhys continued. "Maybe in another decade or two you'll grow into the weapon that Xiang Jao wanted when she took in the spawn of our enemies. You can't fight me, any more than the pathetic humans you spend so much time with could. Your body is as weak and useless as theirs are. I understand you can't kill the spy. But you can leave him to me, and I'll do it for you."

Kaveh lost control. His summ flared out, and he sent a green fireball directly at Rhys.

His ex swore and deflected the flames with another swirl of wind. The two of them faced off, and Kaveh made sure Remi was protected behind him.

Rhys wasn't going to get a chance to hurt Remi again.

Kaveh would make sure of that.

"Enough." The word boomed out above them, and the sun was blotted out by the massive shape of Xiang Jao's body as she descended through the air. She landed with enough force to send a vibration through the earth beneath their feet, and two similar impacts came as Raion and Kaida, the monstertown guardians, landed in a cloud of dust.

She must have wind-walked both of the komainu here, no small feat, given their massive weight.

Her scales spiraled in on themselves, and then Xiang Jao stood in her humanoid alter form, eyes blazing.

"This is not the time for us to be fighting amongst ourselves." Xiang Jao took in the scene, with Kaveh protecting a battered Remi. There was little doubt she understood what Rhys had done, and even less she cared he had done it. "The control object is in use by someone, and there are vast numbers of humans impacted."

"The ratkind spy is lying." Rhys's voice trembled with repressed fury as he gestured toward Remi. "He has to know where it is, and I had no intention of letting him walk free after what he's done."

"Kaveh gave his word that Arimanius's son wouldn't come to harm." Xiang Jao gave Remi an unfriendly look. "As I recall, Remigio Gatti, you also agreed to leave our lands by morning, a minimal request given how you have wronged us."

"Well, I *was* staked to a cactus and tortured when I tried

to leave," Remi drawled out with unnecessary sarcasm. He wasn't backing down.

Kaveh wished he would. He still seethed about Rhys's brutal abuse of Remi, but now that anger was tinged with anxiety. He couldn't fight the matriarch and two guardians and win, but he would if they threatened Remi's safety.

He moved a few steps forward, keeping the bulk of his body between Remi and his ex, and handed Xiang Jao the gold watch piece. Her scaled brows drew in, and her face hardened even more.

She turned to the guardians. "May I ask you to examine our holy artifact? It seems all too convenient that Arimanius's son has turned out to be the Matchmaker's choice for Kaveh."

"Let me assure you, there's been nothing convenient about it as far as I'm concerned." Remi added in that last bit like he didn't care if he made the situation worse.

"There's no need for us to inspect it." Raion spoke with the same infuriating calmness he always exuded.

Kaveh stared at the watch then tried to catch Remi's gaze, but the man refused to look at him. Remi had come here with the intention of seducing him so he could steal the power that allowed Kaveh's clan to control the rift. He had arrived with a hellhound bodyguard, living leathers, and a cyberbug capable of interaction with both human and Riftworld technology. Could he have also brought something that would create an illusion that the Matchmaker amulet had transformed? It would be a brilliant way to entrap a drakone resistant to his psychic abilities. The guardians, however, would be able to see through any such trick. That would mean Remi had faked his shock and fear when the transformed amulet appeared on his wrist.

Kaveh didn't believe that had been an act. He would stake his life on it.

If the guardians told the matriarch Remi wasn't chosen by the Matchmaker, Kaveh would still die to protect him.

Silence hung in the air, and then Kaida spoke. "We knew Remigio Gatti was Kaveh's intended match when we first made his acquaintance. The amulet is not necessary for us to perceive this, but it has utility for younger species such as yourselves."

Relief flooded through Kaveh until Remi chimed in again.

"I'm not anyone's match, soulmate, or one true love." Remi spat the words out. "The Matchmaker can go fuck itself."

Xiang Jao ignored Remi's sacrilegious comment and turned to Rhys. "I share your distress over this development, but your actions were unacceptable. The Matchmaker's choices are not to be interfered with. The consequences can be dire."

"I was trying to do what has to be done." Rhys gestured toward Kaveh and Remi. "Matchmaker or not, we can't tolerate this ratkind creature in our home. Given Kaveh's unnatural tendencies, I'm not surprised this occurred."

"Shut up." Remi tried to push by Kaveh in an ill-advised attempt to confront Rhys. "You treated him like shit when the two of you were together, and there's nothing unnatural about him being ace. You were a total asshole about his orientation then, and you're doing the same thing to him now."

Rhys lunged forward, and Kaveh felt the poisonous flames inside of him ready to leap out.

The gray-scaled drakone jerked to a halt as if he had walked into an invisible wall. Rhys might have impressive wind powers, but the matriarch had hundreds of years and abilities no other drakone in the clan could match. She dropped her hands and paid no attention to the betrayed look her second husband gave her as he retreated.

Instead, she focused on Kaveh.

"I will not allow dissension and conflict to distract us from the current crisis." The matriarch inclined her head in the direction of Raion and Kaida. "The guardians have confirmed that Arimanius's son is your match. I understand your anger. Remi is yours, and Rhys should not have taken matters into his own hands. But we cannot allow Remi's father to use this aberration of the Matchmaker against you and our clan. Take him to the keep, and we will keep him safe there."

"No." Remi shook his head, his voice frantic. "I won't go. There's no way in hell I'll let you trap me inside that place."

He met Kaveh's eyes, a mix of pleading and defiance in his gaze.

Kaveh remembered Remi's panic when he learned the Matchmaker had chosen him, and as painful as the rejection was, he couldn't allow this to happen. Remi didn't deserve to be locked away like some pretty bauble. No, the matriarch didn't want Remi killed outright, but she was fine with imprisoning him and imposing that form of psychological torture.

"I'm not forcing Remi to be with me." Kaveh could hear his voice crack with emotion and strove to keep his tone calm and reasonable. "Matriarch, with all due respect, this is wrong. I don't know why the Matchmaker brought the two of us together, but I do know I'm not supposed to kidnap and lock up the person I'm supposed to love."

Rhys sputtered something, but Xiang Jao gave an inpatient huff and he shut up.

"You don't have a choice." The matriarch sounded colder than Kaveh had ever heard her. "My responsibility lies with our entire clan, and your naive idealism isn't something we can afford right now. You will follow my instructions, or I'll have Rhys wind-walk him back to the keep."

"I'd rather die than let that bastard touch me again." Remi swallowed hard then continued. "I swear, I'll fight every one of you, every minute, every hour, every day. Maybe I can't overpower any of you, but I'll do my damnedest to make all of your lives a living hell."

Kaveh had no idea what to do. His options were limited. He could follow Xiang Jao's orders and drag Remi back to the keep. Remi wouldn't forgive him for that, nor should he. Kaveh could refuse, and then the matriarch would tell Rhys to take Remi.

No. If Rhys dared to touch Remi again, Kaveh would kill him.

He forced himself to take a few long, slow breaths. He couldn't win a fight against his entire clan any more than Remi could.

But he could issue a challenge that couldn't be ignored. He could lay his life on the line for the right to give Remi his freedom.

"I insist on the right of combat." The words were strange in his ears. After all, he had only read them in ancient texts, and he never would have imagined himself saying them out loud. "Matriarch, your second husband has attacked my spouse—my property and my greatest treasure. I demand recompense and vengeance."

Kaveh walked forward until he and Rhys were close enough to touch. The forced proximity felt both intimate and revolting at the same. How had he ever thought he loved Rhys? A myriad of cruel remarks, minor insults, and biting comments came to mind, a personal history Kaveh had tried to repress.

"I challenge you." Kaveh knew his next words could mean he and Remi wouldn't live to see another day. "I demand you face me in a duel over the insult you have given to my property and my honor."

Rhys hadn't moved a muscle as Kaveh approached, barely waiting for the final words of the challenge to leave his lips before he responded. "I accept."

"No." Xiang Jao towered over both of them, a note of agony in her voice. "This can't happen."

Raion gave a low grumble. "The challenge has been issued and accepted. Drakone law is clear in this regard. Kaveh and Rhys will have a duel of honor to decide this matter, with their seconds and supporters in attendance. The winner will do whatever they wish with Remigio Gatti."

He and Rhys would fight a battle as drakones. Rhys was the youngest drakone to achieve his aerial form and the clan's best fighter. Kaveh, Rhys's junior by decades, could opt to either use his one weapon, a poisonous fire that would kill his former lover with a touch, or watch as Rhys killed Remi.

Kaveh squared his shoulders and faced the only mother he had ever known as an enemy, not as a son. "The guardians have spoken. Set the conditions for the duel."

26

The dragon dueling ground, a.k.a. the rodeo arena, was packed.

Remi was set to become the main prize in the Friday mini-rodeo he had heard so much about during the week. Only instead of barrel racing and trick roping, Kaveh and Rhys planned to fight to the death over him.

Shit, had it only been a week since he'd arrived at Moon Star Ranch? It felt like a century.

He walked in from the main ranch building with Raion beside him as a guard. There had been no opportunity to talk to Kaveh and beg him not to lose his life in an asinine display of dragon machismo. No chance to take back all the shit he had spouted about not being dragged off to the keep. No option to do anything but watch as Kaveh faced down his ex-lover, who could turn into a giant flying snake and fight with mini-tornadoes, because Kaveh wanted to save Remi's life and freedom.

The large corral that served to demonstrate rodeo sports was an enclosed oval with metal bleachers on each of the long sides for spectators. The guests and staff should have been freaked out and hiding in their rooms, but they were all here, including the two children who had narrowly escaped becoming phantom snacks at the petting zoo.

The boy and girl jumped up and down and waved at him as he walked with Raion past the spectators, and since that process took forever at the glacial pace the guardian favored, he had little choice but to wave back.

A fight to the death hardly seemed appropriate viewing for young children, but since Remi was the child of two people who weren't exactly parent-of-the-year candidates, he didn't feel he knew enough to judge.

The townies had also turned out in force, sitting a little apart from the ranch crowd on the bleachers. Jessie sat next to José, who had a cast on his leg. They surprised Remi by giving him a friendly wave, apparently unfazed he had turned out to be a Colony spy. Flutterberry lounged on one of the bleachers, and Snow squawked at her then flew off of Remi's arm to perch on the mothcat's back. Remi didn't want the bird to get hurt, but it felt like losing his last friend.

Kaveh had been allowed to have his supporters in attendance, so there were people in the audience who at least didn't want Remi dead. Kat and Lyall had taken seats in the front beside Chrissie, Garreth's wife. She looked anxious and frightened, but when Remi passed by, she gave him a warm smile and told him she was praying for him.

All of the ranch staff appeared to be here as well. Javier was in the stands, sitting next to Jeannette. They both gave Remi a thumbs-up. Now that Remi was facing near-certain death, everyone was willing to be forgiving.

The bleachers on the opposite side held the drakone clan, all in humanoid shapes, which was fortunate for the structural integrity of the metal seats. Xiang Jao sat in the middle with over a dozen of her clan, resplendent in red-

and-gold robes that matched her scales. Her reptilian eyes followed Remi as he crossed the earth floor of the arena, which was still damp from last night's rift storm. As they reached the far end of the corral, Remi realized he was about to be shut in one of the livestock chutes.

"I thought today couldn't get more humiliating, but I guess I was wrong." Remi walked through the open gate of the metal structure, which was a pen constructed of metal bars painted an ugly green that would have clashed with every single one of his outfits. Combined with the brown living leathers he was wearing, he looked and felt like a cow waiting to be roped. Raion closed the gate behind him then sank down on his haunches and went immobile in front of the structure.

Remi had wondered where Garreth was in all of this, since he and his wife owned the ranch the drakones had taken over. That question was answered when the man trotted out on a sleek chestnut horse, his spine ramrod straight and his face determined.

"Good afternoon." Garreth had a great speaking voice, and it carried well in the hushed atmosphere of tension in the arena. He was wearing a long, black duster and matching cowboy hat. "I'd like to welcome all of our guests here today, including those from our neighboring town of Cactus Flower Estates."

He tipped his hat toward Jessie and José and the eclectic assortment of human and rift people around them.

The actual name for the monstertown sounded even sillier out loud.

"We are also honored by the presence of Xiang Jao, Matriarch of the Saguaro Rift drakone clan." Garreth's voice held an edge despite the diplomatic words.

Remi noted that the word "guest" had been left out of the introduction.

"I'd like to take this opportunity to extend my thanks to everyone who helped defend our ranch last night." Garreth tipped his hat to Lyall and Kat, which wasn't that surprising, and did the same to Remi, which was frankly astonishing. "Thanks to them, we have only a few people with minor injuries, and we all know it could have been much worse."

Garreth gave his horse a pat on the neck.

"We often talk about a visit to Moon Star Ranch being a trip to a past world, where the traditional skills of ranchers and wranglers were required for survival," he said. "Today we find ourselves in an alien world, with different rules and customs. The matriarch has assured me that our inclusion inside their piece of the Riftworld is temporary, but for now, we have to abide by drakone laws and tradition."

There was a low, anxious murmur, mostly from the strictly human side. The monstertownies already knew what was coming.

"Two members of our ranch family have been caught up in an ancient and, to me, incomprehensible tradition of combat. That is why we have been asked to bear witness to something similar to an Old West showdown."

Remi wasn't sure why Garreth had included him in the ranch family, but any comfort that might have brought was offset by the disturbing realization that the ranch guests and staff weren't here out of morbid curiosity. They had been ordered here as witnesses on Kaveh's behalf, while the entire drakone clan was here on Rhys's side. That didn't bode well for Kaveh's position in the family, even if this duel didn't end up with him dead or injured enough that he would have to capitulate and hand Remi over to Rhys anyway.

The drakones had the ranch by the balls. The agreement to allow Riftworld water to flow into ranch lands allowed the ranch to continue as it had for decades, and Garreth couldn't piss off the drakones and endanger that arrangement. Not to mention that Garreth, his family, employees, and guests were all trapped inside a fragment of an alien universe ruled by Xiang Jao and the clan elders.

Garreth went on to explain Remi's awful situation concisely, adding that Remi was ratkind. That last bit was probably to reassure the humans they weren't likely to end up locked away in a livestock chute, waiting to be either married off to a monster or killed by one. The crowd's chatter after Garreth finished his speech abruptly cut off, and Remi jerked his head up.

Rhys had entered the arena, Tarasque by his side, and was walking along the ranch side of the audience. The two were accompanied by Kaida.

One guardian and one second. At least that was what Remi thought a duelist's best friend was called. Tarasque was talking in low tones to his fellow husband. Judging by his rigid stance and Rhys's continued head shakes, Remi guessed the older drakone was trying to talk Rhys into something sensible, like not killing Kaveh and torturing Remi again, to death this time.

Rhys lifted his head and locked eyes with Remi, hatred in his gaze. Remi could have tried to drop his gaze and avoid provoking the drakone further.

Instead, he flipped him off.

Rhys took a step toward Remi but was brought up short by the immovable bulk of Kaida. He settled for folding his arms and glowering, his back to the humans and rift people on the ranch side of the bleachers.

Kaveh came walking out along the opposite side of the

arena next, and after a collective inhalation of breath, the crowd burst into applause. Not a polite clap or two, either, but a roar of support that reverberated through the air.

Kat rose to his feet and jogged over to Kaveh's side to be his second. Lyall appeared to be restraining himself from leaving his own seat by glaring at Rhys's back. His eyes were red enough to shoot lasers, and Remi was rather impressed Chrissie not only remained seated next to the infuriated hellhound but even gave him a reassuring pat on the arm. Kaida came over to the center of the arena, her movements faster than Raion's but not by much. After a whispered conversation with Kaveh, Kat walked up to the female guardian, facing off against Tarasque. There was more talking, which Remi couldn't hear but assumed involved both seconds reporting back that the duel was still on.

Remi swallowed, his insides feeling like he had ingested acid. He hadn't expected Kaveh not to go through with it, but this extinguished his last hope of a compromise that would prevent Kaveh from injury or worse at Rhys's clawed hands.

Kaida lumbered toward the chute, which Remi guessed was so she could join Raion as Remi's captor. After several interminable minutes, she reached her destination and came to a stop outside the bars, sinking into absolute stillness next to her fellow guardian as they surveyed the combatants.

Metallic notes rang out through the air, sounding like clashing wind chimes in a gale.

Kaveh turned his back on Rhys, which Remi didn't like at all, and bowed deeply to the matriarch and his clan. Rhys, for his part, kept his own back to the bleachers holding Kaveh's supporters and made no move to bow toward them.

Remi had no idea what the hell this all meant, but a

growl from Raion that sounded like a rock tumbler starting up suggested Rhys had committed a dragon-duel faux pas.

The sound of the chimes cut off, and Rhys attacked.

He wasted little time transforming into his aerial form. Kaveh lobbed a fireball of summ where his ex had been standing, but it was too slow and too off-target.

Remi had seen Kaveh fight off the phantoms at the petting zoo with his poisonous fire, and he could tell this wasn't a serious attempt to kill.

Rhys, unfortunately, had no such moral qualms.

His gray-scaled body twisted up into the air in a gyrating spiral, and three whirling dirt devils spun toward Kaveh. He dodged two, but the third caught him and slammed him backward against the wooden fence surrounding the arena.

Rhys dove down toward him, sending a hail of rocks and dust toward Kaveh and blocking another burst of summ that arced in his direction.

That left Kaveh bleeding from a myriad of cuts, and as he staggered forward, Rhys climbed higher in the air, gathering wind around him. The roar above the arena was so loud it drowned out everything else.

Rhys had created a fucking tornado, and he would kill Kaveh with it.

Remi could do nothing other than grip the ugly green bars of the chute and watch.

The gray drakone dropped to the ground and changed again into his humanoid alter form, gathering airborne debris around him. Although the arena and the people in the bleachers had been protected from the impact of the wind power Rhys was using, likely by the guardians, the same couldn't be said for the surrounding ranch. Torn-up shingles, chunks of lumber, and metal projectiles swirled around Rhys in a deadly whirlwind as he stood facing Kaveh.

A terra-cotta tile flew out of the swirling mass of dirt and debris and sailed by Kaveh's left ear, crashing against the fence. The vet tried to lurch to the right, but Rhys sent a metal rod hurtling toward him, barely missing him.

"Give him to me." Rhys's voice, unnaturally loud over the roar of the wind, held both fury and a note of pleading. Maybe he didn't want to kill his former lover, but it was clear he would do it rather than permit Kaveh to save Remi. Even though Remi had rejected Kaveh's help and refused to consider coming to the keep under his protection, Rhys was going to make his ex suffer for even caring about Remi.

The pompous drakone had patronized Kaveh because he was ace, dumped him, and now was going to end his life because he still had a thing for him and was a jealous prick.

The wind swirling around Rhys compressed into a circle of broken tile shards rotating around his chest. It morphed again into a horizontal vortex of razor-sharp debris, with the narrow end facing Kaveh like the tip of a drill.

Other than the hum of the deadly projectile, all the noise of the battle died away. It was as if even the air in the arena was holding its breath.

"Last chance." Rhys's voice cracked as he said the words.

"I'm not worth your life, Kaveh." Remi only figured out he was shouting after he heard his voice reverberating throughout the arena. "I'm not even worth twisting your ankle. Let the son of a bitch have me. Too many people depend on you, and no one needs me in their life, especially you."

Kaveh locked eyes with Remi, and despite the fear, anger, and host of emotions he must have been feeling, he managed a small smile.

"When this is over, you and I are going to have a long discussion about your sense of self-worth." He turned back to his ex, his face settling into grim determination as he flung both arms out, inviting the killing blow. "I'll never let you hurt Remi again."

Green fire crackled around Kaveh, a last desperate attempt to use his Azdaha abilities to save himself. Rhys sent a hail of projectiles at Kaveh, as the bastard had promised.

And then Snow attacked.

The half-Earth parrot, half-Riftworld phoenix, and all-around little brat launched himself into the air straight at Rhys.

The flap of his wings sent a shower of sparks trailing behind him, flames crackled around his small body, and finally Snow swelled into the size of a California condor and tried to set the entire arena on fire.

Remi dropped to the ground, covering his head with his hands as the searing heat of the flames roared over him and everyone else. He peeked out through the bars of the chute to see Rhys hurling gusts of wind to protect himself from the fireball unleashed by Snow.

There was no sign of Kaveh, and that panicked far him more than the imminent threat of turning into barbecued chinchilla.

Kaida and Raion, who hadn't shown any ability to talk, walk, or make draconian judgments with any speed at all, were suddenly at opposite ends of the arena. The komainu gleamed like their bodies had been dipped in gold, and the raging fires of Snow's fully manifested phoenix alter form beat uselessly against a translucent barrier the guardians had somehow erected above the entire arena.

The screams of alarm from the audience died out as the flames did, and Snow's terrifying size shrank down as he resumed his parrot shape and made an unsteady descent to the ground. Snow landed less than a meter away from Remi, coughed out a smoke ring, and regarded him with puffed-up pride.

A small portal opened up, and a clearly irritated Flutterberry popped out, nudged the bird into the portal with the swipe of a paw, then sprang into it before it winked out of existence.

Remi climbed to his feet, searching for Kaveh.

He could see Rhys, his clothing stained with soot, kneeling on the ground, pawing through a pile of debris.

Remi couldn't make sense of that for a long moment. Then he spotted the shredded and burnt remains of Kaveh's clothing and watched in horror as Rhys picked up a blood-splattered cowboy hat and tossed it aside.

People in the audience overcame their shock and began to stand up, trying to see more. There was a buzz of questions and anxious murmurs and, as it became clear there was no movement in the mass of dirt and fabric where Kaveh had been standing, hoarse cries of grief.

The drakones rose to their feet as well, with Xiang Jao staring down at the field in front of her, her scaled face rigid with repressed emotion.

Remi swayed on his feet. It was over, and Kaveh was dead.

He couldn't cry, he didn't have the energy to rage against Rhys, and he couldn't even care that his life would be over next.

All of this pain and horror was his fault.

Rhys, it appeared, agreed.

The drakone rose to his feet, screaming words to that effect over and over at Remi as he stalked toward the chute. He held something gold and glittering in one hand. It was the cursed Matchmaker artifact that had transformed into a gold Rolex to tell Kaveh Remi was his match, which had led to Kaveh dying in a futile attempt to save him.

The person Remi had been urged him to do something —anything—to try and escape. He could try to run away as a chinchilla or plead his case with the guardians, but he felt he deserved this awful ending to his life. He reached into his living leathers and pulled out his smartwatch.

"Go," he whispered, and Bug's metallic body rose up from the watch's liquid crystal face and flew off toward the stands.

"He dies now." Rhys was in Kaida's impassive stone face, burn marks on his face and upper body now apparent. Snow hadn't held back at his first attempt to be a true phoenix. "The duel is over, and that's what I want. For this lying, thieving rat to get what he deserves."

Kaida remained unmoving for several moments then gave a brief bow. Raion opened the chute gate, and Remi stood face-to-face with Rhys. The drakone's face was contorted by grief and rage as he reached to his waist for a long knife. A bag hung next to it on his belt, swaying as if it contained something heavy. He hadn't needed any weapons to kill Kaveh. It had been slaughter, pure and simple, and Remi was next.

"I'm going to hack off your head and send it to that foul beast you call your father." Rhys grated out the words, the tip of the blade shaking ever so slightly as he pointed it at Remi.

Remi laughed, which was wildly inappropriate and most likely a sign of hysteria. All this drama from Rhys for nothing.

Arimanius, Don of the Colony crime family, would only move on to a different plan to get the drakones' secrets, and take his half-human son's death in stride. Remi had no illusions about his father's sentimentality.

Or his skill at exacting revenge.

"He insists on being called Ari, for your information." Remi had nothing to lose at this point, and enraging the drakone might get this over with faster. He shot a glance at Xiang Jao, who stood frozen, as motionless as one of the guardians. "Unlike your boss, he wouldn't let a jealous asshole murder someone in our clan who was better than him in every possible way."

Rhys lunged at Remi with the knife, but stumbled as the ground underneath his feet rose up like an ocean swell.

Remi reached to grab at the bars, trying to stay on his feet as the earth shuddered.

It was an odd time for an earthquake, and Remi hadn't thought they were common in Arizona. The shaking worsened, and even the drakones became alarmed as the metal bleachers swayed.

The ground behind Rhys exploded, dirt and rocks flying through the air like water from a fountain. A serpentine mass of gleaming blue-black scales twisted out of the earth, and a massive head dominated by two pale fangs dripping with venom loomed over the gray-scaled aerial drakone.

Remi had come close to being eaten by Ceto, an aquatic drakone who could take down an aircraft carrier. He had been tortured and beaten by Rhys, an aerial drakone able to twist the wind into his own personal tornadoes. He had seriously thought a hellhound was about to eat him. This, though, was the most terrifying monster Remi had ever faced.

And the most beautiful.

"Kaveh?" Any doubts about who had showed up to save him disappeared when a drop of liquid from one fang dropped to the ground beside Rhys, flaring into the green flame of summ as it did.

Kaveh was alive and had transformed into an Azdaha earth drakone to kick some ass.

Rhys turned into his aerial shape and launched himself skyward, but he had tried that trick one too many times. The furious dragon that had been the ranch's educated and compassionate veterinarian arced upward, knocking Rhys out of the air with a twist of his muscular body.

Kaveh was enormous and so damn quick.

Rhys, crumpled in the dirt, went back to his humanoid form. As awe-inspiring as the aerial drakones were in flight, they did their fighting at a distance, with their ability to manipulate the air around them. On the ground, they lost their fighting advantage.

The wind started up again, a blast that died within seconds when Kaveh struck hard and fast, pummeling Rhys with clods of earth and rock that flew through the air.

Rhys screamed in pain and terror and tried to scramble away, but Kaveh wrapped his scaled body around him, tightening the force as his ex-lover gasped and begged.

"Stop." Xiang Jao walked across the torn-up earth of the arena and stood with both hands outstretched in a pleading gesture. "Don't do this, Kaveh. This isn't you."

Well, wasn't that rich. She had sat there and watched as Rhys thrashed Kaveh and unleashed a tornado of projectiles, intending to kill him. Now that her boy toy was about to get the same treatment, she wanted to settle the dispute peacefully.

Kaveh gave a low hiss, and a ring of green flame roared up around his coiled body, forcing the matriarch to step back.

The mass of coils shuddered and contracted, and human Kaveh reformed, his hands around Rhys's neck.

He released his hold and allowed the man's groaning body to slide down to the ground.

Kaveh was naked except for a thick coating of dust. He stood, chest heaving, facing a woman Remi knew he thought of as a mother. But the clan had been willing to let Rhys kill Kaveh, and there was no way in hell the Saguaro Rift drakones weren't going to pay for that.

Remi wasn't much use battling dragons, but he knew something about negotiation, even if he was stuck in a livestock chute with two stone lions guarding him like whatever trophy cowboys got when they won the rodeo.

"We have a few conditions to discuss first." Remi caught Lyall's gaze and gave him a quick nod. The hellhound had sworn an oath to not interfere in the duel, but now that it was over, some added muscle couldn't hurt. "Don't we, Kaveh?"

Lyall and Kat both stood up, and the vet assistant accepted Garreth's duster and hat from the ranch owner before the two of them strode out into the arena. Kat helped Kaveh pull the long coat around him and plopped the matching black cowboy hat on his head. Lyall transformed into his hellhound shape, which barely caused a ripple of surprise from the overwhelmed crowd. He put a huge paw on Rhys's chest.

"Yes, we do." Kaveh turned to flash Remi a relieved smile. That, and accepting that the two of them were a "we" set Remi's heart fluttering. "Let's start with agreeing that Remi Gatti is no longer anyone's prisoner."

Xiang Jao gave Remi an appraising look then inclined her head to Kaveh. "I accept the judgment of the Matchmaker, and everyone in my clan will do the same." She didn't mention Rhys by name, but she didn't have to. "The guardians will release Remigio Gatti to your custody."

Remi was all for getting out of his tacky green jail, but there were larger issues to discuss. "There's also the little matter of Moon Star Ranch, Cactus Flower Estates, and a good chunk of Tucson being inside the drakone riftland."

"We don't have the control object." The matriarch's tone held an edge to it, so Lyall put more pressure on Rhys's chest, eliciting a yelp. She let out her breath in a huff. "When we locate it, we will restore the borders."

"I want your word the Saguaro Rift clan will continue its protection of the monstertown and pledge to defend the ranch." Kaveh was getting the hang of this. "During and after this crisis you and the clan created."

"That includes maintaining the water rights to both locations," Remi added. "As well as recognizing the sovereign rights of all relevant local governments and respecting the rights of all sentient species clans, including the ones you don't like."

He was referring to Amanita, Flutterberry, Snow, and even Bug, but he didn't want any of his ratkind relatives left out of this deal either. Hell, he'd throw in the phantoms if they backed off trying to eat everyone.

Xiang Jao stood straighter, her scales gleaming in the sun and her voice echoing with power. "You have my word."

Kaveh exhaled and turned his back to her. He bent down to the ground, ignoring Rhys's panting gasps as he searched for something in the dust. Then he strode over to the live-stock chute, the duster flapping around his heels, Remi's very own cowboy doctor hero.

Raion and Kaida both bowed, and Kaveh bowed back. He threw the gate open wide and pulled Remi into a bear hug. Then he put the Matchmaker Rolex on Remi's wrist and kissed him.

27

"**A**re you hurt?" Kaveh pulled back from embracing Remi, as if he was worried his touch might be unwelcome—frightening, even.

There was no sign of the Azdaha drakone who had burst out of the earth spewing poisonous fire. There was only the Kaveh Remi knew, wearing a concerned expression and worrying about everyone else's feelings.

"I'd say only my pride." Remi looked down at his ripped living leathers, unsure where the blood and damage to the creature ended and his injuries began. His face must look even worse. "But that would be a lie even I couldn't pull off. Better than being dead though, which I would be if it wasn't for you."

"Rhys had no right to touch you." Kaveh's voice was low and hoarse, the fury he had unleashed upon his ex simmering in his words. At least his hands weren't glowing with the green fire of summ. He already had better control over that dangerous weapon, and he had succeeded in changing into his terrifying Azdaha earth form before he was more than thirty Earth years old.

Remi bet that pissed off Kaveh's nasty ex as much as getting his ass kicked in the duel.

Then a thought struck him, and he gave his forehead a whack. Which hurt, a lot. How could it have taken him so long to figure this out?

"You need medical attention and rest." Kaveh reached for his hand, probably worried Remi might try to add to his own bruises again.

"I'm fine." Remi interlaced his fingers into Kaveh's, the touch setting off the same spark of connection he had felt the first time they met, only now he understood it was more than a physical attraction. The warmth and comfort of Kaveh's skin against his was there too. It felt so good to touch Kaveh and to know he was okay and worried about Remi despite all the absolute shit Remi had put the man through. But the two of them had work to do. "Walk with me."

The entire clan of drakones had gathered around the matriarch. Rhys was back on his feet, dusting off his ren faire warrior outfit and not looking nearly battered and cut up enough for Remi's taste.

All of the clan fell silent as Remi approached. He squeezed Kaveh's hand for courage.

Then he pulled his hand loose, went up to Rhys, and poked a finger into the drakone's chest. That produced a few gasps, which was quite gratifying.

"So." Remi adopted the most suggestive and inappropriate tone he could manage. No psychic boost to it though. That would be icky. "Is that a dildo on your belt, or are you happy to see me?"

Rhys jerked back and shot a quick glance at Tarasque and Xiang Jao for support, who both responded with weary expressions. Even Rhys's wife and fellow husband were sick of his shit at this point. "As the matriarch said, we all now accept the Matchmaker's decision. I'm planning to leave immediately for the keep, and you can save your puerile jokes for Kaveh."

"You're not leaving until you show both me and Kaveh what you're carrying on your belt." Remi felt a spurt of panic that he was way off with his guess.

But Rhys's eyes widened in fear and shock.

Remi knew he had him.

Kaveh stood with arms folded, watching Rhys with hard eyes. "Remi asked you to show us what you're carrying. Trust me, I'm not in the mood for jokes."

Rhys hesitated until Tarasque stepped forward and pointed at his fellow husband's belt. Not much of a talker, that one.

Rhys pulled the knife off his belt and offered it to Kaveh. Remi took advantage of that obvious decoy move to go into pickpocket mode. He slid his hand into the odd pouch he had noticed when he had been waiting for Rhys to kill him and lifted out an elongated oval shape.

The control object pulsed with an odd, erratic glow.

It felt heavier than it should for its size, and for a moment, Remi could have sworn a pair of wide-set eyes peered out at him before disappearing into the misty substance within.

Rhys cursed and took a step forward. Remi prudently retreated behind Kaveh, who shoved a hand glowing with summ in Rhys's face.

There was a lot of shouting after that, which subsided when Raion and Kaida put their stone bodies front and center.

"It is the control object." Kaida moved a stony paw over the glowing surface but didn't take it from Remi. "It appears one of your clan removed the device for his own purposes, Matriarch."

Everyone looked at Rhys, and the matriarch drew in a breath with what seemed like true surprise.

"This offense will be dealt with." She came out with that, eventually.

Remi could have been wrong, but he suspected she hadn't known her second husband had unleashed a horde of phantoms so he could control the search for Kaveh's Matchmaker choice. He still blamed her for going along with draining an entire clan's life force to control more territory though.

"I'll take the object and work on restoring the rift boundary," she said.

"I don't think so." Remi held the object higher and addressed Raion and Kaida. "The Colony sent me here to steal this by seducing and tricking Kaveh, and he still fought a duel to save my life. I think he's the one who should keep it."

Raion gave a slow nod. "It is customary for the winner of the duel to dispose of the loser and all of their possessions as they see fit."

"Given that Kaveh has granted his opponent his life, your clan can hardly ask for more." Kaida directed her comment to Xiang Jao with the faintest note of disapproval. "I will work with him to restore the boundary position, and the disposition of the control object will be up to his discretion."

Remi expected more arguing, but the guardians, as usual, got their way. The drakones left to return to the keep, and Kaveh watched them with his lips pressed into a thin line and a protective arm around Remi's shoulder.

Kaveh had made it clear that if it came down to his

wealthy adopted drakone clan or Remi, he was picking the half-human con man whose alter form was a chinchilla.

A terrible choice on his part, but Remi was intensely grateful for it.

With no further extreme winds or draconic earthquakes, the day turned out to be quite pleasant. The sky above was a cloudless blue expanse that faded into purple and gold as the sun began to dip under the horizon. The crowd drifted away after a long line of people came up to express admiration for Kaveh's fighting skills and congratulate Remi for not being dead. It was like the wedding receiving line from hell, but with each handshake or slap on the back, Kaveh seemed to relax more.

Even though his human friends now knew he could turn into a monster, he was *their* monster.

Remi's cousins in crime were long gone, and soon the only people left at the site of the duel were all friends—Kat and Lyall standing a little too close to one another as they spoke, Jeannette and the other wranglers examining the torn-up mounds of desert earth left after Kaveh's earthquake-like arrival, and an animal contingent comprised of Amanita, her colt, and Snow, who popped back through a portal with Flutterberry, flapping sparks off his wings and accepting congratulations on his performance. Even Bug had come out unscathed in all the mayhem, buzzing around the arena looking for any stray plastic.

"You don't need to worry about Rhys anymore." Kaveh spoke softly, which Remi appreciated, since his head was still ringing from the slaps Rhys had dished out. "I let him live out of respect for the matriarch, but everyone in my clan knows I'll kill anyone who threatens you. You'll be safe when you go back to Boston."

"About that." Remi held up his wrist, the gold not-Rolex

glittering in the sun's dying rays. The Matchmaker was many things, but subtle wasn't one of them. "In light of recent events—namely an angry Welsh drakone trying to murder me—I've reconsidered my stance on both Matchmaker pairings and possessive dragon husbands."

Kaveh went still, and Remi bit his lip, dread settling over him.

Mysterious Riftworld matchmaking sentience aside, Kaveh had no reason to want Remi around. He had saved his life, yes, but that had been an obligation, an honor thing. Remi had lied to Kaveh, put his friend Kat in so much danger he had to run off with a hellhound, and ruined his relationship with the only family the Azdaha drakone had ever known.

Remi was, quite possibly, the worst Matchmaker fiancé in history.

"You'd be willing to stay, then?" The hope in Kaveh's tone gave Remi enough courage to meet his gaze. The vet smiled at him, and his grip on Remi's hand tightened.

"I'm not sure why you'd want me to." Remi swallowed a few times because apologies didn't come easy to him and honesty even less so. "I've been so awful to you, and everything I said when we found out I was your match was horrible, not to mention a lie. From the first moment I saw you, I wanted you. Then I found out you were kind, smart, and every bit as brave as the hero of some old Western. And I wanted you even more, but I didn't want to admit it. Snow was right—I am a dirty rat."

"Chinchillas are very clean animals," Kaveh corrected with a grin. "And you can stop trying to put a halo on my head. I wasn't honest with you and a lot of other people I care about either. We're both monsters to many people, whether they're human or from the Riftworld."

"I was thinking." Remi had to get the words out fast because if he slowed down, he'd lose his nerve. "Since my plan to not tell my father I'm your love match has blown up, instead of going back to Boston, I could stay in the monster-town here. I can do my vid streaming in between rift storms and work on my crushing insecurity about being in a real relationship."

Kaveh's whole face lit up, which made him so beautiful Remi wanted to jump him here and now. It would have to wait. Remi wasn't sure he could even walk, much less do complicated sexual gymnastics.

"I'd like to take another stab at dating you—for real this time." Kaveh reached out, and they embraced again, this time pressing together with less frantic worry and more passion. Remi felt more stable than he had anticipated, although that didn't stop him from leaning against Kaveh and feeling the warmth of his muscular chest. He inhaled, breathing in a rich, masculine scent of leather and rain, with a hint of green apple. Even Kaveh's poison ability smelled great.

"We can talk about all of this," Kaveh said. "But first I want you to drink some water and let me make sure your injuries aren't more serious than they look. Then you should lie down and rest."

If Kaveh took Remi to anything resembling a bed, Remi had strong opinions about what he wanted to do in it before they both fell asleep. He brushed a kiss against Kaveh's cheek. "I'm sorry about the break with your family. Rhys is a total jerk, but I think the others only wanted to protect you."

Kaveh's breath hitched at the mention of the drakone clan he had publicly rejected, but he kept steering the two of them in the direction of his pickup truck where he kept a first aid kit. "I have a lot of anger right now. Maybe things will change in the future."

"Well, in addition to dating advice, I'm an expert on dysfunctional family dynamics." Remi released his hold on the vet reluctantly and let Kaveh help him into the passenger seat of the truck. Until the rift boundary moved, the vehicle was little more than a comfortable place to sit. "You've met the worst of my cousins, and don't even get me started on my father. He started this whole mess, trying to steal the control object to manipulate the rift."

Remi still had the damn thing, since the guardians had returned to the monstertown, and Kaveh didn't know any more about it than he did.

"Will your father try to retaliate when he finds out you're not bringing it back to him?" Kaveh pulled a water bottle from inside the truck—because of course he had one ready —and opened up an old-fashioned black leather doctor bag and pulled out a mix of Earth and Riftworld first-aid materials.

"Arimanius is more likely to cut his losses and try to hit Kaveh up for a bride price." That depressingly accurate statement came from Lyall, who had come over to the truck.

Kat was at his side, with Snow on his shoulder. The bird's fiery dramatics had been a setup, of sorts. Lyall and Kat had convinced Flutterberry to help with a distraction if things got bad. No one had expected Snow could fully manifest as a fireball of a phoenix.

Then again, no one, including the man himself, had thought Kaveh could turn into a killer Azdaha dragon.

The hellhound grinned at them. "If your father is too much of a pain in the ass, I'd be willing to give you a discount on assassinating him. Come to think of it, maybe I could make that your wedding gift from me."

"Violence doesn't solve anything." Kat broke in with that, and Lyall gave him a fond look and refrained from his usual comebacks.

Remi didn't need to lean into his powers to guess the hellhound's vow never to get romantically involved with a human might soon be put to the test.

Kat winced in sympathy at Remi. "Kaveh needed to do what he did, but murdering Remi's father isn't justified. Lyall needs to use his powers for good."

"Maybe Lyall should use his powers to get drinks and food for the two of you in the monstertown." Kaveh started cleaning and treating a cut on Remi's forehead. It stung, but it was so nice to have someone take care of him. "Put everything on my tab at the saloon. Thank you, Lyall, for helping with the phantoms and taking care of Remi and Kat. Don't kill anyone on my behalf, but if you ever need help from a drakone, you can come to me."

Lyall gave Remi a pat on the shoulder. "All right, rat boy, I can tell I'm leaving you in good hands. But make sure to tell the rest of your family I'm coming for them, just for laughs."

Remi relaxed, the sharp pain of a cut on his forehead fading as a Riftworld bandage took effect. He was feeling better physically already, and more importantly, the aching void in his chest that had opened up when he left Kaveh was now filled with a warm glow of something that felt like happiness.

Terribly sappy of him, but he didn't care.

Plus, the thought of punking Zale and the Pouch Twins with tales of the hellhound thirsting for their blood cheered him immensely. "I'll enjoy scaring the hell out of them. Go and have a beer with Kat. Snow, only water for you."

The parrot gave an incredulous squawk, and Kat dug out

a Brazil nut from his jeans for him as consolation as he and Lyall walked off together.

"I was worried about a few of the deeper cuts, but everything should heal fine." Kaveh put the doctor's bag away and settled into his seat. "When you're ready to stand, I'd like you to eat and then rest in the cabin for today. We can get you set up in the monstertown tomorrow."

"Food, yes. Rest, later." Remi leaned over to kiss Kaveh, this time on the lips. The two of them drew together, melting deeper into the heat of close contact, and all of the emotional and physical pain of the past several hours faded away. "I'm beginning to think the Matchmaker might actually know what it's doing."

AUTHOR'S NOTE

Thanks so much for reading *Rifted Hearts*, and I hope you enjoyed Kaveh and Remi's story. I love feedback from readers, so please consider leaving a review on Amazon or Goodreads.

Check out the next book in the *Riftworld* series!

Riftworld 0.5

If you're interested in hearing more about Remi's misadventures with Ceto, Sea Queen of the Deep, download the free prequel short story to the Riftworld series, "Witch City Rift", and sign up for M.A. Guglielmo's mailing list to get sneak peeks at further books in the series and special content only for subscribers.

Riftworld 1.5

Curious about the trouble Kat and Lyall got into when they ran off together? Download the free bonus chapter, "Bad Dog Night", and sign up for M.A. Guglielmo's mailing list to get sneak peeks at further books in the series and special content only for subscribers.

FOLLOW M.A. GUGLIELMO

Linktree: https://linktr.ee/Aphemia66

ALSO BY M.A. GUGLIELMO

The Riftworld Series

"Witch City Rift" Book .5

Rifted Hearts Book 1

Bad Dog Night, Book 1.5

On A Rift's Edge Book 2

The From Smokeless Fire series

Summoned

Soul to Steal

Price to Pay

The Blessed Series

Prince of Shadows

ACKNOWLEDGMENTS

Every book is a different writing journey, and the path that led to *Rifted Hearts* was made possible by the love and support of many people. My daughters Chiara and Sabrina deserve all of my gratitude for putting up with the time I spend writing, my use of them as a sounding board for tricky sentences, and giving me the Gen Z perspective on life and the world their generation will inherit. *Rifted Hearts* imagines a relatively benign future after a series of apocalyptic events, one fantastical and the others all too real. I hope we can do more in the present to make a better future world.

I'd like to thank my virtual assistant, proofreader, and all-around book cheerleader K.J. Harrowick for her advice and critiques. The novel is immeasurably better thanks to the stellar developmental and copyediting skills of Jeni Chappelle. My thanks go out to Dar at Wicked Smart Designs for the beautiful cover.

I'm grateful for help from the writing community, including my fellow authors in the Rhode Island Romance Writers group, as well as those in the Association of Rhode Island Authors. Portions of this book were workshopped during classes at Grub Street in Boston, and I'd like to thank the instructors there and my fellow students. I 'd also like to thank Teri Schiller for her advice about the medical care of horses.

A special shout out is needed for my Riftworld Street

Team members, who've provided beta reading feedback, left reviews, and shared their enthusiasm about the book and its characters. In no particular order, I'd like to thank: Rose McClain, Gary Lee Webb, Barbara, Jennifer DiSclafani, Claire Pacey, Kimberly Irish-Tarbox, Kennedy Hopkins, MesmAhryze, Amy Nutting, Graham Ellis, Maria Lozano, Crystal June, Sky, Jessica D., Tracy Seymour, Gordon Rodmell, Christina Lowry, Caroline, Ashley Brown, Cindy Damon, Amber Barnhardt, Lauren Gavlin, Patty Taylor, Jammie Rose, Fern Slater-Walters, Elaina Harding, Crystal Anderson, Sabrina, Toni Whitmire, Hanna Skovgaard, Zurisadai, Naomi Bynum, Natalie Malone, Teresa Jordan, Gabrielle Sims, Patrizia Müller, Clara, Julie, Zenda, Katie Anderson, Aziza Evans, Shelby Boheen, Marlys Frisby, Susan Barbee, Book.Nerd, Donna Bruno,Ida Umphers, Trina Jones, Sophia Harlow, Arren Mercado, Amber Pate, GrammaT, Shelley Coats, Samantha Basks, Sara M. Hiltunen, Deborah P., Jill McCarn, and Patty Taylor.

The Riftworld's animals are based on my real-life encounters with Earth species ranging from a misbehaving rescue parrot to the opinionated horses at a dude ranch. I'm eternally grateful for all the companion animals who make our lives better, and the veterinary professionals who care for them.

ABOUT THE AUTHOR

M.A. Guglielmo is a neurosurgeon, mother of two awesome daughters, and a lifelong fan of speculative fiction. Her Italian grandmother may or may not have been able to cast the evil eye on difficult neighbors, and Maria loves telling a good story, especially if magical curses and witty villains are involved.

After having the wits scared out of her by ghost tales told to her over a campfire in the Moroccan Sahara, she's come up with a plan to travel to all the potential settings for her novels. Since those include the mountain-ringed home of the Jinn and a future dystopia complete with monster portals, some items on her bucket list might be harder to achieve than others.

Maria is always dreaming of the stories that will come out of her next travel destination.